Baby Grape and the River Folk

To the Readers at the Butler Library

Thank you.

Baby Grape
and the River Folk

Thom Rogers

Mill City Press
Minneapolis, MN

Mill City Press, Inc.
212 3rd Avenue North, Suite 570
Minneapolis, MN 55401
612.455.2294
www.millcitypublishing.com

ISBN - 1-934937-25-8
ISBN - 978-1-934937-25-9
LCCN - 2008934115

Cover Design and typeset by Sophie Chi
Cover Art and interior drawings by Emily Zuzack

Printed in the United States of America

Contents

2-1

~the rain and the river~

The rain poured all night and the river started to swell. Toby sat huddled on a barrel, slouched over the barge's rudder. The barge in front of his and the one in tow were invisible in the dark. Toby watched the front and rear towlines, both lit with lanterns. He could barely see the glow of the lamps in the rain, but the light gleamed on the wet surface of the towlines and helped him to navigate his barge as he steered to keep the lines straight—ahead and behind.

Toby's barge carried several large barrels of whiskey, some large canvas bags of dyed wool, lumber shorts, grain sacks, and the cart—with its wheels removed. Inside the covered cart were Gina, the two Indian girls named Jaynee and Robin, and the girls' dog.

Toby wasn't sure if the wetness on his cheek didn't share rain and tears; he was still saddened by the loss of Bea the mule. He knew the sharp sting of grief would pass, just as it had started to after the recent loss of his father.

Gina had crawled out from the dry cover of the cart to talk to Toby twice during the long night and had given him her dry coat to wear. She rubbed his arms and shoulders briskly to help warm him, but that quickly faded. Toby was cold to the bone, shivering like he'd never be warm again.

He tried to imagine how much rain was pouring into the funnel-shaped river valley, the water rising and rushing to chase them downriver to Pittsburgh. He guessed that the twenty miles behind him were swelling to dangerous levels, which would require them to travel a much faster river than he and the others had wanted.

He knew that Ernie and Ella, the couple that owned the three barges and the supplies onboard, were old hands at floating the river. Pete and Eula rode in the last barge, and Toby had begun to realize that they were equally proficient at "barge running." He felt safe to be tied between the two barges with the four adults in charge. They all were such nice folk, and Toby felt it was "the pure hand of God," as people say, that had put him with them on this trip.

In fact, he doubted he would have made it through the ordeals of this journey without the help of everybody on the barges. He was beginning to understand the true value of friendship. He realized that any one of these people would put their lives before his to save him. It had taken some ordeals to prove it. Toby liked this bunch of people and knew that they were a sort of family. And as Ernie had put it, they "could do anything together."

Toby felt the front of the barge pull left. He leaned hard into the rudder and steered into the towline. Then he felt it pull Pete's barge into tow behind him. Water sloshed across the floor of the barge, getting deeper and deeper. Toby guessed that daylight—if there was to be any with this storm—shouldn't be too far off and hoped it would come soon. The rain and river would feel more manageable in the light, he thought.

Again, the barge pulled hard to the left. Toby heard a shout. He recognized it as Ella's voice. She yelled, "Toby, hard left! Hard left! Tell Pete!"

Toby pulled on the rudder and turned his head to shout behind him. "Hard" was all he got out when his barge crashed into something solid. He almost lost his balance as the front of the barge lifted and the entire thing tilted. It came to an abrupt halt until Pete's barge plowed into him from behind! This knocked Toby to his knees and he heard the girls screaming.

Pete's barge slid up and onto the middle barge, and Toby was just able to scramble ahead of it. Everything came to a complete halt. Toby heard more shouts in the dark. Eula was the first one to him, as she'd been on the front of the trailing barge. Her boat had been in tow thirty feet behind Toby's, and now she stood at his side! As Pete approached them, the lantern dropped onto the deck and broke, spilling oil and fire onto the barge!

The flaming oil floated across the deck and spread towards the barrels of whiskey. Toby knew they would explode if the fire got to their contents. But as quickly as the fire washed over the deck it went out, scattered by the rain and the water on the deck. Toby figured the lamp must have been pretty low on oil to begin with.

"Toby, you ok?" Eula asked, gripping the wet sleeve of his coat and leaning into his face to be heard over the pounding rain.

It took a moment for Toby's eyes to adjust to the darkness and for him to see Eula by the light of the other lantern. "Yes…." Toby replied as he turned to the cart. It had slipped off the crates and now sat at the edge of the barge, at an angle not too healthy for its occupants!

"Gina, Gina!" Toby yelled, and went to the cart.

"We're ok…." Gina crawled out from under the cover of the cart and had Robin in tow. She had the look of deep sleep, but the cold rain cured that. Jaynee was behind the others and stood under the oilskin, out of the rain. Only their profiles were visible in the darkness, but everyone seemed to be fine.

Eula went to the front of Toby's barge and shouted to Ernie and Ella. That's when she noticed the towrope hanging loosely into the water. She yelled again and paused for a reply. None came…. Pete's barge began to swing away from its perch on the back of Toby's. Eula took a last look at the others and, satisfied that they were ok, hopped onto the barge with her husband…

◊ ◊ ◊

2-2

~the rainy wait~

Toby and Gina realized that the cart was in an even more precarious position than before and that they needed to get to it quickly to pull it back onto the barge. Jaynee realized the same thing and jumped down onto the deck. Little Robin stood off to the side while the other three tugged at the cart. It was stuck. They changed positions and tried again. They grabbed it together, and with one concentrated effort, managed to budge it a little, but not far enough. Toby leaned over the edge of the barge and lifted again. He was on his knees and held the axle of the cart in one hand. It was then that the rear of Pete's barge rammed against the middle boat again, knocking the girls down. Then Toby and the cart slipped off the barge and into the water.

The last thing Toby heard as he slipped under the water was Gina's scream. His feet touched the rocks that the barge was hung up on, but they were slippery. He couldn't gain any purchase with his feet. He realized that the cart was turning in his grasp and let go of the axle. But then he felt a tug; the axle was tangled in his coat sleeve and wasn't going to let him swim to the surface!

Toby's one arm was at the surface and he waved it frantically. He could turn his head so his face was just at the surface of the river. He gasped for a breath and yelled to Gina: "Gina, I'm caught!" He coughed water and drew another breath. The cart slipped again and he felt the jacket tighten about his wrist. With another breath he turned into the water and tried to slide off the coat. It was buttoned up! Each button took a lifetime of fumbling to undo. He turned his face upwards again, but this time he had to strain to break the surface for another breath. He groped at the buttons again and had all but one undone....

Everything was moving again! The barge was slipping off the rocks and the cart moved once more, pulling Toby further beneath the water's surface. He had just this last breath with which to get free! The button was loose and he slipped the coat from his shoulder. Now he pulled his free arm around and pushed the other sleeve down, but soon realized that the axle had twisted the coat so tightly around his wrist that he couldn't get free!

Something hit his leg and then grabbed his arm. He felt a hand groping him and feeling its way across his chest. He grabbed the hand and pushed it to the tangled sleeve. He was starting to convulse for air. He wasn't going to make it! More tugs on his sleeve and he realized that it was being cut with a knife.

Thank you, Gina!, was his last thought as he blacked out. But seconds later he felt the rain pounding on his face. He coughed up water and gasped for air. He was too exhausted to do anything but try to float. He felt hands pulling at him, a bare arm around his neck, and his body being pulled across the surface of the water.

Toby was in a dreamlike state; his head swam with half-formed thoughts. He heard his name spoken as he tried to help pull himself onto shore. The rain was fiercer now than it had been. Toby lie on the ground, still coughing up water. He was left alone for several moments and then the arms pulled at him again. He crawled up the muddy bank and felt himself being guided forward. He realized that the rain was only hitting his legs now; he was underneath something. *Gina, oh, Gina*, he thought, but couldn't speak. He was about to collapse when he felt her on top of him. Toby felt her hands opening the front of his shirt and pants, and then felt her naked skin up against his ice cold flesh, warming him. He felt a warm liquid across his stomach; she had peed on him and was now laying herself on top of him again. He was starting to get some feeling back in his body and his teeth stopped chattering. Then he passed out...

◊ ◊ ◊

2-3

~a morning's surprise~

Toby woke coughing. Every muscle in his body was stiff and ached from the cold. He was now lying on his side, her body curled in against his, with the back of her body against his entire length. Her hair was matted against his face and chest. When he felt her stir, he slipped his arm over her chest and hugged her. He kissed her neck and she pressed the side of her head against his face. He was more grateful to her than he'd ever been. They slipped back into sleep again, and neither moved for a long while.

Toby woke up aroused, with his hand on her chest. Several moments passed before he realized that something wasn't quite right. He curled his fingers and felt the mountain lion's claw necklace. It was Jaynee! Toby froze in place. He slowly withdrew his hand from her chest and placed it on her hip. He couldn't push her away; she had just risked her life to save him. But if he could just back away from her body he'd be able to relax and maybe gain control of himself.

He thought of how wrong this would seem to Gina and how it betrayed the bond they had created over the last several months. But he was now in a situation he couldn't solve. He wanted to stand up and move around, but he liked being warm. Plus, it was still raining and he knew he would just get a "cold wet" on him again. Right now he was wet but warm, and he could survive this way.

Toby remembered that Gina had once told him that the right thing to do in difficult situations was "whatever it took to survive." With that he relaxed and soon slipped back to sleep.

Jaynee was the first to move the next time they woke up, and Toby came to when he felt her move away from him. When he opened his eyes he saw her looking at him. She smiled.

They were under a large rock at the river's edge; raindrops marked the water's surface. Toby realized that it must be daylight, as he could see across the river to the other side. He noticed that the water was much higher than it had been. He got to his knees beside Jaynee and turned to face out of the "shelter."

Toby remembered climbing up a bank to this spot the night before, but now the water's edge was less than two feet from where they knelt. He looked down the river to where the others had floated, but there was nobody in sight!

He held his hand out from under the overhanging rock and gathered some of the rain in his palm. He drank some rainwater and then used a second helping to wash his face. Jaynee helped herself to a drink and then looked at Toby again. He realized for the first time how pretty she was. Her shiny black hair hung down past her shoulders and seemed nearly dry. She smiled again and Toby saw how white her teeth were. Her dark eyes looked at him and he knew she wanted to say something. Instead, she pursed her lips and turned to look downriver again. Toby touched her arm and said, "Thank you."

They remained that way for some time as Toby wondered how far downstream the others were and if they had tied up. *Could they tie up in the fast moving water?*, he wondered. *Of course they would try! They wouldn't leave the two of us here—would they?*

Over Jaynee's shoulder, Toby watched a tree limb floating by and judged the speed of the water. It was faster than he could walk; and *that* wasn't good for the barges' travel. He was hungry and knew that Jaynee must be, as well. They couldn't stay here; the others wouldn't be able to return to them against the fast water. They would have to start down the river themselves—and the sooner the better!

Toby touched Jaynee's arm and she turned to him. "We need to go...." Her eyes were soft and quizzical. Toby walked his fingers across his palm and pointed downriver. Jaynee nodded her understanding.

He stood and realized too late that his pants were still unbuttoned as they fell down. He grabbed at them and tried to pull them back up. Jaynee giggled and stepped out from underneath the overhanging rock. With a beet red face, Toby grinned at her and started to lead them downriver.

The rain continued as a drizzle for the rest of the morning. They were soaked, cold, and famished when Jaynee stepped to the side of the trail and climbed up the hillside. Toby stopped and watched her; he thought she was going to relieve herself. But about twenty feet away she pulled out Gina's knife and knelt down. Toby was puzzled by her activities. He climbed the wet, slippery bank and joined her. Jaynee was pulling roots from the ground, first one, then another, and then several more. Each one looked like a human form, complete with legs and arms. With six of the roots in hand, Jaynee wiped the dirt from the knife on her deer hide tunic and stood up. Toby reminded himself to tell Gina to get the girls some underpants when they got to Pittsburgh. (Or maybe not!)

Jaynee found a small rivulet of clean rainwater to rinse off the tubers and handed two of them to Toby to eat. She seemed to relish each bite, but he cupped water in his hand to drink with the food.

About an hour later, he was feeling much stronger than he had for quite some time. As he followed Jaynee through the forest, he watched her wet tunic clinging to her body. He started to have other ideas besides hurrying to find the others. Toby had no idea how old she was, but he figured her to be about four-teen—or maybe older—since she was more filled out than his sister at home.

Jaynee stopped abruptly and squatted to the ground. Toby followed her lead and she looked back at him with great terror in her eyes! She covered her mouth with her hands and he knew not to make a sound. In the silence he heard snuffling noises. Jaynee's hand rocked back and forth as she motioned him to move towards the river, about twenty feet away. They quickly covered the distance and stood at the edge of the fast-moving, muddy water.

At his side, Jaynee hunched her back and held her fingers in a claw-like pose. Toby knew she meant a bear and watched in the direction of the snuffling noises. She slipped the remaining roots into her tunic and put the knife into the rope belt that Gina had made for her. Then they both stepped quietly into the cold river and swam away from shore until they felt the current pulling them downstream. It was an effortless way to travel, and if the water hadn't been so cold, it would have been the best way to find the others.

They floated around a long curve in the river and could now see quite a distance ahead. The others were still nowhere to be seen! Toby guessed it was a couple of miles to the next turn in the river and wondered if they could keep floating until they reached it. But his teeth started to chatter and he saw that Jaynee was in the same shape. He figured they were at least a mile from the bear and hoped it was going north. Either way, they weren't going much further this way. He nodded his head towards the near bank and they swam ashore.

The drizzle had stopped now, and the air temperature was climbing fast despite the day's rain. It wasn't as bad a day as Toby had thought it would be. He watched as Jaynee silently removed her tunic and sat naked on a rock. After several stunned moments, Toby removed his clothes and sat down on a nearby rock, facing slightly away from her.

Toby busied himself with looking at the sky and noted that it was still overcast. He realized that it would probably rain again, which didn't thrill him. But he was thrilled at the sight of Jaynee sitting there. She squeezed water out of her tunic and Toby watched as her breasts moved. He quickly picked up his shirt and began wringing it out—glad to have something to cover his telltale desire for her. He glanced around and tried to think of something else.

After an hour they were sufficiently warm and continued the journey south along the river's edge. They came upon a fish wedged in a small pool of land-locked water. They cleaned it and carried it on a stick, hoping to build a fire later if they didn't find the others soon.

They finally made it to the next bend in the river—a couple of miles from their last river swim—and still none of the others appeared! Toby kept looking northward and trying to see if there was more rain to come, but the sky was slowly clearing now.

The couple's pace slowed as they got tired and the afternoon air suddenly got cooler. Toby's feet hurt and his legs were stiff, so he sat down for a mo-ment. Jaynee came over and sat beside him—a little too close! He could smell something: Was it her clothing or the fish on a stick? Jaynee kept looking at two hilltops in the distance and then behind them into the woods on their side of the river.

Toby watched her for awhile and then began following her gaze from one hill to another. She had a plan, but the language barrier prevented her from telling him about it. With some rudimentary sign language she indicated some-thing that Toby guessed meant "cave."

Jaynee gathered some small stones and motioned for Toby to get off of the large rock he was sitting on. With the stones, she made an arrow that pointed into the woods. Toby wasn't sure that leaving the river was a good idea and shook his head. She held out her hand to stop him and pointed to the sky. "It's *not* going to rain again," Toby said. But she nodded and made more hand signs. After awhile Toby realized she was describing food, shelter, and a fire! He wasn't sure what all was going to happen, but those things sounded good to him…

◊ ◊ ◊

2-4

~getting lucky~

For the next hour, they walked diagonally up from the river's edge. Toby was glad for the change of scenery from the river as they walked in the forest. The large trees were spaced far apart, and the ground moss and ferns were soaking wet and cool. The drop in temperature made Toby think longingly of how much warmer the air was along the river. But he followed Jaynee, and they soon were on more level ground than any they had traveled so far.

To their right was a cliff side. Ahead of them was a rock face. Toby then saw the cave entrance. The area around the entrance was cleared and appeared to be used frequently. Toby approached cautiously, letting Jaynee enter first. It was a wedge space about ten feet across that then narrowed to a point about twenty feet in. The ground inside was a light sand—and dry as a bone! Several pieces of wood were strewn about on the floor. A circle of rocks was there also, showing the charred remains of many previous fires.

Toby saw that it was good and smiled at Jaynee. She smiled back and pushed the "fish-on-a-stick" into the sandy floor. She pulled at the closest tree limb and began to break off twigs to start a fire. When Toby stepped forward she waved him off. He realized that she considered it *her duty* to make the meal.

She pointed to the wood and then motioned for him to go and find some more. He furrowed his brow and tried to imagine a dry stick of wood anywhere in the forest after such a rain, but he left and scoured the nearby area. He decided to just get anything he could find and shouldered several limbs.

After some struggle with two twelve-foot limbs, he dragged them into the cave. Jaynee looked up and gave him another of those great smiles and motioned for him to put the wood on the other side of the cave. The evening sun was fading, but the fire lit up the cave with a warm glow. Jaynee had the fish cooking by the fire and the flickering light danced on the rocks. Suddenly Toby realized that the wood he brought in was for others to use—and that visitors always left dry wood for the cave's next occupants.

They warmed themselves by the fire and steam rose from their clothing. When the fish was cooked, she offered a side to him. Toby accepted it and sat cross-legged to eat. So did she!

He turned away from her and continued to eat slowly. He wished they could talk; he missed talking to Gina (or in most cases listening). Finally, when he finished eating he nodded and rubbed his stomach. "Thank you, Jaynee." He smiled.

"Good," she replied.

Toby was shocked at her reply. He stood and walked over to her. "Good?" he said.

"Good...." she said again, smiling at him.

"You can speak?"

"Good?" she said again. He realized that it was probably the only word she had picked up from Gina. Then he realized that she had probably picked it up from him, as he was always saying "That's good."

Jaynee pulled the hot rocks from the fire with another stick and buried them in the sand as he'd seen her do another time. Then she went outside and came back several minutes later. She drug one of the limbs he'd brought in closer to the fire, took off her tunic, and hung it to dry. Then she lay down on the hot sand and turned towards the fire.

Toby repeated the same motions of going outside the cave to relieve himself and returning to strip and hang his own clothes up beside hers. He lay down behind her, watching the fire's light dancing on the cave walls.

Without turning to him she asked again, "Good?"

Toby nuzzled her neck and said, "Very good!"

They parted only twice during the night, and Toby woke with the mosquitoes biting on his butt. By the time he was dressed he was still scratching it vigorously. Jaynee laughed at him as he scratched and said to her, "Not Good! NOT good!"

They walked the rest of the morning and Toby spent most of the time thinking about how two women could do things so differently…. He was glad to know the differences, and wondered where all this was going to lead.

As they rounded another curve in the river they saw one of the barges tied up to the shoreline! There didn't seem to be anybody else around, though. Toby was so excited as he hurried to the shore ahead that he didn't notice the sad look on Jaynee's face as she followed him…

◊ ◊ ◊

2-5

~another passenger~

Toby was first to reach the barge and pulled hard on the heavy towrope that secured it to a rock on shore. He managed to pull it in far enough to wade out to it and crawl aboard. He saw a note tied to the rudder arm and wiped his hands on his dry shirt before he picked it up to read. Some scrawled words were smeared from the rain, but he managed to read Ella's handwriting:

Toby, everyone is fine, we had to go ahead.
Will be waiting down stream about 2 miles.
I know you can bring the barge with Jaynee's help.
Gina misses you.

Ella.

Toby smiled at the note and looked at Jaynee climbing onto the barge. He took her hand to help her up and showed her the note. "They're ok," he said, smiling broadly. "It's all GOOD!"

"Good," Jaynee said without much enthusiasm and then walked to the front of the barge. Toby watched her go and wondered what was wrong. She was so happy this morning, and now this. He pulled in the towrope and coiled it onto the floor of the barge.

He wagged the rudder several times and the barge moved a tiny bit. He had it moving after several more tries and guided it into the flow of the river. They began to move downstream at a leisurely pace.

Jaynee sat on the front of the barge and dangled her feet in the water. She didn't turn around to look at Toby until he whistled to her an hour later. His stomach was growling. She reluctantly stood up and came to the rear of the barge, looking at him without any emotion. He patted his stomach and pointed to hers. She shrugged and went to the goods stored under the canvases. She pulled back the tarp and then froze with her arm in midair. Toby saw that something was wrong and let go of the rudder to go to her side.

He stopped short when saw the huge snake sitting on top of the barrel—coiled and ready to strike! It must have crawled up under the tarp to soak up the warmth and was now startled. Toby stepped back and looked across the deck. He wished for his whip. He was frantic; he looked all over the deck but found nothing he could use as a weapon. He knew that the others had probably left him something, maybe a rifle—or an axe!—but everything was under other tarps and he wasn't going to lift any!

The heavy towrope was his only option. Toby picked it up and left about three feet dangling from his hand as he stepped forward. He saw Jaynee's hand drooping from the weight of the heavy tarp and knew her arm was getting tired…. He had to move fast! But what would he do?

He started to swing the rope in a circle above his head and moved towards the snake. "I never want to see another snake!" he murmured through clenched teeth. He tried to think through the snake's possible moves and which way Jaynee would have to move to get away. *But what would the snake do?* He would have to make the first strike do the trick. He realized that Jaynee had no idea what was about to happen when the rope's movements caught the snake's attention. It turned its head towards the swinging rope and Toby moved around so that Jaynee could see him.

In just another step Toby drew the full attention of the snake away from the stoic girl and she slammed the tarp onto the snake's head. It wiggled and thrashed around. Jaynee had it by the body, gripping it tightly. Toby reached the snake and whopped it with the heavy rope. It continued to move and Jaynee seemed to be losing her grip on it! Toby moved to strike it again but the snake whipped itself loose.

Jaynee leapt back; she grabbed her hand and squealed. She jumped on top of another pile of stored goods and Toby followed her. He saw the large puncture marks and blood on her hand! Toby turned towards the snake and saw it drop onto the deck, slither to the edge of the barge, and disappear into the river.

Toby felt another snake below the canvas and pointed out its outline to Jaynee. She nodded with tears in her eyes. Toby wished this snake would just crawl away too, but he knew there wasn't much hope for that at this point. He knew he had to deal with this snake first before figuring out what to do with Jaynee.

He decided that the snake probably couldn't bite them through the canvas unless it was bunched up and it was lucky. But, he wondered, *how many more are there*? Toby took the knife from Jaynee's waist and stabbed the snake. After several minutes of thrashing around it was still. Toby took Jaynee to the back of the barge and sat her on the small barrel so he could look at her hand.

He tried to remember what Gina had told him about Lew's story of cutting open a snake bite and sucking out the poison. He steeled himself against the idea of doing this to Jaynee when she fell off the barrel and passed out on the deck.

Toby grabbed her hand and turned it towards him, thinking of how the poison was working its way into her. He did what he thought he remembered and made a deep diagonal cut into the bite mark and then another across it. He repeated the pattern on the other puncture and had two neatly cut, bleeding X's.

He put the webbed part of her hand into his mouth and sucked as hard as he could. When he felt something burning his tongue, he spat out the blood and poison and then sucked again. He kept it up until his mouth hurt and the wound wasn't bleeding anymore. Toby was shaking all over and sat down on the barrel for a quick rest, still watching the area for more snakes.

He decided the best thing was to find the others as soon as possible, so he used the rudder to put them back into the middle of the river. He kept one eye on the river and one on Jaynee. When her hand started to bleed again he cut the bottom of his pant leg to make a bandage. Her skin felt cold. He decided to take a chance with a tarp and cover her up. He whipped off the tarp, ready to throw it back if he had to. But when he saw that it was safe, he covered Jaynee with it and hoped she was sleeping comfortably.

Toby watched the river change color in the late afternoon light. When he felt that they had gone the two miles, he hoped he'd see the others soon, but there was still another expanse of empty river ahead.

Now, all Toby could do was sit and wait. He steered the barge into the center of the river's current. He noticed that the watermark on the rocks was receding and nearly a foot of foam-like markings were left drying in the air. He was getting closer now to the next turn in the river and became impatient at the wait. He wanted to see what was ahead…

◊ ◊ ◊

2-6

~a river of thoughts~

The river journey was a bundle of mixed emotions for Toby, and his mind raced from one thought to another. He continued to keep one eye on Jaynee and the other on the river's course.

Jaynee was delirious from the snake bite and threw up twice in the first hour. When she woke up, Toby brought her water, which she drank greedily. Her hair was matted and had lost its usual shine; it was greasy from the sweat that covered her from head to toe. She managed to keep her eyes on Toby for a few seconds at a time between lapsing into short fits of restless sleep.

But those periods of sleep erupted into wakefulness and dry heaving. Toby had nothing else to give her and thought it odd that the others hadn't left some food. He wondered if it was somewhere that he hadn't looked, but he wasn't too crazy about looking under any more tarps just now.

When Jaynee settled into some more restful sleep, Toby began to feel the weariness in his own body; he hadn't had a full night's rest since they'd left the sandbar. His thoughts eventually left him considering all that he had yet to face. He'd lost the cart, Bea, *and* the money! What was he going to do to repay it? He wouldn't have anything to give to his mother and sisters. He wondered how long it would take to repay everything he'd lost. Plus, Mr. Rodgers had promised to give his pay to Toby's family while Toby was away. How would he work off *that* debt?

Now Toby was starting to feel "a lot sick" himself from the stress of it all. Jaynee rolled out from under the tarp and lie on the deck. Toby figured she was just too warm and let her sleep. His mind kept turning his own problems over and over: *This isn't fair! How can I work off all these debts and keep my family fed? And NOW I have to worry about Gina, Jaynee, and Robin, too! It's not fair!*

Toby hung over the rudder and stared into the water. He couldn't sink the feeling of what was bothering him. None of it was really his fault, but at face value it did seem to be his responsibility to make things right. He knew he simply couldn't afford to ignore their needs. Everybody around him was looking to him to be "the man" and make it all work out. But still....

He wondered what kind of money Ella and Ernie would pay him and if it would come close to being enough to repay everything else. There didn't seem to be any way to resolve all that troubled him.

Another turn in the river and still no sight of the others, which added to his sinking feeling. *Where is everybody?*, Toby wondered. The banks of the river hadn't changed; they were still very steep, climbing up several hundred feet on both sides, and really didn't afford a place to land the other barges. The river had slowed down now and was no longer as swollen or rapid as it had been from the heavy rains. Toby liked being back on the barge and thought: *If Jaynee hadn't been bitten, today would have been quite nice—actually!*

His eyes flashed from the river's downstream glitter to the green of the hillsides. *What if Jaynee and I just went ashore and traveled the country? I wouldn't have to face anybody and wouldn't have to work—forever!—to pay back the debt.*

Thinking this way just caused him to slump deeper into the gloom of his situation. He couldn't leave it all; he still had his sense of fairness and what his father had taught him of right and wrong. He sighed deeply and absentmindedly pulled on the rudder to bring them back into the center of the river. His thoughts had taken him from the duty at hand and the barge was too far to the left, nearing the shallows.

A loud noise fully woke him to reality. The front of the barge was hooked on something. It took a moment before it started to swing around. Before Toby could catch things with the rudder, he was turned around and the barge was backing itself down the river! He pushed hard to his right and realized that was the wrong way! He was back in midstream and wondered if it wouldn't be just as well to let it go that way.

After about half an hour of standing half-turned around, he decided it wasn't a good idea and pulled hard on the rudder. Then he noticed that the river made a sharp turn up ahead.

No!, he thought. *This isn't a good place to try to turn!* He pushed again and managed to get the barge turned, still backing itself downriver. Jaynee was coughing, holding her side with her good hand…. A moment later she threw up again. Toby wanted to help her—get her some water to rinse out her mouth and to put on her forehead. But he was just "a heap busy" at the moment!

He steered the craft as best he could, watching as both sides of the river narrowed and the current picked up speed. The horseshoe shape of the river's curve was probably nothing to seasoned boatmen, but it was a tough situation for Toby as he worried about Jaynee *and* about steering backward.

His fear and temper were just about reaching their limits when he heard someone whistle! Toby swiveled his head to the far shore and saw the others! Gina stood on the flat land about ten feet above the water level and waved to him.

His relief quickly turned to anger again and Toby wondered, *NOW WHAT?! How the hell am I going to toss the anchor, steer this barge, and not step in the puke on the deck? Damn it!* His anger was definitely steaming to a head now.

Gina had seen all the trouble and called to the others. But when they ran to her side, Toby saw them laughing at his predicament and that just made him angrier! He pushed hard on the rudder and felt the barge turning slowly around. The shoreline closed in rapidly and he reset the rudder to the opposite side and pushed again. The barge came around quickly—all at once! Then in a perfect sweep, the lumbering, floating mass aligned itself just right with the other barges, slipped between them, and locked into place!

Pete jumped from his barge onto Toby's and tied it off. He clasped a hand on his shoulder and said, "Great landing, Tob'!" Then he saw Jaynee lying on the deck and rushed over to her. "When did she get bit!?!" Pete asked. As Toby filled him in, the others arrived and listened with concern. Pete lifted Jaynee and they all started for the campsite. Gina tried to hold Toby's arm, but he ripped it away and walked off in a different direction…

◊ ◊ ◊

2-7

~a faithful friend~

Gina followed Toby at a distance and didn't say a word. When he found a fallen log, he sat down. The dog was at Toby's side instantly, with its head in his lap. Without thinking, Toby stroked its head and looked back at the river. His eyes went to the campsite and he saw what a nice camp the others had made. They'd tied tarps to trees as tents, a nice fire burned, and a cooking pot steamed. Toby thought of how hungry—and how tired!—he was.

In a soft tone, Gina asked, "Toby?"

"Not now…. I just want left alone!"

"We could talk…."

"NOT NOW!" The dog shrank back when Toby raised his voice, but he continued to stroke its head and stare at the sun shimmering on the river. Gina started to say something again but backed away and returned to the camp when he gave her a sharp look.

The dog tired of the petting and lay down at Toby's feet. Toby was peeling bark from a small twig with his teeth and spitting out the pieces to the ground when Pete and Ernie approached.

"That was one fine piece of navigation you did, Toby! And Jaynee is going to be fine. Her hand will be useless for a week, but it should work ok—in time," Ernie said.

Toby just nodded and continued chewing on the twig. He didn't look at the men. His anger had subsided, but his mind was made up.

Finally, he looked up and saw Gina approaching just as he began to speak: "I can't do this! I've had it! *Every day* is a struggle for life and death! I'm tired of snakes, mountain lions, KILLING!...” He looked directly at Gina and then back to the ground. “…and I just want to go home. I want to go home *every night*! I want to see my family! I want to walk the streets of the city and watch the people doing the things they do…. I want to sit on the porch and, and—COUGH!” He smiled at the ridiculousness of what he’d just said as he continued to stare at the ground, glassy-eyed. “Yeah, I want to *cough* from the smoke—I *miss* the smoke!” He tossed the well-chewed twig onto the ground and startled the dog, which walked over to the twig and began sniffing at it.

“Toby, you’re tired, and you’ve done more than anybody should have to do; but you DID it, and you should be proud!” Ernie spoke in a quiet, firm voice. “Toby, *you saved Jaynee’s life*….”

“…She told us what you did,” Gina chimed in hesitantly. “And *Toby*, it did save her life!”

“That’s my point: I don’t want to do this!” Toby looked back up at the three of them and tried to make it clear how adamantly he felt about this. “I’m not cut out to be…THIS! Whatever this is! What if I’d not been able to save her, what if she’d died? I can’t live with THAT! Don’t you understand? This life isn’t mine.” Toby broke off another twig and fondled it as he continued. “It’s too serious. One mistake and people can die!” He shook his head and looked away.

Ernie put his hand on Toby’s shoulder and squeezed it as he stood up, looking at Pete and tilting a subtle nod back towards camp. Pete gave Toby a nod and followed Ernie. Gina watched as the others left and then turned to Toby and knelt down at his feet. She said nothing and sat as quietly as the dog.

Toby ignored Gina. He silently poked holes in the soft soil with another short stick and glanced from the river to the sky and back to the ground. He hadn’t looked at Gina at all, and he had no desire to, as it might soften his resolve.

“Toby…I….I want to say something.”

He cut her off and said, “*Not now*, Gina, I need to just think this out….”

Gina left without saying anything but returned shortly and handed Toby a bowl of stew. He didn’t accept it right away, and then let it sit in his lap for a few minutes until she left again.

When it was just him and the dog, he started to eat slowly, but he soon found he was scraping the bottom of the bowl and looked to the campfire for more…. Slowly he rose and walked to the camp, where the women smiled and greeted him. Jaynee was sitting up with a bowl on her lap. Her dark brown eyes studied Toby. She almost seemed to be back to normal, but he could tell she was still weak.

Gina stood across the fire from them, her arms crossed over her chest. She watched the look on Jaynee's face and then slid her gaze to Toby. Finally, she turned and walked to the river's edge.

The men and women chatted about the rest of the trip back to the city. Robin, who had been sitting beside her sister and quietly playing with the dog, stood and walked over to Toby. She put her arm around his neck and kissed his cheek. He looked at her and couldn't help himself; he smiled and gave her a hug. He tickled her tummy. As she giggled, Toby blew a raspberry on her neck.

His resolve was beginning to melt…

◊ ◊ ◊

2-8

~a partial answer~

Toby took another bowl of stew, some bread, and the ever-present (and ever-hungry) dog and returned to the edge of the water. The day was spectacular, despite his mood. The afternoon sky was perfectly blue and cloudless. Toby ate quietly, softening the hard bread in the stew's gravy. Even then, he still had to chew at it for awhile to swallow it. He stared at the river, noticing that he could only see the bottom about a foot from the bank as the muddy water hadn't cleared yet. He saw a crawfish moving along and thought of the ones he ate earlier on this trip. *They weren't so bad*, he thought. *I'd eat 'em again.* He smiled as he thought about the exploding pot and how he'd chased the crawfish around the field....

As he finished the last of the stew, he soaked a heel of bread in the sauce and tossed it to the dog. In one quick slurp the dog caught and swallowed it. With a wag of its tail and a shift from one paw to the next, the dog waited for another treat. Toby smiled and said, "I don't even know your name, you mangy cur...." He reached out and curled a finger under the dog's chin. Its fur was wet and sticky with slobber. The dog seemed to love Toby's affection as much as he loved the food! "You don't ask for much, do ya?" Toby said. He thought about how easy it was to make the dog happy and how it seemed to be content with whatever circumstances came along. It reminded Toby of Bea. This critter made such a small demand of him, and yet made such a large contribution to them all. Something suddenly occurred to Toby: why was he fighting the events of the trip? What about "the acceptance of events" that he had admired in Bea and now in the dog?

"Toby." It was Gina's voice. "Toby, I *have* to talk to you—before we go any further. You have to know some things and I want to tell you while we're alone." She took a seat on the ground near him, her body turned slightly towards the river. "Some of this we talked about before, but so much else has happened since then.... I...I jus' want it all out in the open. I know you're thinkin' some things over right now and I think it's important for you to know all there is to know....

"When we left Lucca's farm—it's true: I did want to go to find Luke." Toby turned to the river and watched it flowing past. Gina knew that Luke wasn't a subject Toby wanted to hear about again, but she went on. "But he wasn't the only reason I wanted to leave there. Toby, I *had* to get away from that horrible place! I had to get away from Lew and Lucca, the beatings and the 'other stuff.' I would have—no!—*should have* walked away before you came to the farm. So when I found out you were goin' to the Landing, I knew it was my chance.

"I know now it wasn't love with Luke—it's just he was the only other man I knew near my age.... Toby, I would've been a prisoner with him, too." She paused for a moment and cleared her throat. "Ella called it 'in-fat-shoo-a-shun' and I think she was right, even though I never understood it before. It all changed after being with you for jus' a couple o' days. Maybe when we.... When I did that 'snake-squat' and you helped me.... I don't know.... The nights we spent together were somethin' different for me. Different than what I knew before. Tender. Everythin' before that was jus' rough farm hands."

She turned and looked over at the others before she continued. "I was like Jaynee and Robin, taught the same way they were, that I wasn't worth anything. I jus' didn't know any different. But you taught me that truth and honesty is better when you share it with others. And that damn honor code you live by...."

Toby turned and studied her face, waiting for her to continue. "That way of 'keeping your word' to others was somethin' different than jus' tellin' the truth. And not walkin' away when things got too hard...."

Gina was now petting the dog as she spoke. "I know you wouldn't hurt someone just for the fun of it—and *that* was somethin' new to me! You don't understand that. I never had that before; I was too young when I was with me mum and then she turned hard after my brother died....

"And I trus' you with my life, Toby. You saved me—mor'n once! So how could I not trust you now? You saved me from…that life on the farm, from Lew and Lucca—and from Luke, too. And there was the snake, and then the mountain lion. That was the bravest thing I ever saw! You jumped in front of me to save me…. You're the bravest man I ever knew!"

Toby felt embarrassed and kept his eyes on the river. It was a moment before Gina spoke again. "I know that you felt sure that your mum would take us in when we get to your family, but it's a lot to ask! The girls and me…. And we're not gonna exactly fit in, well, maybe not at first…. Anyway, I want your promise on somethin', okay?"

There was a pause before he looked at her and she silently waited for him to reply.

"You have to promise, if for ANY reason you don't want me—I mean us," she said, glancing at the girls. "You HAVE to tell me. Promise me this! We might not be able to fit in, and the girls might not take to the city…."

Toby studied her face for a moment and without an answer he returned to studying the river. He wanted to tell her about the night with Jaynee, to tell her that he never expected it to happen, and that he probably wouldn't have lived through the night if it hadn't been for her. But the more he thought about it, the more uneasy it made him. He turned to Gina, but she didn't seem disturbed at the pause and continued talking.

"I will ALWAYS try my best, and the girls will too—or I'll beat 'em!" She erupted with a laugh. He smiled and waited. "Ella promised to teach us some manners and the ways of girls in the city. How we should act—for you! An' I love the way she and Ernie get along. I…. They are so much in love—so much alike!" Toby slowly nodded in agreement. He chewed the inside of his lower lip and gazed into the ripples of the water where he spied the crawfish again.

"…You have to swear this to me," Gina went on. "It's *that* important…. I know you don't want to ever leave the city again, and go back to livin' the way we have. The cold and hunger, I didn't mind it so much! I could do it again, but not without you!" There was another long pause. She was obviously getting worked up (as she was petting the dog hard enough to rub the fur off of its back). "I jus' couldn't stand the quiet like the three days you didn't talk to me, near Alum Rock. We were lost—and hungry. It was all so awful! And I had my curse upon me…."

Toby considered the phrase but still didn't understand it. He remembered hearing his mother and sister talking about it once, but they got quiet when he walked into the kitchen. He just continued nodding as Gina continued talking.

"Oh! I just need to quit worryin' about how it all might go...." She wrung her hands together, chewed her lip, and squirmed in her seat on the ground. "Toby, I only know that you are the only man I will ever love! Even if I.... If we part, I just won't love anybody ever again...." Her confidence was wilting and she was getting nervous waiting for him to reply. She began to dread his response and drew a deep breath as she waited.

Toby finally spoke. "Gina, I have nothing. I have LESS than nothing, 'cause I owe them for a cart, the whiskey still, and a mule—I mean *Bea*!" (He was determined never to forget her name!) "...and I have no idea of how long it might take to pay back the debt...." He trailed off and shrugged. He picked up a small stone and tossed it at the crawfish, which stood up, underwater, and held it's pinchers towards the tiny rock as it settled to the bottom

"But Toby, I have even less than that! Don't you understand?"

He nodded, but didn't say anything.

"I'm not worried, I know *exactly* what I'm gonna do...."

Just then, the dog woke from its daze, looked behind them and wagged its tail. Ernie nodded to Gina as an apology for the interruption and spoke to Toby. "Pete and I have been watchin' the river and figgur that the water will start droppin' fast. We figgur that the river is runnin' at a fast walk—and at that speed we could start tonight and be in the city by noon tomorrow!" Ernie smiled at them and added, "Ella and the others, well, we got a lot of business to do, and we want to get there as quick as we can. Besides, if we don't take this high water we might have some hard travel near the Ford as it gets pretty shallow. We got our lights and the near-full moon to make the river—before she drops.... When that river drops, it could take *two* days to make it."

Ernie smiled again and said, "We better eat the last of that stew before we go...." He was already several strides ahead of them, but Toby quickly caught up and plied him with questions. Gina walked behind them, listening and wishing she had answers, too.

(The mutt followed them and its nose to the smell of the stew...)

◊ ◊ ◊

2-9

~fast food and a forest of chimneys~

Toby noticed the shrug that Gina gave Ella as they were standing near the fire and mopping up the last of the stew. He smiled at Jaynee, who was learning to eat with one hand. The other, bandaged, was too tender to touch. Gina hovered over her and offered help, but Jaynee refused.

Toby sat with his new appendages—the dog and Robin—at his side. Both of them were eating big helpings of the stew, and Toby tried to imagine where Robin could put all that food. He shared an occasional smile with her and winked at Jaynee when no one was watching. Quietly, she smiled back and put away another spoonful of stew.

The adults finished eating while Toby and Gina went to the river's edge and quickly packed away everything they'd brought ashore. They rigged the lights on poles cut from small trees and fastened them to the front of the barges. When all this was done and Pete was satisfied his barge was ready, he and Eula went aboard and waited on the others.

Ernie and Ella had their barge ready next. Now everyone was waiting on Toby and Gina, as they were the last ones to get settled in with their crew. Finally, when all was ready, they hoisted the anchors and Ernie began fishtailing the rudder to move them to the center of the river. Toby duplicated the motion and looked back to Pete and watched him moving his barge the same way.

It wasn't long before Toby felt the current of the river and the uneven pulling of the ropes connecting the three barges. Soon, the ropes evened out and the barges moved along silently. Pete began singing a song, and before long Eula, Ernie, and Ella joined in. Toby didn't recognize it, but he hummed along and repeated phrases as he learned them.

Darkness slipped in before he realized it. His eyes had gradually adjusted to the fading light until it was nearly pitch black, just before the moon rose to shine down on the river. Each crew lit their barge lanterns and the night was warm and dreamy. Soon stars began to emerge and Toby allowed himself to relax and enjoy the river night.

From behind him, he heard Pete whistling softly. Toby knew this tune and hummed along. The air filled with the choruses of insects, birds, and other wildlife, making it seem as if they, too, were singing. Gina sat with the dog and Robin, each of them with their heads on her lap. Toby couldn't see Jaynee in the darkness, but he knew she was seated against some of the cargo, facing him. He knew she was awake and that she was watching him. (It was more that he could *feel* it rather than *see* it). Toby wondered if she would be as talkative as Gina when she learned the language. He knew Robin would be a "yacker" given the way she and Gina carried on, but that didn't bother him.

God, the river's nice!, Toby thought. He wondered what it would be like to manage a steamboat on the river. *Could I do it with this crew?* He thought about the girls as workers. They worked harder than most men he knew. They didn't mind the steady pace that it took to load a barge, and their only limits were the strength required for heavy work—and that "curse" thing that Gina had mentioned, which Toby hadn't quite figured out.

When the girls fell asleep, Gina came to sit on a barrel beside Toby. The night air grew colder and Toby shivered. Gina noticed and got up so she could hug him from behind. He felt her warm chest pressing into his back and realized he was getting warmer—rather quickly! When Gina started to say something, he cut her off with a "Shhh!…" She took the hint and kept quiet the rest of the night. When it was near dawn, Gina went back to the lump on the floor of the barge. A tangle of legs (four with fur and four without) protruded from under a tarp. She crawled in to join them.

Toby rubbed his arms and swung them from side to side to stay warm. He noticed that one of the lanterns was just about out and that the other was getting dim, but it was the same on both of the other barges. It was, as Toby guessed, the darkness before the dawn. Just as the lanterns faded out all together, the dawn broke over their left shoulders. When it was light enough to see the others and the shoreline on both sides, Toby saw that they were perfectly centered in the river. Ernie stood on the front barge, giving his full attention to the river ahead.

They were making a broad swing around another curve and were still making good time. Toby watched the riverbanks and tried to estimate the speed they were making by picking two spots on the bank and counting how long it took to get from one to the other. He figured their speed to be eight miles per hour and wondered how far it was to home. Would he go first to the shop, or to his house? He really wanted to see his family and spend time with them, but he knew if he started telling them about his adventure(s)—well, it would take all day! He thought about their responses to his stories and smiled. Oh, and his mother's cooking! She would feed him to no end!

The morning sun rose higher in the sky and the girls began to stir under the tarp. The dog was up and seated beside Toby. He could feel it looking at him for more food. Damn! And that didn't account for the others being hungry, too! Toby thought again of how difficult it would be to get by with all of them relying on him.

Ahead, Ernie was pulling on the rudder/oar and drifting the barge towards the right-hand shoreline. Toby watched his movements and imitated the drifting. They were within ten feet of the bank when Toby heard Pete's anchor splash into the water. Toby threw his in next and Ernie dropped the last one. All seemed to find a hold into the river's bottom and the barges stopped.

Ernie and Pete jumped into the thigh-high water and waded ashore. They walked into the thick brush along the river's bank and reappeared a few moments later to sit along the shore. Ella, Eula, and Gina (who was carrying little Robin) were next to wade ashore and disappear into the brush. But while the other women were in the brush, Jaynee rose and squatted over the river-side of the barge. Toby was embarrassed and turned away. He began to wonder if she might do that in the middle of a street, *in the city*—at some time *not* as convenient as this!

When she finished her business, she moved down the side of the barge and rinsed her unbandaged hand and face in the river's water. She cupped her hand and drew it to her to drink. She made a funny face, spit out the water, and shot Toby a look of distaste. He smiled and wondered how she could taste a difference in the water so easily. Was it the taste of smoke in the water, even this far from town?

The others waited for him to go ashore and find a spot suitable to relieve himself. By the time he returned to the riverbank everyone had already gotten back on their barges and was looking at him.

"Let's get a move on Toby, your momma's waitin'!" Ernie shouted to him.

Toby waved and shouted back, "NOT NEARLY AS LONG AS I HAVE!"

He pulled himself up onto the barge and lifted the rope to the anchor.

It wasn't too long until he heard Ernie and Ella talking in surprised voices. They'd gone maybe two more miles and were just rounding another curve in the river. Toby thought he recognized the hills across the river and knew they were getting close to Pittsburgh. He strained to hear what Ernie and Ella were so worked up about. They kept leaning over to see around the bend in the river.

Several very long moments passed as his barge drifted to the spot where their concerns had started. Then Toby saw it!

It wasn't right! He squinted and tried to make out something he could recognize in the skyline. Nothing made sense. His gaze drifted from one area to another and then back to Ernie and Ella. By then Pete and Eula were also standing, transfixed by what they saw. Everyone had stopped fishtailing the rudders. Nobody said a word as they drifted slowly ahead.

It looked like a dead forest! Where Toby expected to see whole buildings, there were only walls of brick—and freestanding stone chimneys. It was like this in the entire city! Everything was burned beyond belief! As they moved closer, Toby realized that the bridge had burned away, leaving only its stone bases. Other boats were drifting along the river. Most seemed to be there with a purpose, as their workers moved along the decks. People were also visible on-shore, working along the streets and building areas. Some of the buildings had been used to support tent-like hovels to shelter people. Clothing was hung on ropes, and some people just sat on the rubble. It reminded Toby of the people back at Parker's Landing. He thought about the fires Ella had told him about and how the people were left with nothing! *Left with nothing*, Toby thought. *Much like me!*

Gina and the girls also stared at the burnt city in shock. They hadn't seen Pittsburgh before, but this was obviously not what they were expecting. They glanced between Toby and the horror of the sights onshore. They all turned quickly when Ernie gave a sharp whistle. He waved them to the shore and pointed to a clearing along the bank. Toby landed the barge against the bank with such precision that everyone looked at him in surprise. Pete deftly guided his barge in beside Toby.

They tied up the barges and ran a shore-rope to a heavy stump. Still, no one spoke as they looked up the bank towards the devastation. About fifty feet downstream, an old man with a fishing pole sat with his feet soaking in the river. Wordlessly, the group made their way to him and greeted him respectfully.

He was slow to respond. When Ernie asked him what happened to the city, the man finally looked at each of the others, one at a time…

◊ ◊ ◊

2-10

~a tale of two cities~

Ernie asked about the city again, but the man was still surveying the group. All the while, he continued to rinse out one of his socks and wring it dry before carefully hanging it over his boot. He didn't speak until he'd looked over the adults, then Toby and Gina, and finally Jaynee and Robin. He studied the Indian girls at great length before saying, "You bunch look a little travel worn. Guess you don't know about what's happened."

"We don't," Ernie said. "We just got here on the barges...." He nodded his head towards the rafts. "We came in from the north. What happened?"

The old man turned and looked back at the city. "Burned...."

"I can SEE that. When did it happen? Why? How did it start? Were you here?"

"Too many questions...." The old man shook water out of his last sock and hung it over his other boot. "Damn straight I was here! Helped as much as I could—we all did! People runnin' all around, couldn't see for all the smoke, and it all went up in *five hours*! ALL GONE—in five hours! Some washwoman, she had a fire goin', washin' up folks' clothes, an' the wind kicked it up. It ain't rained an' everythin' was tinder-dry an' jus' ready to burn.... We helped each other loadin' and carryin', but it just went too fast!"

The man shook his head and pulled his feet from the river. He wiped the water from them and wiggled his toes. "ONLY ONE DEAD!" he said loudly, looking at the women again. "Heart gave out, I figgur." He shook the water from his hands and rubbed his face. Then he took out a scarf and began wiping the dirt from his face and neck. He stopped and looked again at Jaynee and Robin. He squinted his eyes, studied them, and then turned to Ernie and said,

"Injins?"

Ernie nodded and asked, "Do you know of the market district?"

"Gone...."

Ella spoke over Ernie's next question, "Fourth Street? To the Liberty...."

"All gone!"

Ella looked devastated and for the first time the man realized that she and her group had been affected by the fire, too. He changed his tune to a more respectful tone. "Sorry ma'am! Sorry folks...."

Toby leaned around Gina and asked, "But, when did all this hap—"

"April tenth—Thursday! Round about noon. They figgur the loss at over TWELVE MILLION! And—was over a thousand buildings—gone! Them folks didn't have time to get any of their belongin's! SHAME it was!" The man rolled his head around on his shoulders as if to pull out some stiffness. "Shame it was...started on Ferry and Front Streets...."

That's only half a block from my shop, Toby thought, slack-jawed. He looked wide-eyed at Gina, but spoke to the man. "Sir? Nothing is left in that area?"

"Boy, look around—there's NOTHIN'! It's all gone! Keer over to da Mon'," he said, motioning towards the Monongahela River.

"How 'bout the South Side?" Pete asked as he held Eula's shaking hand.

"Most of it's ok, but the bridge burnt...."

The adults look at each other in disbelief. "Burned completely?"

"GONE!" The old man was getting tired of the questions and wanted to be left alone. "...Went up in ten minutes. A lot o' folk hadta leave their stuff right there and run ahead o' the fire!" He looked up and down the river before he continued. "You got supplies on them barges?"

Ernie nodded, looking at the others and then towards their parked barges.

"I'd guard 'em if I was you folk; there are still a lot of folk in need, an' a lot of people lookin' for anythin' to steal....mostly punks!"

Toby immediately thought of the boy who had attacked him before he and Lew had left the city. He tried to remember what date they'd started out. *The fire was on April 10, the man said,* Toby thought. *We must've left close to then, maybe within a day or two....* His thoughts were interrupted when Ernie spoke.

"Pete, can you and Eula back off with the barges and get anchored in the river?"

Pete nodded slowly, staring at the ground, thinking it through. "...Ain't gonna get that dinner you promised us—for awhile, anyway...." He smiled, turned, and made his way back to the barges.

Ernie added one more thing: "Get all three guns loaded and keep them on your barge...."

Pete waved his arm without turning. Eula gave one last look over her shoulder and then followed her husband.

"Toby, get yourself—and Gina—over to your family's house and see how things are. The girls will come with us...." Ernie thought for a second and then added, "No, you better take them along, too."

Toby nodded and started up the cluttered bank. Gina curled a finger towards Jaynee and Robin, motioning them to follow. The dog clambered through piles of debris, sniffing at everything.

"Meet us back here as quick as you can!" Ernie yelled to them. Toby heard Ernie shout something else to Pete, but he didn't stop to listen. He wanted to get to his mother's house as fast as he could. He knew the others would follow him and easily keep pace if he ran, but he was somewhat comforted in knowing that only one person had died. So he thought it best to make a fast walk of it.

They picked their way through paths of fallen bricks and piles of useless debris. The bricks that had fallen from the walls had been sorted and were ready for use in new buildings. Toby's stomach growled, and he realized that the barge crew hadn't eaten since last night. He didn't have a cent on him, so he turned to Gina and asked, "You have any money?"

She reached into her only pocket and pulled out their last two coins: a nickel and a half-cent. He sighed and took them. They would buy a loaf of bread and some dried meat. He wondered if anyone was around to sell anything. He looked across the area and saw a woman carrying a large basket with a cloth over it.

Gina was entranced with the entire scene. She tried to imagine what had been here before the fire. *So many buildings!*, she pondered. Toby looked back at the girls when he remembered that they were barefoot. There were a lot of sharp objects in the debris, but the girls seemed unconcerned. He'd noticed before how tough their feet were, but he just wasn't sure about them walking around the city with it like this....

All around them, brick layers perched on scaffolding, and their helpers tended them. Younger men carried hods loaded with bricks and mortar up planks to the masons. Some of the men hooted at the girls, and Toby scowled at the men for their ignorant comments towards "his crew."

As they approached a crowded area, Toby noticed two men running across the scaffolding. Just as he looked up, they jumped down and landed in front of Toby and the girls. It took a moment for Toby to recognize the leader with a purple scar across his cheek—just where Toby had left it! Toby reached behind his back and pulled the whip from his waistband, but he didn't show it. Gina reacted in a split second, reading Toby's mind. They stopped and warily waited for the others to act.

"SO! He returns—and with a pack of *girls*!" the cocky leader announced. "...And what are those two?" He motioned at the Indian girls.

"They're people you don't want to mess with!" snarled Toby. His fingers curled tightly around the whip handle. The other kid stood behind his leader. He seemed to lack courage, but grinned at them. Gina stepped to Toby's side and looked defiant. Her stance showed her fearless strength as she gazed at the two boys.

"Maybe you need another lesson—a mark to match the one you earned down the street!" Toby let the whip unfurl from his hand and the coils dropped to the ground by his feet.

The scarred boy's eyes widened and he stepped back. "You still gotta answer for that!"

"Sure, I'll answer for it. Whaddaya askin'?" Toby flipped the whip out without taking his eyes from the older boy's face. Gina curled her finger on her thigh, pulling up her dress to reveal the knife holder. The two boys gaped at her legs as she drew the knife from its sheath. She'd spent some time during the trip sharpening it on a stone, and its edge gleamed threateningly in the sun.

From the corner of his eye, Toby saw Jaynee step into the circle. The dog was at her side, letting out a deep-throated growl. Jaynee cradled several bricks in her wounded arm and hefted one in her good hand, ready to throw it.

Another boy in the opposing gang was still standing on the scaffolding, watching the scene below, but he backed away from the edge. He wasn't about to jump into the fight.

"Since you don't seem to have any questions, I guess we'll pass." Toby raised an eyebrow, and motioned for Gina to go. She still held the knife menacingly and walked past the boys without so much as a glance. Next went Jaynee, who dropped a brick near the leader's foot. He jumped back and said nothing. Robin followed, wiggling her butt and shooting the boys a look of defiance. Toby and the dog brought up the rear and they all continued the trip across town. Toby never looked back. He knew something inside him had changed. He smiled and spoke confidently to others on the street—always keeping an eye on his crew...

◊ ◊ ◊

2-11

~home and a family~

Toby and the girls crossed what was left of the city and ignored any more jeers and stares. A young girl, dressed rather poorly and carrying a wicker basket, walked ahead of them. Toby increased his pace and caught up with her. She turned around to look at him. Toby looked back in astonishment! He recognized her at once as the girl who worked in her parents' bakery, a shop he and his family had often visited.

Toby had his first crush on her, but she'd always ignored him. He remembered how nice she had always looked. His sisters called her a "Prima Donna" because she always acted like she was better than everyone else. The girls used to imitate her in the kitchen as they helped their mother cook, making prissy faces and pretending to be afraid to touch the food—giggling all the while.

Now she was filthy. Her fingernails were caked with dirt and her hair looked as dirty as the dark blue jumper she wore. Her eyes had a vacant look to them. Toby was shocked at her appearance and swallowed hard before speaking. He wondered why he'd been attracted to her before. Now, she was a blank looking young woman—with as little appeal to him as a woman could have. Toby realized how small she really was. Without her parents' store to strut around in, she was just another waif.

He looked at Gina and realized that she noticed his concern about the girl, so he winked at her and spoke to the girl. "Alicia? It's Toby! I see the fire...I mean, you...Uh, your folks' store burned?"

She looked at him dumbly, as if it was the first time she'd ever seen him, and simply nodded. She silently pulled back a corner of the basket's cloth and showed him the loaves of bread she had to offer. There was his favorite:

twisted rolls with sugar and cinnamon in them. He took eight and asked how much. She took the nickel and gave him a penny in return. Toby passed out the rolls and noticed a burnt one on the bottom. "Can I buy that one too?"

She looked at the one he pointed to and replied, "That one's my lunch…."

"It's for the dog, and you can eat one that isn't burned." He smiled, but she didn't seem to notice or care. She handed him the roll and glanced around. Without another word, she wandered over to some workers across the cleared way.

Toby watched her depart and munched on his roll. When he felt the eyes of the others on him, he led on. The dog had already wolfed down its roll and was now at Robin's elbow, its eyes fixed on the roll she was drooling over. They made it to the street where the Howard & Rodgers Company had been. Nothing much remained. Some metal and anvils were still standing where they'd been when Toby had left that morning—so long ago. They continued walking to the storefront anyway, and Toby described the area to Gina.

"…It was all shops. Here was the iron shop, and there—Fenlon's Livery Stable. Some leather shops—for harness making, and over here was where my father worked—where I worked." When they reached the front of the copperworks they saw a sign which read:

We will be rebuilding in this same area. If you wish to contact Mr. Rodgers please write care of Postmaster, Town Center of Pittsburgh.

Toby was quiet for some time, just taking it all in. A long wall of brick ran along the back of the site, and a kiln where they heat-treated the metals was still standing. He thought about all the men without work and with families to feed.

He heard a couple of men talking inside so he went to the doorway and peered beyond it. "Abe?" Toby called. He stepped inside and saw the old man tipping a charred timber out of the way. Another man was helping. "ABE!" Toby called louder and caught his attention. Abe looked at Toby for a long moment, smiled, and then ambled over to where Toby stood smiling back.

"My word...." Abe whispered as he studied Toby. "You're back!?! We didn't know what to think. We had word that Lew got into some trouble—that he killt someone in Butler! We figgur'd you'd been arrested. Mr. Rodgers was gonna send someone out to see what happened. But then there was the fire, and...." His voice trailed off with a sweep of his large "paw," indicating all the charred remains from the fire.

Toby didn't know the other man, but shook his hand and nodded to him. "Where's Mr. Rodgers? Is he safe? How bad is it—for him? And what of Mr. Howard?" Toby was firing off questions faster than Old Abe could answer. He held up another paw and stopped Toby.

"You been home?" Abe asked in a quiet voice full of concern.

Toby felt a pang of something that bothered him. It was the way that Abe had asked it. "What of my home?" He looked at Abe and the other man for answers, but they were quiet and their faces told him nothing.

"Go home, Toby. But—" here Abe gripped Toby's arm. "Stop back. I wanna hear it all...." Toby had a sense of dread, but simply nodded and turned to leave. Gina and the girls had stepped up behind him and he pushed past them, winding his way onto the street.

Toby took a long look at things and began to trot in the direction of his home. The girls matched his pace and the dog brought up the rear. Even as Toby ran faster, his crew kept up with him. They were all in tremendous shape, and had no problem making the distance in good time. To onlookers they looked like a pack of dogs on the trail of something. They ran a course across the city streets for awhile until Toby started to slow down again. Another half a city block and it was all the same. Just the blank stares of the burned out brick buildings looking back at them. Several families sat in makeshift shelters, squatters on their own property where their houses had been.

Toby suddenly stopped and went no further. He was standing in front of what was formerly his own house. There was nothing there to greet him except for the chimney, which was only half standing.

His shoulders dropped and he heaved to catch his breath. He realized that while he was gone his family had suffered as much as—if not more than—he had on his travels. *Where had they all gone?* He whipped around, looking for something to tell him; somebody to help him find an answer....

"Toby?" a voice said.

Toby spun around and saw a man that he vaguely recognized walking in his direction. He thought it was one of his old neighbors from a few houses down.

"Toby, sweet Lord! We thought you had died. Nobody knew anything of you! You look so well!" The man said hurriedly. "We all tried to find out...but with the fire and all...."

Toby nodded and hurriedly asked, "But what of them? Momma and my sisters?"

"They're fine!" the man said.

Toby relaxed a little. He realized he was shaking and tried to stand properly. He felt like he was going to topple over. Gina was beside him and put her hand under his arm, curling her fingers into the crook of his elbow as she listened to the man talk.

"They didn't have any work. As you can figgur, they had to go find somethin' to do for pay—like everybody else! Toby, they stayed on as long as they could. But they went to stay with your momma's sister, Madeline." The man sounded so sorry for Toby it was like he was apologizing.

Toby nodded, his eyes glazing over as he listened. "Didn't Mr. Rodgers pay them the money he was supposed to?"

"Course he did! But after a couple of weeks...after the fire, nobody had money.... The men weren't getting paid, and there was little food being brought into the city. It's just the wrong time of the year for crops, you know!"

Toby was still nodding. "...When did they finally leave?"

"Two weeks ago I 'spect. Took a boat down the Ohio to the town where your aunt is...."

Toby thanked the man profusely and backed away, still thinking about what had happened. He thanked the man again over his shoulder and started the long walk back to the barges. Back to his home...

◊ ◊ ◊

2-12

~left holding the bag~

Toby led the others through the debris-strewn streets and made a short-cut across town to the barges. He was about thirty feet ahead of the others and kicked at the dust as he walked along. Gina had fallen back to walk with the girls and decided to leave him with his thoughts.

Maybe I could borrow the rowboat and go downriver to see everybody. Ernie and Ella could spare it, Toby thought. *I could earn some money as I went; sleep in the boat. And in a week I could be there....* He looked back and made sure that the others were still with him. *What about them? I can't just walk away, that's not an answer. I've got to think through this....* His thoughts kept nagging him and he chewed on the inside of his cheek as he thought. *There was the cart—and the gold! We could go back to get it and use the money till we earn it back to pay Mr. Rodgers. And what of the pay Gina and I have coming for working on the river? Oh, but Ernie might not be able to sell some of the goods we brought downriver, and he might not be able to pay us right now....*

He thought through a bunch of different scenarios and the possible outcome of each. He decided it was best for him to stick with his "river family" for now and hope that his sisters and mom were safe. He thought to send a letter to them right away. He couldn't hear the others talking anymore and turned to see what they were doing. Gina was sitting on a pile of brick and had her boot off. She rubbed her foot and was putting the boot back on when he heard a shout.

Toby turned back to the direction he'd been walking and saw several men coming towards him. He shaded his eyes and realized in an instant what was happening. It was the kid he'd whipped, a couple of his buddies, and a man that looked like a sheriff! Toby froze for a split second and then turned and started for the girls. When he was within ten feet of them he shouted, "Gina, get the girls back to the barges! Don't get caught and don't tell them anything if you do…. I'll meet you all back there—probably after dark! Don't lead them to the boats! Understand?"

Gina was lacing up her boot and quickly tied it. As soon as her foot hit the ground she raced off in a different direction from Toby, motioning Jaynee and Robin to follow her. There was the sound of a police whistle-horn and shouting. The guys with the sheriff began to chase the girls, but they had a hundred feet head start and started to blend into the fire wreckage.

Toby headed away from the river and straight down the street. It was filled with carts and wagons where people had stopped working to eat their lunches. Everyone watched as Toby raced past, and he realized that he couldn't hide from all those eyes. How far could he run? He knew that his travels had put him in the best condition of his life, and he felt he could cover a couple of miles. But if he crossed any of the three rivers, it would be a trap to get back.

He looked over his shoulder as he ran. He no longer saw anyone chasing him, so he slowed his pace a little. He rounded a corner onto another empty street and decided to look for a place to hide. He could wait until dark and then travel back to the others. But maybe it would be better to get closer to the river….

He looked to each side of the street and noticed an abundance of partially caved-in basements. He could hide there!

"Over there!" a woman shrieked and pointed at Toby. A man on horseback rode towards him, but Toby darted into the rubble, knowing that the horse and rider couldn't follow. He stumbled behind a wall; the loose bricks were hard to walk across. The streets had been cleared and the rider could circle the block too quickly for Toby to chance getting to another area. He was safe—so far! The long wall beside him gave him good cover, so he ducked down and ran as best he could all hunched over.

"There's a reward for anybody that finds the boy!" Toby heard the man shout. *This is gonna get ugly,* he thought, realizing that a lot of desperate people would now be hunting him for the reward. Unless he could blend in with the others and circumvent the chase, he would really have to dig himself in—somewhere!

To make things more difficult, it was broad daylight, and people would have plenty of time to search the area thoroughly. Toby still had plenty of strength and knew he could outrun all of them—except the horses! He cursed and ducked through holes in the brick walls as he went. There were just too many people working along the streets. He couldn't get too far, even if he could change his appearance.

Could he hide in one of the drays? Or a wagon? Maybe under a crate? What would be the best? He squatted down and leaned against the wall. He was in the shade now and it wasn't too bad right here. But could he stay hidden long enough? He wasn't but twenty feet from the cleared street and knew that someone on horseback would be able to see him. But he could probably hide from most people on foot....

He watched a wagon passing and wondered if he could run to it and hop in without being seen. No! There were too many people standing nearby and someone would spot a quick movement. Staying right where he was seemed better than any attempt to move. He felt like a trapped rabbit with a pack of dogs circling around and slowly closing in.

He noticed a low spot in the crater he was kneeling in, so he picked up some loose bricks and quietly built up a wall to help him stay hidden. Some bricks pulled loose easily, but others were wedged tight. Toby wiggled them loose and the mortar crumbled. It was hard on his fingers, but he worked feverishly.

He put his knee down as he was pulling on a stuck brick and everything collapsed beneath him! He dropped about ten feet and landed on a solid floor. The jolt stunned him and he sat motionless, waiting for the pain of a broken bone to start. He regained his breath and recovered from the shock while he waited for his eyes to adjust to the dark. Gradually he saw the outline of an arch and a tunnel disappearing into the distant darkness.

He heard voices above him and moved to the archway. Someone's shadow passed by the opening above and Toby listened. "Nothin' here but another rat hole!" He was sure it was the voice of the boy he'd whipped—that thief! How was it that he'd tried to steal Toby's pocketknife, and yet *Toby* was the one on the run? He stood slowly and dusted himself off. He wondered about the others: Had they made it away? Would anybody think that they were going to the river? It would be very difficult for Gina and two Indian girls to make it far without being noticed. But he figured that if he could count on anyone to make it, it was them!

He cursed under his breath—at the situation, and at himself. He'd just answered his own dilemma. They *were* the best people he could count on! How could he ever consider not being a part of them? He realized that Pittsburgh was no longer his home. And without his family here, the city held little interest for him. He knew that there would be a lot of work here for some time to come, and they could make a good deal of money for a hard day's work. It was an opportunity that he saw as a great start for him and the girls, but sooner or later someone would figure out who he was. Then he'd probably have to spend some time in jail—for something that wasn't his fault! No, he would go downriver with the others and then haul goods back upriver again.... But first he had to get out of here!

He looked down the dark tunnel and realized it headed in the general direction of the river, sloping as it went. Toby started walking and thought of stories he'd heard about tunnels under the streets that drained rainwater from the city into the rivers. But which river did this one lead to? How far was it to the river and how would he make it in total darkness?

Just as it was getting very dark, Toby noticed a glow of light about twenty feet ahead! He walked towards it and realized that there would be a lot of holes at each surface opening and where the floor—or ceiling!—had caved in. He walked quickly, but carefully. The floor was wet and slippery. Everything, including the walls and floor, was caked in a black film. He recognized the black stuff as soot from the fire.

The distances between openings of daylight were long, but he could still see his way. He wondered: *Am I getting close to the river? And how will the tunnel end when it gets there? Will it be above the water's surface or below?* He was most worried if he could get out that way and about how far he might have to swim.

He stopped and rubbed his face from weariness, not realizing that his hands and clothes were covered with the black soot. Now his face was covered, as well. He looked ahead and saw more daylight. He thought of the time of day and figured it to be mid-afternoon. He had about four more hours to get as close as he could to the river and decide how to get out. He guessed that most of the people would work until dark and that some would camp out on the streets. He'd have to avoid them somehow.

◊ ◊ ◊

He heard something scurrying and thought of the rats that must have hidden in this tunnel when the fire hit. *How hungry would they be? And how aggressive?* He shuddered and moved ahead.

He'd been walking hunched over for several hours now, and his back ached. He squatted down, straightened his back, and stayed in that position for some time. While he stretched, he thought about the open fields he'd seen up north. He longed for the green valleys and the crystal clear water of the streams. On the river he'd be able to lie with Gina on the deck at night and watch the stars. Thinking of Gina made him think of his nights with Jaynee. Would there more nights with her, too? He had to put that out of his mind! He stood back up and kept walking.

Toby let his hands drift along the walls to keep himself centered in the tunnel until the next lighted area. He perked up when he saw it ahead—until he heard voices! Toby stopped and listened. He was too far away to understand what was being said, so he gingerly stepped forward. The voices grew louder. Toby strained to hear them and was startled when he heard the "clank-clank" of a shovel or pick against brick. He continued his stealthy advance until he was about twenty feet from the workers. Two lanterns hung over their work area, and the men were looking at a hole they'd punched into the sidewall of the tunnel.

"It can't be mor'n two feet more!" said one of the men.

"That's what you said before we dug *these* two feet in!" The other man was puffing for air and leaning on his shovel. "We'll just blow it! Put some dynamite in the center and blow it!"

"WE CAN'T! Dammit, they'll hear us! And they'll probably reach it before we do.... We have to make it through—tonight!"

"But what if we're off? What if it's over that way—or that?!" In the lantern light, Toby saw the man wave his arms in both directions before throwing down his pick and stepping back.

"Damn you! I told you I measured it mor'n once, and I tell you *it's here!*" The man wiped a cloth across the back of his neck and took a lantern to hold against the opening.

"We blow it! Listen to me! *No*, listen!" He pulled at the other man's arm, turning him around. "I told you the door was closed—but it wasn't locked. The gold is TWO FEET from HERE! The safe was a good one, and I'll bet the bags aren't even burned! We blow a hole in and get out before they figure out what happened!"

"And what if the whole building is lying on top of it!? Then what?"

"It won't be! Yesterday they were starting to clear the debris and I saw that it was mostly out of the way…."

"All right. Blow it!" The man stepped back and offered the other man space to get by.

"We only have about thirty seconds of fuse and we'll have to get out fast!" He started ramming the bricks with a steel bar, slowly breaking them apart. He created an opening and kept going until he had to reach into the hole to pull out the loose bricks. They kept at it for another half hour and then sat down on the brick pile they'd created. One of the lanterns was nearly out of oil and flickered. They sat in silence for another ten minutes.

Finally, one of them said: "We'll do it just after dark, that's about an hour from now. If I weren't so dang tired I'd just keep punchin' at the brick…."

"Why wait? We can just blow it and use the tunnels to get away—like we talked about."

"Cause I think there will still be people working on the other side of the wall."

Some more time passed as Toby waited for them to set up the explosives and get ready to finish their "work." He was tired of waiting, tired of hiding, and worried about the dynamite!

"Okay, it's set!" one of the men said. "When I light it, let's each take a different tunnel. Grab a lantern and get ready…."

Toby hadn't considered that someone would be running towards him! He looked back and wondered how far he would have to retreat. He cursed silently and turned, ready to run when the others did so they wouldn't hear him. He was already backing down the tunnel when he heard, "Run!" He spun around, and with his hands still on the slimy walls, he ran hard. The explosion echoed through the tunnel and made his ears ring. He turned and started back up the tunnel. There in the distance was one of the men lying in the black slime. He seemed unconscious and wasn't moving. The lantern lie beside him, barely lit.

Toby figured it was his only chance to get past the man and down the tunnel—but he had to move now! He picked up the lantern and started moving up the tunnel. He got to the blast hole just as the other man was stepping into it. "Hold the light and wait here," the man said as he entered the hole.

Toby stood there for a moment, considering taking the lantern and running before somebody from above came by or the other man came out. But just then, Toby heard the man climbing back towards him. The man extended his arm from the opening and shoved a moderate sized bag towards Toby. "Quick—take this!" he said, glancing at Toby. "What the hell? Did you fall in the mud?" Before Toby could do anything the man was backing into the hole again and had left him holding the bag....

When Toby heard noise from above, he stuffed the bag inside his shirt and ran, carrying the lantern with him. Behind him he heard voices talking and then shouting. He guessed that the others from above had just gotten to the man lying in the slime. Toby kept running until he was out of earshot, but the last thing he heard was a gunshot...

◊ ◊ ◊

2-13

~filthy-stinking-rich!~

When Toby climbed out of the storm tunnel, it was dark and no one was nearby. He figured that he was about a quarter of a mile away from the scene of the crime and not too far from the river. It was a dark night, with clouds covering the moon and stars. He was still carrying the lantern, but it was ever so close to going out. He figured that his running was sloshing the last of the oil onto the wick and allowing it to burn a little longer.

Toby saw that he was about two blocks from the water and silently made his way to the river. He passed by a campsite, where people were standing around the fire and talking loudly. "I heard the explosion, an' I thought it was someone bustin' up some walls, when I heard men talking about somebody stealin' somethin'. I waited and some men rode up on horseback. It was the sheriff. I guess he was still in the area—lookin' for that kid!"

They shuffled around the fire as Toby slunk by, still listening to the man talking.

"I guess somebody used some dynamite to get to a safe and steal some gold...."

"They caught 'em?"

"You bet, got 'em both! And I figgur they're gonna be earless when they get done wif 'em." A couple of the men laughed.

"Suits 'em right! Stealin' from folks that are burned out! Got nothin' left, an' folks steal." This made Toby stop in his tracks and think about the money he was carrying.

"Ain't that big a problem. The money wasn't *really* bein' stolen! Not from the one who owned it, anyway."

"What!?!" Another man joined the conversation. "How so?"

The second man laughed loudly and continued telling the story. "I heard one o' the thieves confess that he was workin' for the man who OWNED the money and he wanted it stolen—so's he could collect insurance." The others howled. "Yep, stealin' his own money!"

And he gave it to me, Toby thought with a grin as he turned and hurried towards the river's edge. When he reached the barges, the others were standing around a bonfire, all of them quiet. Each one seemed lost in his or her thoughts and stared at the fire. Toby got closer and noticed the girls weren't there! Toby quickened his approach. When the others heard his whispered greeting, they seemed immediately grateful.

"Toby!" Ernie was the first to recognize him in his filthy condition.

The first words out of Toby's mouth were: "Where are the girls?" He said it in a demanding, breathless tone.

Ella answered before anyone else could. "They're fine! They're across the river. They beat the men chasing them and we sent them across. But how are you? My God! We thought you were lost...or caught!"

"I'm good, but they're gonna be lookin' for me.... I should go to the girls...."

"Toby—you need to know something...." Ernie stopped smiling and sounded gravely serious. "Ella and I are broke. We lost the house in the fire and it's gonna take the bank awhile to rebuild. Our money was there and we have to wait for them to put numbers to each account." Ernie raked his fingers through his hair and looked at Pete and the women. "We don't have the money to pay the balance on the new boats, and we can't sell the goods we have on the barges, as most of our buyers are broke, too."

Toby stepped closer to the fire and the others noticed how bad he really looked.

Ella stepped to his side and hesitated, but put her arm over his shoulder. "Gina told us about your home, and your family being gone. I'm sorry!" Toby nodded to her, but his mind was racing in another direction....

"How much money do you need to pay off the balance on the steamboats?" He listened to his own voice as though it were someone else's.

"Just over a thousand dollars," Ernie answered. "Why?"

Toby reached inside his shirt and pulled out the heavy bag he'd carried from the tunnel. "Will this help?"

Everyone squatted around the flat rock and counted out the gold coins, placing them in neat stacks. They totaled just over fourteen hundred dollars! Ernie and Pete just looked at Toby and shook their heads as he explained how he got the gold and told them the story he heard at the fire.

Then Ernie spoke: "Toby, you've saved us all—again! And with this—it makes you a full partner! You now get a full third of everything we take in!" Ernie reached over and put his hand on Toby's forearm. "Tob', it's a *lot* of money we're talking about! And if we do things right, all of us are going to be very wealthy people in the next few years. Pete and I had made a lot of plans before we found out we were—temporarily— broke! And now we can go on as we planned..... But that'll wait until tomorrow! We've got some others to see about selling out our loads, and then...and then we're headin' upriver in the morning. It's gonna be some exciting times on the river for us all!"

They were all smiling, mesmerized by the fire and the glitter of the gold, when Pete looked at his new partner and said, "Toby, you stink..."

$$\Diamond \Diamond \Diamond$$

2-14

~a double crossing~

Their laughter was loud enough to be heard across the river. Ella offered to row Toby across and meet with the girls. Despite his financial good fortune, he was lonesome. And with his family gone from town, he desperately wanted to see "his girls." Ella broke the silence in the rowboat by whispering: "Toby, we have made so many plans, but the men will tell you about all that. It's just so much that you've done! That money is gonna pay for the boats! Oh God, I could kiss you!"

Toby smiled to himself in the dark and looked to the far shore. "It was all such...such dumb luck," he said. "I dunno. We just seemed to be so lucky.... I hope it lasts...."

"You sound like you didn't do a thing at all, Toby. But you've done *a lot*! And Ernie wasn't kidding you about the money to be made. You saw the immigrants. There'll be many that want to head north from here. Many of them won't be able to leave Pittsburgh to travel down the Ohio River westward. There simply isn't enough left to provide boats and wagons—and supplies. So they're gonna change their minds and go our way. *That's* what we're planning on! They'll have to head upriver or cross land. And *we* have the boats to pull the barges back north. We can haul them and still tow barges loaded with supplies to sell at the Landing...."

Toby straightened up in the seat and took the oars from Ella. "I guess that *will* make a lot of money.... And we can bring a lot of goods back—once they get the city put back together." He thought about the things that people at both ends of the river would need. "I just hope we all can move as much as we're planning. It just seems that EVERY plan I made in the past two months caved in on me...." He dipped the oars in the water and gave a great pull. He glanced behind him and saw the girls' campfire near the shoreline on the north side of the river.

"...I know it seems like that now," Ella said. "But let me ask you this. Think of what you were doing—just two months ago.... *Now* you've got yourself a position, a *boat*, three girls to help you, and a *full partnership!*"

Toby nodded at her words. "I know. And I *am* very happy with it all. I'm just still worried about my mom and sisters...." He trailed off, wondering how soon he'd see them again.

"Of course. And they're probably worried about you. You should send them a long letter tomorrow! I'll bring you paper and ink.... To the left some; there are rocks near the shoreline.... I want to take the girls and get them some good traveling and work clothes. I'll come get them in the morning and take them with me. In the meantime, I guess you're gonna get some extra rest—*and a bath in the river I hope!*"

Ella and Toby laughed and he heard the voices of the girls greeting them. It was nice to see them glowing in the light of the fire. He was also glad to see that they had set up the campsite already. Gina and Jaynee were there to catch them and tie up the rowboat when it bounced to a stop on the shoreline. Gina hugged Toby as he stepped out of the boat and Jaynee smiled her rare smile; he could see the pleasure in her eyes.

Gina and Ella talked as Toby and Jaynee walked back to the center of the camp. Toby went directly to Robin. He checked on her sleeping face and covered her with the blanket. Jaynee watched in silence, but Toby saw her smile.

Toby heard a shriek of joy as Ella and Gina climbed up the bank and approached camp. He looked puzzled and turned to watch. Gina hopped to his side and grabbed his arm. "Toby, Ella's gonna take us to BUY clothes!" He nodded and smiled at her exuberance. "We'll have NEW clothes to wear! Oh, Toby, I never had *new clothes* before! And the girls will get some, too. And we'll have some to wear as the crew on *your boat*—Captain! Uh.... Toby, you stink!"

Ella barked out a laugh and added, "We already tol' him that!"

"I was in a sewer...." he replied in a tired voice, still smiling.

"Well, maybe you should get in the river and clean up. Besides, we've got a lot to do!" Gina paced near the fire. "We should wake up Robin and get her in the boat; and that way we could get an earlier start in the morning....and be ready earlier!" She was still talking to herself when Toby looked again at Jaynee. Her eyes had never left Toby, and she didn't seem interested in what was going on with Gina.

Ella interrupted Gina's running on and said, "Gina, you should stay and I'll come and get you—early!"

"But you can save rowing across again! And besides, when Toby gets cleaned up, he'll probably want to get some sleep...." Toby nodded his agreement. He was tired and wanted to lie down.

Gina was determined to go back across the river—tonight! She wasn't about to wait until the morning. She picked up her blanket and then pointed to Jaynee and her blanket and motioned for her to go to the boat. Jaynee shook her head in silence, stepped back, and pointed to the cooking pot and then to Toby. She wanted to stay and feed him! Gina thought for a brief moment and realized that *she* should be feeding him. "Oh, I'm sorry Tob', I didn't think...."

"You go ahead. I do want to clean up, eat, and get rested. I know how much this means...." Before he could finish the sentence, Gina hugged him and gave him a peck on the cheek. She turned and grabbed her blanket, picked up the sleeping Robin, and set off for the boat.

Ella was stunned, but gave into Gina's eagerness. She pursed her lips and spoke to Toby: "You both be alright? We could come and get you, too?" Toby shook his head. Ella looked at Jaynee, who nodded and turned away from the fire even though she didn't understand what was being said. Finally, Ella said, "We'll be back in the afternoon. And I'll get clothes for you, too, Tob'—and for Jaynee...."

Jaynee and Toby watched as Ella, Gina, and Robin pulled away from the shore and began rowing back across the river. Toby sat by the fire and unlaced his boots. Before he had them off, Jaynee handed him a hot bowl of some kind of fish chowder or stew. Toby sat silently, enjoying the quiet night and sipping at the broth. Then he felt Jaynee approach him from behind. She had another bowl of water and a cloth. She knelt down in front of him, pulled off his socks, and began washing his feet....

He finished the stew and set the bowl down beside the fire. Jaynee silently removed his shirt and washed his chest and arms, his back, neck, and face. He relaxed and let it all happen. Later he was lying under the blanket, naked, with Jaynee next to him. There was something nice about the quiet of the evening and the wordless love of this girl...

◊ ◊ ◊

2-15

~a run upriver~

Toby watched Jaynee as she made breakfast and turned his freshly washed clothing to dry near the fire. He was wrapped in the blanket, turning the old pages of the newspaper Ernie had given him. It was a copy of the *Pittsburgh Chronicle-Telegraph* and it covered the events of the Great Fire. Toby had read it through several times already. He squinted in the morning sun and held the paper into the light. He read it aloud, paraphrasing the written reports. "...over 6,000 homes destroyed...caused by a washer woman's fire...a quirky wind moved fire through the ramshackle houses built beside forges and factories.... No one killed! A firestorm they had fought and lost...impelled by the hand of the Destroying Angel.... The flight of a fiery-flying Serpent.... Five hours of fire covering 50 to 60 acres." Toby looked up and saw that Jaynee was watching him as he spoke. Quickly she looked back at the clothing and fussed with them.

"…people running, some screaming, others hallowing, warning the people to fly for their lives. Carts, drays, furniture wagons, omnibuses, horses and all, and every kind of vehicle, crowded the streets to an excess, which made it difficult for each to escape, and threatened destruction to all...!" Toby looked again at the remains of the city and tried to imagine the fire. He shook his head and put down the paper as Jaynee handed him his pants and socks. He pulled them on and smiled at Jaynee as she handed him the clean shirt. This he hung over his knee and then tied his boots. When he was dressed—except for his shirt—he turned over the paper and continued reading.

"...Sullen people with determined Spirit...gazing along the scene, lost by non-existent streets....Winds blowing hot coals with such intensity that complete buildings burned in half an hour...." Toby looked up at Jaynee and said, "The ENTIRE Monongahela Bridge burnt in TEN MINUTES!" He noticed her quick glance towards him when he pronounced the name of the river. *Of course*, he thought. *It's an Indian name.* "Jayne," Toby said, using the English version of her name for the first time. "Do you know *Monongahela?*"

She paused and then nodded. She said the word back to him, and even though she pronounced it slightly differently, it was the same word. He pointed to the river and said it again. She smiled and nodded.

Toby nodded and continued reading aloud: "Market Street, Diamond Alley, and Fifth Street.... Only one in ten saved anything.... The sufferers bore their calamities with manly firmness.... The more complete destruction of any ward we think was never known.... A long line of burnt timbers across the river, between the naked piers, is all that remains of the bridge.... Piles of furniture, bedding, and the last of personal belongings scattered across the hillsides...."

Toby was still holding the paper and looked again at the city. From the corner of his eye he saw Jayne drop to a squat and stare into the woods behind him. He folded the paper and put it down beside him. Without seeming to be alarmed, he pulled on his shirt and acted as if nothing was wrong. He kept his eyes on Jayne's stillness as he stepped to pick up the whip. Everything was silent. He turned and watched the woods in the direction she was looking. He saw nothing and heard nothing, but he knew Jayne was never wrong when she heard something. Slowly he sank to a squat beside her and waited.

Nothing moved. Even the birds were quiet. Neither one of them moved a muscle as they watched. Silently, Jayne picked up a bowl of water and poured it on the small cooking fire. It hissed and steamed as the fire died. Still not a sound came from anywhere else. Toby was about to stand and go to the edge of the woods when he heard the sound of a small twig breaking from the footfall of someone—or something—in the woods nearby....

Toby focused his gaze on the spot the noise came from and saw a small movement in the shadows. He nudged Jayne's arm and nodded at the woods. She nodded and then pointed in a different direction. He held up two fingers with a questioning look. She shook her head and held up three fingers.

Three of them?, Toby thought. *Who are they? And why are they trying to sneak up on us?* Toby nudged Jayne again and pointed to the woods to their left. She nodded and stoop-ran silently into the brush, away from their camp.

Toby followed her, but just twenty paces in they ran into a large man who caught Jayne across the neck and had her wrapped into him in one quick movement. Toby was too close to pull out the whip, but he saw the flash of Jayne's knife slash the underside of the man's forearm.

He screamed a curse and yanked Jayne's hair. The knife slashed again and the man withdrew his hold quickly. They heard two other men crashing through the woods in their direction! The man was still cursing Jayne loudly and shouting directions to the others.

Jayne hesitated a split second before running into the woods with Toby at her heels. They covered fifty yards in silence and were barely short of breath when they stopped to listen. They could hear someone heading in the direction they'd come so they took another tangent.

Toby was the first to squat and Jayne joined him as they heard a man run by. He was panting and stumbling, not anywhere near the physical shape Toby and Jayne were in. It gave Toby some hope that they could get through this. He still wanted to know *who* they were and *why* they were chasing them.

With practiced stealth, they moved along silently, keeping the winded pursuer ahead of them, ready to change directions in a heartbeat. Finally, the man stopped and cursed. He turned around and slapped his hat against his thigh and wiped the sweat from his face. Slowly he returned to the area where the chase had begun. Toby pointed to his ear and motioned for Jayne to follow him back and listen to the men's conversation....

When they crept up on the camp—from a different direction—they could hear the men clearly. The man Jayne had cut grimaced in pain and rocked back and forth, holding his wound. "That evil bitch cut me—*twice*! Damn that hurts!" He spoke to the other man who was wrapping a cloth around his cut forearm. "...I'll kill her! I'll cut *both* her arms *off*! Then I'll beat her with them! Damn. Won't it quit bleeding?"

Toby turned his head and watched Jayne's face. There was a fierce look in her eyes. She glared at the man, her eyes burning and her jaw muscles tensing.

"I think we're not gonna catch 'em," said the third man. "An' we had better get you to the doctor.... Damn, I wanted to catch 'em! 'Specially the boy. We could sure use that reward!"

That turned Toby's head back to the fire. *Reward! Great, just great....* He'd temporarily forgotten about the price on his head.

"The girl'll fetch a good price, too.... The sheriff'll put it up there—on an Indian girl!"

"*Damn right!* And that'll make it more for us to get—when we get 'em *both*!"

"Help me up and get me to the doc, 'fore I bleed to death," said the first man. "That bitch!" he added again. The other two each took an arm and walked him back to the river.

Toby guessed that they had a boat somewhere and would be gone in minutes. He suddenly saw clearly what to do. He spoke softly to Jayne and used his hands to gesture so she'd understand: "Grab the blankets. Then we run to boat.... Cross river!" She grabbed his hands and finally said to him, "Tobay, I understand you!" With that she dashed into the cleared spot and grabbed both blankets. Toby was too stunned to say anything and followed her as quietly as he could. *She understands AND speaks English!?!*

They could see the two men struggling to help the third man walk. Jayne and Toby had no problem circling them and gaining distance to the shore of the river. With one glance up and then to the west, they saw the boat and dashed to it. Jayne reached it first, tossed in the blankets, and motioned Toby to get in. He had no sooner made the center seat and grabbed the oars when she untied the rope and was pushing the boat away from shore. She tossed the rope into the boat and followed it. As she lifted her leg over the side of the boat, Toby pulled hard on the oars and began to swing the boat around.

They heard the men shouting as they reached the water's edge and saw Toby and Jayne escaping. One man dropped the arm of the other and ran into the water. He began swimming and seemed determined to catch them. Toby knew he could row faster than the man could swim and wasn't worried.

Still, the man was a powerful swimmer and was closing the distance. But when he lifted his head and looked at them, Jayne took her knife and stuck it into the top board of the boat's rail. It was then that the man realized what waited him if he did reach the boat...

2-16

~the double crossing—again!~

Toby started to sweat but didn't slow his rowing. In between oar pulls, he looked at Jayne. She was still half turned in her seat, watching the man in the water and the two on shore.

"What—How much...." He gasped for a breath. "How much can you understand or speak?" he stammered.

"All that you say...." Jayne replied in a casual voice. She watched the swimmer heading back to the far shore and then turned back to Toby's surprised face. "Yes, I speak English. It took me time to...remember words, the way to say things...." She spoke slowly and with an accent different from Toby's, but he could clearly understand her. "Tobay. My mother was a white woman taken by the Indians. I was four! I forgot it all—until I listen to you and the others talking. Then I remember, and it became quicker.... I was afraid. Or scared. I don't know. For my people, it isn't right for woman to speak...." As she spoke, she looked behind him to their destination on the other shore, then to him, then behind her again.

"There was times I wanted to say something, but I was comfort-tible *not* talking.... Theee...the other women? They make a lot of talk." She shrugged and smiled.

Toby's expression changed from awe to a smile as he nodded to her.

"Tobay, I am happy to be with you and NOT speak."

Toby had slowed his rowing and let her explanations sink in. "Then you... when we spent the days traveling together? You, uh, never wanted to talk to me?"

Jayne looked a little sad at his question. She shrugged and looked into the water. She drew a long breath before she spoke, "Yes. And no." She looked back again and saw the men, still standing on the north shore. They were stranded, and the man she'd cut was sitting on the ground....

"Tobay, don't tell thee...others. I have a reesonzz. And it might be good for you that I listen when others don't know that I understand. Don't ask me right now to explain; but I weel!"

"We might not even see the others," Toby said. "They're all out—busy getting the boats and supplies...." Toby half turned and looked at the shoreline. The boat had drifted with the current and was downstream about fifty yards from where the others should be. He cut the boat and had to pull harder to cut across the current. He studied Jayne's face and knew anybody on shore would realize they were talking if he tried to say much more to her at the moment.

As the boat bumped into the gritty shoreline, they were both near standing and ready to step out. Toby paused and tossed the line to Jayne, who caught it with one hand and looped it around a rock to finish anchoring the boat. They were a street away from the barges, which was what Toby wanted the men on the other side of the river to see. He hoped they might not connect them with Ernie and the others!

Jayne almost led Toby in a fast walk as they headed one block inland and then turned left towards the barges. A lot of men were working in the area and many of them noticed Jayne's confident strides. *She's a very good looking woman*, Toby thought. On top of that, her leather tunic made her noticeable, as it was cut much shorter than what people considered proper. As they walked, the men continued to stare and some of them outright leered at her!

Toby saw her in a different light now. Her face seemed to shine with a half-smile, and he wondered if it was because they shared a secret. He thought of the ways that they had "read each others' minds" back when they hadn't spoken, and how they could "sense" each others' thoughts without any need to communicate further. He wanted to keep that, but he also wondered why she wanted to remain quiet. Regardless, he matched her silent strides down the street.

They rounded the cleared street and stopped to see if anyone was watching them. When they saw that the coast was clear, they headed to the campsite. They reached the barges, and just as Toby had predicted, the rest of the crew were gone. Toby paced around, mumbling to himself about what to do next.

Neither one of them could stay in the city any longer. They needed to let the others know and then get away.... *But to where?* With rewards being offered for both of them now, they wouldn't stand a chance of not being caught, even for a day.

Toby paced some more and started to get tense. Then something caught his eye and gave him an idea! A cornerstone from a building sat on its side in a pile of rubble. "We'll leave a message....on this!" Toby said. Jayne stepped out of his way as he searched for something to write with.

He returned after several minutes with a rock that was darker than the cornerstone. He set the cornerstone on end in the center of the campsite, and he and Jayne squatted in front of it. They looked at the rock in silence and tried to figure out what to write.

Toby tested the writing rock by making a mark on the cornerstone and then rubbing it with his fingers to see how well it held up. It should work. Toby nodded and turned the stone a little to find a flat surface. He drew the compass symbol for North and then two parallel wavy lines below it to indicate the river. "Think they'll understand it?" he asked Jayne as he drew back to look at the message.

Without a word she took the writing rock from him, wiped the dirt from another part of the cornerstone, and wrote her message: the symbol of a bird, a few marks Toby didn't recognize, and then "2 2 PL".

Toby mused at the markings before he offered his guess: "Two to Parker's Landing?"

Jayne dropped the small rock, took Toby's face in her hands, and kissed him full on the mouth. "You are smart man, Tobay! We go now!" She looked around to see who was nearby and started walking to the barges. Toby followed and looked at the tarp-covered goods on the barge ahead, thinking about what they should take with them.

Jayne took a lantern and looked under a tarp before fully pulling it back. At first they didn't see much that would be of use to them, but then they saw the butt of a rifle. Toby pulled it out and poked through some bags until he found ammunition. They soon found the bag of dried meat, some grain, a cooking pot, and another blanket. Toby took another flint from the crate near the rudder. *OK,* he thought. *Fire, a cooking pot, some food...What else? River water to drink....*"What else?" he said out loud. "A cover!" He searched for something to keep them dry from the rain. "Jayne, find us some kind of cover—for rain." She was already pulling out a piece of oilcloth and folding it up.

Nothing else came to mind. He knew it would be hard for them; they'd have to row the boat the whole way. They would take as much time as they could and hope Ernie and the others caught up with them before they suffered too much hardship. Jayne was standing and ready to go, but Toby took a last look around. She nodded to him, her way of saying that all was ready. They walked quickly back to the rowboat.

When they were in the boat, untying the rope, they heard someone say: "I think it *is* them." Both of them lowered their heads and Jayne took the oars. Without a sound she had the small boat heading out to the center of the river. Toby watched the north shore; he wanted to see that the men who had chased them earlier were gone, but they were still standing on the shore looking directly at them!

"Maybe this isn't a good plan, Jayne! They'll know which direction we're goin'." She shook her head slowly as she watched the men on the other shore.

"We give them something else to think about...." Jayne said. "Wee go as far as wee can. Far as they can see, and we get off on this side—make them think we go south. When it ez dark, we go north...."

Toby smiled at her cunning and leaned back to get some rest. A hundred questions rose in his mind. There were so many things he wanted to ask her, but he knew there would be time for that later. He decided to get some sleep, as he'd take over rowing when it got dark so they could make a good distance upriver that night. He pulled down his hat to cover his face and shade his eyes from the sun—but not so far that he couldn't watch Jayne. Her tunic was getting soaked with sweat and he watched her breasts swaying underneath it as she pulled hard on the oars. From under the blanket, Toby peeked at her face and saw that she was looking at his body, too.

*What a great country this is....*was his last thought as he drifted off to sleep…

◊ ◊ ◊

2-17

~a good partner and a good plan~

They banked the boat when they reached a spot on the south side of the river that looked safe. Jayne stepped onto shore and pulled the boat towards her—with Toby still inside it! He had started to stand just as she started to pull, and he nearly lost his balance and fell into the water. *My God!*, he thought. *She is so strong!* Her physical ability continued to amaze him. It seemed that they were all getting into fantastic shape. He noticed his own body and how hard his muscles were now. His chest and arms had filled out in the last two months. As he carried the rifle, he noticed how light it felt. He was comfortable carrying it, and having it with him gave him a sense of comfort.

Jayne walked in a large circle and studied the surroundings. The trees covered the area well and it didn't seem like there was any chance of running into anyone here. She returned and knelt down near some dried wood. She pulled out her knife and the dried, salted beef. She cut two long strips and handed one to Toby. He started to sit down when he saw a two-foot long branch that looked like a wishbone. He considered it for a second, and then stooped down to pick it up. With the beef strip in one hand and the branch in the other, he sat down across from Jayne.

He looked over his shoulder at the river for a moment and then swiveled the stick so that its long leg matched the direction of the river. "Jayne," he said as he gathered dirt into a mound in between the "legs" of the forked branch. When he finished it, he looked downriver to check on the men again. "We are here." He punched a hole in the mound with his finger. "The river behind me is the Allegheny...." Jayne nodded. He pointed at the other long leg and said, "That is the Monongahela...." Again, she nodded. "They both come together and form the Ohio...." He touched the short end of the wishbone.

"Ohh-high-ohh," she repeated slowly.

Toby reached across the mound and poked another hole in the ground on her side. "That—is the place where the others are...the boatyard. It's about four miles from here, and it's across that river. We would have to run—hard!—to get across the hill." He pointed at the mound. "And when we get there, there are cliffs we'd have to climb down to get to the river.... Of course, if they've gone, we'd have to run back here to meet up with them...." Toby scratched his neck and thought about it.

He wanted so badly to join up with the others. He wanted to be on "his" tug and head north with the whole crew. He got sidetracked in these thoughts so long that Jayne lowered her head into his line of vision to get his attention. Toby caught himself and blinked several times before he continued. "Otherwise, we could go back to the barges at night—and catch them there!" He stabbed the dirt at the location of the imaginary boats.

"Tobay...." Jayne drew her index finger along the branch to the juncture and then back up the other limb to the spot he'd marked as their location. "... they MUST come past us—here! To us. It's good we stay here...and wait.... Or we go north. They cannot get past us on river!"

Toby shook his head. "We need them to find this boat—here! And then they will think we went south, remember? If we leave *with* the boat, they'll start looking upriver for us." Toby shook his head slowly before speaking again. "We could cut the boat loose and let them guess where we came ashore."

"Tobay, they saw the boat, at the edge of water—*here*! They might swim to it and come after us, before the others come...." Jayne waited for him to consider her thoughts. She stood and walked to the bank, looking past the trees to where they'd left the men. "...and Tobay? There is a boat going to them now!"

Toby hopped to his feet and joined her, both of them hidden by the trees. They stood frozen, watching.

"...If they go across the river, they'll get horses and ride us down," Toby said quietly. "And if they come this way with that boat, they can still chase us upriver.... With all of them, they could row all night. We couldn't get ahead of them."

"Tobay, the man I cut, they have to take him to doctor. He can't make the trip with them...."

Toby considered this for a moment and then stepped away from Jayne. "I can't kill them; it's not like what happened upriver! They jus' don't know why I'm wanted. They're jus' doin' what they're told! It's their job!"

Jayne spat her next words at him: "They want the money! That's ALL the white man wants!"

Toby looked at her for a moment, wondering if she included him in that statement. Her eyes swiveled back downriver. "I know what they will do," she said finally. "They will leave one man to gather others to help. Then *he* will bring others on horses. But two men will come in boat."

Toby hadn't considered this. In an instant he realized she was right! They didn't stand much of a chance on land, and probably even less in the boat!

"Tobay, we make a path to the south. Let them follow us, then we go around them and return to the boat."

"Jayne, they won't leave the boat here! They'll take it back downriver!"

"Then we walk north...."

"It's nearly a hundred miles!" Toby was frustrated and walked in a little circle. He raised his arms and let them fall, slapping against his thighs. "A hundred miles!?" he said again. He felt like someone had just put a heavy saddle on him.

Jayne smiled and looked at him, "Don't worry, you—li'l Grape." Toby shot her a surprised look; he didn't know she'd picked up on Gina's nickname for him. Jayne ignored it and kept talking. "I will feed you, carry you, dress you in the morning—and keep you warm at night!" She gave him a mischievous smile and turned to gather up the gear they'd brought...

◊ ◊ ◊

2-18

~the figure eight~

Toby and Jayne waited several hours in the shade along the river, watching the opposite bank downstream. Toby was absentmindedly drawing a figure eight in the sand when it suddenly occurred to him what they needed to do.

"Jayne! We need to run this path.... We let them come onshore, see us, then we run south. When we make sure that they're following, we'll go apart and run this 'figure eight' path *across* the direction we were headed!" He made the shape in the sand again and looked up at her. She nodded slowly, glancing downstream again.

"Then, when we get back to the path, we head south and make two large circles and come back to the boats!" Again, she looked at the pattern in the sand and nodded.

"We'll meet here and pick up our stuff. We should hide everything now— the blankets and the pot. Then we'll take their boat with us, and cut it loose upstream...."

"They cross now!" Jayne said, leaning away from the bush they were hiding behind. "They go across to barges."

"They'll go and drop off the man that you...." Toby hesitated for a second. He didn't want to remind himself *or* her of the earlier knife incident. "...the man that's hurt. Keep watchin'. I'm sure two of the men will head this way."

Toby went to hide the gear and then made footprints in the clearing to the south. When he returned ten minutes later he squatted beside her. He peered around her and saw it: The two men were now *four*! And they were rowing hard to get to them.

"This is gonna get difficult," Toby said. "Whatever happens, meet me back here! And we'll probably have to run hard."

Jayne's eyes hadn't left the boat as it closed in on them. "Tobay…two have guns. They are hunting *us*! We go now!" Jayne stood and pulled the draw-strings loose on each side of her tunic. Toby sucked in a breath as he watched and wished they were anywhere else. *We will be soon,* he thought as he stood and carefully stayed out of the sight of the men in the boat. He followed her up the bank and watched those hips swaying....

Once they reached the top of the bank, they looked back and stepped into a clearing. Toby waited until one of the men spotted them and pointed. Then he turned and began his run south. It was a slight uphill trek and they pushed themselves hard. Jayne was still in the lead, but Toby had no problem keeping pace with her. They made sure to trample grass and break small limbs along their way. It would take a complete idiot to miss the markings on their trail. Toby reached another clearing and looked back. They had gone over half a mile, and he saw the first man's head crest the riverbank.

"Jayne, as soon as we get into the woods again, we turn and make the fig-ure eight." She was stooping and running faster now. *This one can run like a deer,* he thought, admiring her sleek beauty as she crossed the last of the open area. Toby ran a few side steps while looking back and saw the second man pointing in their direction.

Another quarter of a mile and they split into different directions. Toby ran as fast as he could, hopping over fallen trees, sunken ground, and small bushes. He kicked up a rabbit and the poor critter dashed ahead of him, barely able to get out of his way.

Toby was starting to get winded and slowed his pace a bit. He guessed that he'd crossed another half mile and began to round the top of the figure eight in his mind. By the time the chasers ran out of their tracks, they would go back and then find the place where they separated.

He was closing his half of the figure eight when he had to stop and drop. He'd nearly run into a man slowly walking along the first path. The man held his gun with both hands and was intently looking at the ground, searching for footprints. Toby used the moments to catch his breath. Slowly, and in silence, he stood up. He saw the man about fifty feet to his left.

Toby was half-squatted among some ferns when he saw Jayne's head directly across from him. He saw her looking at him, so he held up one finger and pointed at the man. He then shrugged his shoulders and shook his head to indicate that was all he knew. Jayne held up two fingers and pointed past the man they could still see. Only their eyes moved as they waited till the man disappeared.

They had lost several moments and Toby was getting upset. It was now! He stood and motioned for Jayne to make the crossing with him. They passed the original path and set out in opposite directions, again moving as quickly and as quietly as they could.

Toby passed a short tree where a bird swooped, pecking at him and squawking loudly. Toby waved his arms and ran on. The bird returned to its nest but the sound of gunshot startled it again.

"He's here. Headin' downriver!"

Toby was now running as fast as he could and had outdistanced the man behind him. Sweat soaked his clothes and ran into his eyes, burning them. He tried to wipe it away. He figured he was now approaching a quarter mile from where he'd been seen and knew Jayne would have heard the gunshot, which would give her an idea of where he and the others were.

It's time to get to the boats, he thought. *Will the men keep heading that direction and give me a chance to double back?* He was gasping for air now but still making good distance. The damp underbrush in the wooded area softened any sound of his running feet, and he felt sure no one was near. He could see the edge of the river and realized that he was a little east of where he needed to be. When he broke out of the tree line, he dropped over the bank and was at the river's edge.

Jayne was already there. (*That figures!*) Toby hurried to her and saw a frown on her face. She was tugging at something on the boat's edge. When Toby reached the boats, he saw what she was tearing at. The men had locked them together with a short piece of chain and a padlock!

Toby studied it for a moment and then grinned and motioned for Jayne to get into the boat closest to her. She cut the tie rope loose. Toby gave her a smile that she didn't see, as her eyes were watching the bank. Toby lifted the front of both boats and pushed as hard as he could before swinging his feet over the bow of the empty boat. Once inside, he grabbed his oar. He jerked his thumb backward as Jayne had her oar in the water. She pulled hard on her oar and he pushed his, causing the boat(s) to turn in the water.

Soon they were pointed upstream and began matching their oar pulls. The boats were moving and they were gaining distance. Despite the current that tried pushing them back, they were increasing the distance to the shore. Within ten minutes, they were half a mile from the shoreline and were getting tired. But as they shared glances—and matching tugs on the oars—all while sweating and panting, it was if they were mutually agreeing to a common goal. Toby could feel that his rowing was stronger than hers, causing the boat to "crab." He lessened his pull and tried matching hers when they heard another gunshot.

Toby looked at the shore and saw the man stand up. *He'd been there— not far from the boats—all along?!* Toby was puzzled. The man aimed and took another sighting, but it wasn't anywhere near them. *What's he firing at?* Several more shots rang out, and then the oddest thing of all happened: The man waved!

It was getting dark, but Toby was sure that's what he saw. He looked at Jayne and noticed she was studying the situation, too. She turned to him and shrugged. "A friend?" she said. The shoreline was just light enough for Toby to see the man pointing downstream! *What is going on?...*

◊ ◊ ◊

2-19

~a little overboard~

Gina paced the deck of the new steam-powered tug. This was the boat that she and Toby were to run on the river. It was a nice looking boat, and she enjoyed the smell of the fresh paint. She also liked that it had plenty space. There was a small deck on the front that was about a twelve foot triangle; a rear deck about twenty feet long curved beyond the twelve foot width of the bow area. Midway, a twelve by sixteen cabin was separated into the boiler steam-engine room and a smaller room, fashioned for living quarters. Above them, connected with a ladder, was the steerage cabin. It was a small area surrounded by windows, and its back wall adjoined the smokestack.

Robin and the dog played on the bow deck, both unconcerned with the others' efforts to make the boat ready for their trip upriver towards Foxburg. Robin had had a couple of restless nights since she'd been separated from Jayne and Toby. After sitting up the past two nights holding Robin and rocking her to sleep, Gina didn't pay much attention to her today. She was agitated with the delays and the talk of needing some part for the third boat. They said all this might take *another week*! Gina paced back and forth, looking up at the steerage cabin. Glass windows wrapped along the sides and front, and the wood was painted white with black trim.

Some workers were still putting the finishing touches on the other two boats. Gina watched the activity on the other tugs and saw Ernie, Ella, Pete, and Eula huddled together, talking. Ella looked up at Gina and nodded. She patted Ernie's arm and climbed over the railing onto the boat where Gina stood.

She crossed the deck and stood along the railing beside Gina. "Gettin' antsy?" she asked.

Gina was gnawing on a stub of fingernail and dropped her hand to reply. "Yes! I'm gettin' afraid for Toby and Jayne.... They've been gone for two days."

"Well, I've got *good news—and bad.*"

Gina looked at her a moment before responding. "...And?"

"Pete saw them last night! They were headin' upriver in two rowboats, and the search party thinks they went south." She laughed and then continued. "Pete waved to 'em, but it was gettin' dark. He was the last to see 'em, and he was shootin' downriver!" She laughed again and looked back at the others. "Pete has the search party headin' south. Maybe clear down the Ohio!"

Gina was so relieved that she let out a laugh and beamed. She imagined Toby and Jayne rowing away in the dark, laughing as they went.... "But they didn't have any food—or much to help 'em travel with...." Her concerns changed the tone of her voice from laughing to serious.

Ella squeezed her forearm and smiled. "Can you think of either of *those two* gettin' captured?" Gina was quiet and stared into the distance. Ella moved her head into Gina's field of vision. "And!" she said. "Since Toby has a rifle and Jayne's with him, well I can't see them starvin'...."

Gina was still staring past Ella, lost in worry. She wasn't particularly worried about them being safe. She was more jealous of Jayne being where *she* should be—at Toby's side. She began pacing again, but not far from Ella's position. She circled twice before she came back and saw Ella watching her closely.

Gina asked her, "There was some bad news...?"

"The foundry can't pour the brass to make another propeller for another week...." Her voice tapered off as she let the words sink into Gina's thoughts.

"Another WEEK!?!" Gina's voice was shrill. She dropped her arms to her sides, slapping her thighs. She paced the deck again and circled three more times before speaking. "Ella, *we* could take this boat and go pick them up, couldn't we!?" Her eyes implored Ella as much as her words did.

Robin turned her head and dropped the cloth she and the dog were playing with. She sensed that Gina was unhappy and walked over to her. Once beside Gina, she put her wet, grubby hand into Gina's and looked up at her. Robin's hair was matted again with sweaty tangles and dog slobber—a far cry from the neatly brushed hair Gina had so carefully done for her that morning. Even the one—and only—dress they'd bought for her was messy and covered with muddy dog prints.

Gina smiled at the little girl and returned her attention to Ella. "Can't we run upriver and take them some supplies?"

Ella knew what the real question was: *Will you take me upriver and let me go with them?* She shook her head slowly and leaned on the railing. "Gina, I don't have the experience with the boat. That's what we're gonna do for the next couple of days—learn it! The men are discussin' that right now. We should be over there too, case them men-folk decide to do somethin' wrong!" Gina missed the joke and sighed, but followed Ella across the railings of the adjoining boats. She shooed Robin back to the front of the boat and paused a moment as the little one pouted and finally rejoined the dog.

The others opened the discussion circle and made room for the two women to join them. Ella gave Ernie a pointed look, and he understood the mood Gina was in. He immediately took charge of the situation and put his arm over Gina's shoulder. "We have one delay to wait on, and in the meantime we are gonna practice movin' these tugs, keepin' the fires and the boiler's steam up, and learnin' how to operate 'em." He was addressing all of them, but everyone else knew the ropes and watched Gina, hoping for the anxiety of youth to fade.

Gina remained quiet and studied the deck planking, but listened intently to Ernie's description of how the tug operated. Once in a while Pete offered information he'd gained on the boat's behavior in the water.

The rest of the morning was filled with long lectures from the men as they went overboard describing simple things to the women. Several times, Gina saw Ella and Eula roll their eyes behind the men's backs. She shared a few covert grins with them and kept glancing back to the dog and Robin…

◊ ◊ ◊

2-20

~what's a poor boy to do?~

Toby crawled out of the water and gave a soft whistle. He turned in the pitch darkness to the sound of the reply whistle. Jayne approached him and draped the blanket over his shoulders. He shivered a little and drew it tightly around him.

He had just finished swimming back from cutting the boats loose in the middle of the river. He hoped they would make a good distance downstream before anyone discovered them; and he hoped that anyone who did would think that he and Jayne were headed in that direction. If anybody checked, they would know that his family was downriver and would figure he'd gone to see them.

He was still shivering when he felt Jayne open the blanket and step inside against him. It took less than a minute for him to completely forget his condition and to realize a new one. Jayne could warm him in seconds. His breathing was quick and shallow, as was hers. Her warm skin bonded to his, and it seemed like they would stand this way all night.

When he was warmed to the point of sweating, he felt Jayne's arms slip from his back and trace along his arm until she found his hand. The next thing he knew she was leading him into the woods. To his surprise, she had built a small fire in a little depression in the ground. He hadn't even seen the fire's glow in the trees. *This girl is amazing*, Toby thought.

Jayne's blanket was already laid out on the ground on top of some leaves she'd gathered for a cushion. She released his hand and went to the blanket. Once there, she untied the lacing on her tunic and pulled it loose. It dropped to her feet and she gracefully stepped from it. The firelight illuminated her brilliantly white teeth as she flashed Toby that rare and beautiful smile of hers. Her dark eyes were glued to his as she lowered herself to the waiting blanket.

Some time later, the two watched the fire and each slipped into an exhausted, restful sleep.

◊ ◊ ◊

Toby woke when he heard a shuffle nearby. It was almost daylight and Jayne was near the fire, still without her tunic. He watched her back muscles as she fumbled with something. He could see small sticks leaning over the low fire. Each held a small piece of something cooking over the flames.

He stretched and rubbed his eyes and then rolled to a sitting position. "Smells good...." he said through a parched throat. He cleared his throat and coughed.

Jayne turned and gave him one of the most beautiful smiles he'd ever seen from her. He looked at the freckles that blended into the tanned skin across her cheekbones. *Boy!* He was in trouble. At the moment there was no other woman so beautiful. He shook his head and blinked at her, but she just smiled again and turned back to the fire.

"Come. Eat!" Jayne handed him a charred stick. He blew on it before putting it into his mouth. The meat was flavorful and chewy, but he couldn't identify it. She handed him another stick and he took it without pausing. He was so hungry. But then, he was always starving any morning he woke up with Jayne by his side! He moved closer to the fire and pulled another bite from the stick.

He studied the uniformity of the meat and decided it looked like a small finger! He quickly looked at her hands to count her fingers, but then noticed the snail shells lying off to the side. *Snails?*, he thought. *I didn't know you could eat snails! NO-body eats snails!* He paused only for a moment and then shrugged and popped another snail in his mouth.

Jayne chewed hers slowly as she scanned the forest floor. Birds chirped in the distance, and Toby thought maybe they were jealous of his meal! They could hear other small movements in the distance as well, but nothing to worry about. The woods were waking up as the sunlight streamed through the trees. Toby mused on how each subtle sound in the forest was the giving up of life to become a meal. A bird "pecked" an insect from the bark of a tree, or a frog "slurped" a passing bug. Energy, shamelessly and simply, traded one form for another.

Toby thought about the summer sun and the early July heat that would probably follow the cool morning. The day would be hot! They sat in silence, finishing breakfast and watching the forest. After awhile, Jayne asked, "Tobay, will they bring boats today?"

"I don't know, Jayne. I don't want to stay around here too long...."

"I don't want to stay here...too. We can leave messages, along the river for others to follow...."

"What kind of message?" Toby looked around and finally fixed his gaze on her.

She laid three fingers on the back of her hand and pointed to the rocks. "We stack three stones and one small stone to show the direction we go."

"How will the others spot three small rocks?"

Jayne looked at him, wondering if he was making fun of her. When she decided he wasn't, she said in a matter-of-fact voice, "Robin will know."

Toby nodded and started to roll up the blanket when Jayne playfully jumped onto his back and rolled into his embrace on the bed of leaves....

◊ ◊ ◊

Awhile later they were walking along the wooded shoreline and Jayne found the right spot for their message. She walked to the water's edge and looked around. She bent down and picked up a stone about the size of her head and set it on top of a larger stone just above the surface of the river. Then she looked about till she found another suitable stone to place on top of that. When she was satisfied that they wouldn't slide off, she stepped back onto the shore. She found a four-foot stick and pushed it into the silt at the base of the bottom stone. The limb slanted northward to indicate their planned direction.

The morning sun came across the river and was very hot for as early as it was. Jayne looked into the sky and studied the clouds for several minutes before speaking. "Tobay, rain tonight. Maybe late afternoon.... Storms. They will last maybe two days...."

"We should find shelter—or make one! What about those rock faces over there?" He pointed to some bare rocks along the hillside that were visible through the trees. "Do you think we might find cover there?"

"Rocks have faces?" She looked so innocent when she asked him.

"Uh, maybe," he said. He smiled and jutted his jaw, giving her an up-nod towards the hillside again. "How about those, further north?"

Puzzled by his smirk, she turned slowly and dragged her gaze towards some hills about two miles away. "Better chance—there...." She raised her arm and pointed to another spot further up.

They walked through the growing humidity and the thicker trees. Smaller trees were ahead, and that meant heavier ground brush. And that meant harder travel!

The heat caused Jayne to stop and undo the laces on the top of her tunic. She rolled it down and tied it around her waist, making a short skirt. She looked up at Toby staring at her. She smiled and said, "Better."

Toby gulped. Even though he was getting used to her, it was a shock. "It sure is!" He smiled again as he offered her the lead and watched her shapely figure in front of him.

◊ ◊ ◊

The day got hotter as they crawled through areas of heavy brush and thorny briars. They sweated and slapped at the pesky deerflies and mosquitoes that followed them. Finally, the brush gave way to a larger opening, a sort of meadow covered with wild flowers and ferns. It was a beautiful summer sight. Jayne was about ten feet in front of Toby when she dropped under the flowers and was out of sight. Toby stopped in his tracks and feared that something had happened to her.

He approached slowly. He saw Jayne pushing something into her mouth as her other hand groped the small plants. She was picking bright red straw-berries! They picked and ate berries for the next hour. They filled his hat and her cooking pot with the fruit, finally stopping when Toby thought he never wanted to see another strawberry again.

Jayne sat on the ground, one hand on top of her full stomach. Her hands were red, as were her cheeks, chin, and chest—all stained with the red berry juice. She was licking the stickiness from her fingers when she noticed Toby laughing at her. It took a moment to sink in, but she realized why he was laughing and pointed at the stains on *his* face and hands.

After a good laugh, Toby looked at the sky and noticed how it had changed while they'd been picking berries. "Jayne," Toby said, using the English version of her name for the first time. "We need to get on and find a place to shelter." He pointed to the sky. She nodded in sullen agreement.

After walking for another mile, they found a wide stream with clear water coming down from the hillside to their left. They put down their belongings and washed off in the cool water.

They felt refreshed and energized after crossing the stream. Here the forest changed: There was less brush along the ground, which made travel easier. They quickly made up the time they'd lost and walked along the base of the hill looking for some type of shelter.

After an hour, they came to a path that seemed worn by occasional use. It showed hoof prints and signs of people walking in the now-dried mud. They paused only a minute before deciding to follow it.

The path rose up about thirty feet and then leveled off. When they reached the top, they found a clearing with a fire pit. Large trees ringed the area. It was a spooky sort of place, quiet and deserted. Jayne stopped and listened as Toby slid the rifle off his shoulder and lifted the rolling block to check the cartridge inside.

They walked around slowly and found a small fenced area that was used as a chicken pen—complete with several dead chickens inside! They walked some more and saw the roof of a small building tucked into the hillside, hidden from the center of the clearing. Toby walked closer and Jayne followed at a distance, keeping an eye on everything behind them.

When they approached the front of the rock house, Toby called out to the opened doorway. He waited and then said again, "Hello?"

He slid his eyes to Jayne. She was still watching behind them and glancing in every direction. It was deathly still.

As Toby approached the doorway, he heard a low, throaty growl…

◊ ◊ ◊

2-21

~a growl greeting~

Toby listened at the door and waited for something to happen. After the growl slowed and became quiet again, he pushed open the door with the barrel of the rifle. It took a quick minute for his eyes to adjust, but then he saw a large dog trying to get up on its feet.

Toby stepped inside once he realized that the dog couldn't stand. It was mangy—all skin and bones. Toby searched the rest of the cabin without moving. He swept his eyes through the room and returned them to the dog. Jayne stepped in behind him and looked it over. The dog's head wobbled, and it slowly slipped back down onto its front paws. Behind the dog, on a bed covered with a shabby blanket, lie the remains of what looked like an ancient mummy. White hair lie across the face, and the slack jaw made it look like the woman was trying to scream.

It appeared that death had been painful and took her life in a struggle.

Jayne stepped around Toby and started to the bed, but stopped when the dog growled again. Its head lolled and its eyes were unfocused. Jayne said something in Indian to the dog in a small, soothing voice, and drew closer as she spoke. Some more words and a couple of steps closer.... The dog thumped its tail once on the floor, using up the last of its energy to resist her charm. Jayne knelt down beside the dog and looked closely. She saw quills sticking out of its opened mouth, piercing his tongue, lips, and the roof of its mouth.

She immediately motioned Toby to kneel down beside her. "Tobay, we must help. He can't eat—can't drink!" Her voice was very soft now, and the dog let her pet his shoulder. It whimpered and sighed. Toby realized that the dog had probably not moved in days; he was lying in a puddle of his own urine-mud on the dirt floor.

"Tobay, look for something to pinch the spears. They have small hooks on them and are strongly stuck...."

Toby stood and began to search the inside of the cabin. The dog's eyes followed him without protest as Jayne continued stroking him. Toby could find nothing that would help. But he wouldn't quit. He turned over everything in the place, but that wasn't much. He found some dried, crushed leaves inside clay pots on the wall shelves. They smelled good, but they weren't what he was looking for.

Finally, he spied several metal tools hanging on nails pounded into a post beside the stone fireplace and cooking area. There was a rudimentary hammer, a chisel, and a pair of pincher pliers. Toby took the pliers and knelt beside Jayne and the dog.

Jayne had the trust of the dog now and tenderly held his muzzle. Toby wasn't sure just what to do, but Jayne spoke: "Gently put the pliers on a 'sticker,' then pull it back—hard and quick!" (They both knew the word "sticker" was wrong, but chose to ignore it at the moment. It wasn't time for English lessons.)

Toby's hand shook as he pinched the first quill and determined the proper direction to pull it straight out. He drew a deep breath and pulled hard. The dog jerked, but Jayne's grip was too much for the dog's remaining strength. Toby pinched another and pulled again. The barbed quills left small holes in the dog's lips, tongue, and gums. With each pull, the dog seemed to relax a bit. During the final five pulls, the dog began to lick at the sore spots inside his mouth. By the time Toby finished pulling out quills, the dog's tail thumped the ground. Jayne brought a clay pot with rainwater to the dog. Within minutes, he was much more alert, but still unable to stand.

Some green, smoked meat hung from a piece of rope tied to a ceiling pole. Toby sliced off several pieces as Jayne used the flint and steel to start a fire. She had it going before Toby had emptied the pot and chopped the meat into fine shreds. They sat and watched the cooking pot heat up, and Jayne took some of the dried herbs and put them into the pot. "I will be back," Jayne said as she turned and went outside.

The dog lifted his head and watched her leave. Then he watched Toby until Jayne returned with some leafy plants in her hand. "I saw these when we came in, so I will use them in the stew." Just the word "stew" made Toby's mouth water. He remembered the Sunday stew that he used to have at home, the whole family gathered at the table....

Jayne was looking at Toby and noticed the far-away look and sadness in his eyes, so she quickly said, "Tobay, it will rain, maybe two days, and we need dry wood to keep us warm...and to cook with."

Toby was now back in the present and nodded to her. He smiled and replied, "I'll get enough to cook with—and *I'll* keep you warm!" He winked and went to the door. Jayne smiled and began humming what sounded to Toby like an Indian song.

After his third trip, Toby stopped and looked in the pot. It smelled great. He put a finger in the broth and tasted it. *Wonderful!*

"Jayne? What should we do with her? There is still some daylight.... I could start and dig a grave." He looked at the woman's frail body and then at the dog, still lying beside her.

"We eat first, and then I will prepare her for her to...live in the ground... as you dig...."

Jayne gave the dog the first bowl of stew and Toby the second. He sat on a bench and ate while watching the dog lap up the last of what was in its bowl. Toby ate slowly and soon noticed the dog staring at him. Toby still had half a bowl left. He carried it over to the dog's bowl and dumped it in. "There you go—*you...Beggar!*"

The dog looked up, and Toby saw how quickly its eyes had cleared. He smiled and the dog thumped its tail. "We'll see...." Toby said as he walked outside to get a shovel he'd seen in the lean-to beside the hut—or cabin; he wasn't sure what to call that little building. Toby saw that the hut's roof was made of sod and hoped it didn't leak! The wind had grown stronger and changed, now coming from the east.

Toby chose a spot near the top of the hill and looked around. There was another mound of dirt there, about the size of a grave! Toby went to it and saw a small cross, just two twigs tied together. It looked like it had been dug within the last month and Toby guessed it to be the woman's husband.

He cleared off some leaves and began digging. With grim determination and his jaw locked in place, he struggled for nearly an hour. He knew he couldn't dig a deep hole with the time constraint he had, but he was finally satisfied that it was deep enough to keep wild animals from digging up the body and feasting on it.

"Tobay"! He turned to see Jayne beckoning him to join her. He stabbed the shovel into the mound of dirt, took one last look at the grave, and then went to her.

He noticed the worried look on her face as he approached and she pointed at "Beggar." The dog was now sitting and had moved closer to the cot that held the woman's body.

"He won't let me finish with her. I try everything, but he won't move." Jayne and Toby approached Beggar. Toby squatted to the dog and rubbed behind its ear. He thumped his tail, but wouldn't move. Toby backed up, patted his leg, and said, "Can you carry her?"

"Yes, she's very light!"

Toby took the whip from his waistband and tied one end around the dog's neck. Then he stepped back, coaxing the dog with a tug and a plea. "Come, Beggar!" The dog still didn't have the strength to resist Toby's steady pull, but watched intently as Jayne picked up the woman's body.

The four of them went to the top of the small hill, and Toby jumped into the grave. Jayne handed the wrapped body to him. He placed it gently into the soft dirt and then climbed out. Beggar was now standing at the very edge of the hole and looked at the lifeless body of his owner. He pawed at the edge of the grave and acted as if he wanted to jump in. Jayne held the end of the whip-leash, kneeling beside the dog.

Toby lifted the first shovel of dirt and let it slip into the hole. The dog stayed put, so Toby continued shoveling in more dirt. Jayne chanted what Toby figured was a prayer for the dead, and he felt the beauty and sadness of the words as he shoveled. The dog watched everything, his eyes moving from the grave, to Toby, and to Jayne.

When Toby was nearly finished, the first of the rain drops fell. Toby patted the mound of dirt with the shovel to pack it down and make sure the rain wouldn't wash it away. When he finished, he untied the dog and placed his hand on Jayne's shoulder. She was still kneeling and used his arm to pull herself up. They turned and hurried back to the building as the rain drops increased. As Jayne entered the hut (cabin?), Toby turned and looked back to the top of the hill. Beggar was now lying on top of the mound, looking back at Toby. Toby called, but Beggar remained there.

"What was the prayer you hummed?" Toby asked. He sat down on the log bench and patted the spot beside him as an offer for Jayne to sit, but she shook her head and went to the bed. She began to pull off the cut grass and leaves that had been soiled by the old woman's passing.

She carried an armload to the fire and pushed it in by the handful. They silently watched the fire consume the gift. The smoke filled the hut and smelled horrible! Both Jayne and Toby coughed and choked, leaning back from the smoke. Toby grabbed one of their blankets and flapped it around to clear the air.

Lightning struck nearby, and they both jerked their heads towards the door. Toby stepped over and looked again at the top of the hill. A tree near the grave had been struck and was burning. Toby peered into the rain to see the dog, but couldn't find him. "Beggar!" Toby hollered as he stepped into the rain.

"Beggar!" Toby waited a moment and then ran to the top of the hill. In the near darkness, he scrambled across the wet leaves and saw that the dog was pinned under part of the tree that had fallen on top of the grave.

Even in the dark, Toby didn't have to go any closer; he knew the dog was crushed and dead. Still, he stooped in the rain and petted Beggar's head, admiring his loyalty to his master. Toby was no longer in a hurry to get back to the hut, as he was already drenched and thinking of Bea…

◊ ◊ ◊

2-22

~the long rain~

Toby was seated on the log bench again and pulled off his wet clothes. He felt numb. *What was the purpose of saving that dog from starving if he was just going to die anyway?* He tossed his boot on the floor and Jayne turned to look at him. She didn't say a word, but she needed to tell him something.

"Tobay?" she nearly whispered. She turned from the fire and waited for him to finish unlacing the other boot. He didn't answer, but slammed his boot onto the floor. Finally, he looked up at to her and waited for her to speak.

"Tobay, this place has magic...." she said, nodding to affirm it. "I felt it when I touched the woman. Her body was waiting for me...."

Toby snorted at her and pulled at his wet hair, trying to squeeze water from it. He tried to pull off his soaking shirt, which was hanging off of one shoulder but stuck to his wet skin. He jerked at it in frustration and ended up wrestling madly to get it off. Finally, he yanked it off over his head and slammed it onto the dirt floor, creating a little puddle of mud around it.

Lightning struck again and the crack was deafening. Toby's face shone in the flash and Jayne jumped. As her eyes adjusted to the dark room again, she said in a louder voice, "Tobay, her spirit went into me!" Jayne shuddered as she thought about what she had just said.

Toby was now on his feet, pulling at the laces on his pants. He looked at her in the dim firelight and was struck by how serious—and frightened—she was!

"Jayne?" He paused and waited for a reply. None came. She had her back to him now and was poking at the fire with a small stick.

"Jayne, what do you mean: her spirit *went into you*?" She didn't reply, but he could see her shiver again. He knelt down behind her and wrapped his arms around her.

In one firm, sweeping motion, she pushed him away and stood. She spun around and bent at the waist. He saw the tears welling in her eyes before she spoke. "Tobay, you don't know this..." She shook her fist angrily—not at him, but at what she was feeling. "....Nothing is worse than this! She is a wee... a wish...." Jayne was frustrated at not remembering the words. Finally, she said, "She was—is! Is witch! And now she is with me! *IN ME. Inside me!*" Now she clasped both her fists against her chest.

Again, Toby tried to reach for her and she slapped his hand away. "Jayne, that doesn't happen! It just doesn't!" But as soon as he said it he heard the uncertainty in his own voice. "Jayne, it can't happen.... It's not possible. They can't just move into your body!" He looked around and tried not to imagine what she suggested.

"Tobay, *you do not understand* these ways. When I entered this hut, I knew. I could feel it. Our medicine man—the Indian doctor—spoke to me of this. He said I had 'the way' in me, and that others would try to use me...."

Toby stared at Jayne intently without speaking. He wanted to tell her his own beliefs, but realized this one of hers was much stronger.

The rain continued to pour and the ceiling started to drip. Several small trickles of water glistened in the firelight and began to pool in the center of the floor.

Toby backed up and sat on the bench again, rubbing his hands on his face in weariness. He took a deep breath and decided to play this out to find out what Jayne thought was going to happen now. Minutes passed slowly and the summer storm began to really pick up. Toby knew that it could sustain the powerful wind, rain, and lightning for some time. After another twenty minutes passed with only the sound of the storm, Toby's patience ran out. "So what do we do?" he asked.

"You must not touch me! THAT is very impor...important! You must not LOOK at me too long. TOBAY! LISTEN! Hear me! It could be dangerous to you."

Toby sighed and looked at the fire. *It's going to be a long rain*, he pondered as he looked at her legs glistening in the fire's light...

◊ ◊ ◊

2-23

~the right way to leave~

Gina practically wore a rut in the new finish of the deck. She'd paced nearly nonstop, even during the last three days of rain. At the moment, she was leaning over the railing and staring into the muddy water. The morning passed without any word from the others, and she looked to the front of the tug and watched Robin glaring into the water, too.

The child sat motionless, with a blank stare on her face and her arm around the shoulder of the dog. She seemed to be talking to the water and shaking her head. After watching her for several minutes, Gina continued to pace back and forth. It was now over a week since Toby and Jayne left the campsite after Ella had come to take her and Robin shopping. They'd had no news of them except for Pete's report about them taking the rowboats and heading north.

Gina was desperate to know anything about Toby and Jayne. She'd imagine them drowning in the river at night or being lost somewhere, and then she'd settle her mind knowing that both of those things were almost impossible. Still, her desire for Toby and her runaway imagination of Jayne and Toby together ate at her night and day. Two nights ago, she was ready to unhitch the tug, fire up the boiler, and steal away to look for them. But her loyalty to the others, and their constant reassurances of "how competent and skilled the other two are" settled her down.

The boat builder had given them many hours of instruction, making them pay attention to details of how the boat worked, how delicate the boiling temperatures were, and the need for lubrication on certain parts. They practiced firing the boilers and steering the boats. They moved the barges around The

Point upriver to where they were now at the boatyard. On several occasions, they even pulled the barges, maneuvered them to the shoreline, and tied them off.

All of that, combined with the heavy work required to load firewood, keep a good fire going, keep the steam up, *and* operate the boat made Gina sleep well, but it didn't quench the fire of her own needs. She suffered silently, thinking of Toby no matter how tired she was. And everything reminded her of him—even the way the morning sunlight glimmered like it had when they were traveling together. Her mind drifted back to the many events of their days on the road and she smiled, flooded with warmth at the thought of the love they had shared.

She so desperately wanted to lie beside Toby and talk, like they'd done so many times before. Her only jealous comfort was that Jayne couldn't speak English. At least that part of Toby would be reserved for her!

But then Gina worried: What if that made their relationship purely physical? *That* thought overshadowed everything else. Gina knew that Toby could not miss Jayne's rare beauty. And he was such an accomplished lover—she had seen to that!

She slammed her fist onto the railing. She turned around and nearly tripped over Robin, who had approached silently and was now standing at her side. Gina caught herself on the railing and regained her balance.

"Oh, Robin! I'm…. Did I hurt you?" She squatted down, put her hands on the little girl's shoulders, and instantly saw the tears. "What's wrong, are you hurt?"

Robin's tears were welling up faster than she could blink them away. "Jayne…hurt! Jayne hurt!" she said in a halting voice.

"What are you talking about? Robin?" Gina's face became more concerned, which scared Robin into shedding more tears. Gina tried to recover from the shock of hearing Robin speak English and had to calm herself down before she could console the girl "What are you talking about? What happened?"

"I talk—Jayne…. She…." Robin looked around as if the words were written somewhere for her to read, and then she looked sternly into Gina's eyes and continued to try to explain. "…She sick! Hurt!"

"How do you KNOW this? Why do you say this? What about Toby? Is HE all right?" Gina realized that she was gripping Robin's shoulders very hard when she felt the small girl trying to wrench herself free. As soon as she realized that she was hurting her, she quickly hugged Robin to her and stroked her hair. After a moment, she held Robin at arm's length and asked again, "Tell me what, I mean, *how do you know this*?"

She realized that her voice was so loud that it scared Robin. Gina took a breath and smiled before she spoke again. "Robin, tell me...what you saw!"

In a rather calm and unconcerned voice, Robin said, "I talk Jayne. I see her. She sick!" Robin's eyes were drier now, and she spoke as if she'd just come from seeing her sister on the other boat.

Gina gently shook her head and kept her gaze riveted on Robin's face, her mouth hanging open. She waited quietly, blinking in disbelief at what she was hearing. "How did you—talk? What did she say?" Gina was confused at her own question; what was she expecting for an answer? How could Robin have spoken to Jayne?

"I see Jayne—there, in water.... She say she sick. She no her—she...." Robin glanced around again, looking for a way to explain herself. "She—old woman in...!" Robin started to tremble again.

Gina's hands drifted away from Robin's shoulders and dropped to her sides. She was into "feeling" for a solution, rather than thinking through things rationally. Robin was looking up at her, and the dog was shifting at the tension in the air.

Gina stepped past the smaller pair and began pacing again. She looked at the stoker fire burning in the boiler and then towards the living cabin, thinking of the food they had stored onboard the day before. There was plenty! She could cast off, back out the tug, turn it, and be heading upriver in no time.

"We need fire!" Gina was talking to herself and went to the wood supply. She picked through the wood and gathered dry pieces to toss into the firebox. The flames began to lick at the dry wood, and the heat rose. Gina was now looking at the smoke stack and watched the pressure building in the boiler. It would take about five minutes to get up a good head of steam before they could get the boat moving.

Gina was talking too fast for Robin to understand a word, but Gina sensed that the youngster was ready to do whatever they were going to do. The Indian girl had been like a sad, caged animal for a week. Both of them had, in fact. And now they were loose and ready to go!

Gina pointed to the rope on the front of the tug's mooring and waited for Robin's reply. The little one smiled in a heartbeat and went forward to wait for Gina's signal. Gina climbed the ladder and went inside the small steering cabin. She leaned out and studied the smoke's pattern. It was nearing the right color. She thought through the lessons that the captain had given her. Slowly she pushed the power arm ahead and felt the shudder of steam gushing into the piston chamber.

As the boat moved forward, Gina looked at Robin and gave her a nod. Robin pulled at the mooring rope. When it loosened, she removed it and tossed it towards shore, even though most of it ended up in the river.

Gina pulled the power arm back and felt the shift as the tug reversed and pulled away from the dock. As they were slowly reversing and turning, she felt her own power: She was going to rescue Toby! And she would help Jayne! At that moment, she wished she felt differently about Jayne, but she couldn't help herself and how territorial she felt towards Toby.

She was just turning the boat and aligning the bow into the straights of the river when she saw the others running along the bank, waving and shouting. She couldn't hear them and didn't care. There was no time to discuss anything. (She was on a mission!)

She raised her arm and pointed upriver. The last thing she saw was Ernie throwing his hat—hard—onto the ground. The others stood with their hands on their hips, and Gina knew that this wasn't the right way to leave, but she couldn't help herself....

Gina stole one more glance at the others over her shoulder as the boat's power climbed and she began to feel the speed increase. She felt confident that her training had been thorough. After all, she'd had to guide the tug around the base of the bridge piers and return back to the dock. This time she sailed between them and watched the currents for signs of shallow waters.

As the tug approached some men who were working on the structure, they turned and looked at her in surprise. They couldn't believe their eyes: *a woman at the wheel*! She heard their hoots and catcalls, but Gina just gave little Robin a big grin. She gave the men two long toots on the steam whistle. They watched as the tug passed below them and then waved their hats.

Robin danced around the bow deck, and the dog barked loudly. Captain Gina stood proudly at the wheel, her hair blowing in the wind, her hands steady on the wheel. Nothing had ever been like this in her life! She cut back on the steam and the vessel slowed as they passed another tug pulling two barges. Then she turned into the river to her right—the Allegheny! It was upriver now: back to the wilderness—their home!

Tears—either from the wind or from happiness—welled up in Gina's eyes as she spun the wheel, heading for the center of the river. This time she pushed the power lever forward as far as it would go....

◊ ◊ ◊

It wasn't two hours after they'd passed the convergence of the three rivers and were headed north on the Allegheny when Robin was at the front railing, pointing to the shore and jumping up and down. Gina could hear her squeals above the sounds of the steam engine and the propeller churning in the water. She turned the tug, slowed the power arm, and judged the craft's forward motion against the current. Next, she pulled at the rope strung across the ceiling of the steering cabin, and the steam whistle sounded: *FWOOP, FWOOP, FWOOOOOOP!*

Robin loved the sound and gave Gina a broad grin. She watched the water ahead for submerged rocks, all the while dancing her little "wiggle dance" in excitement. Gina moved the craft forward at its slowest pace, and they were nearly ashore when Robin leapt from the railing onto the muddy bank. She ran to the three stacked rocks, the stone marker that Jayne had left for her, showing what direction she and Toby had gone. Robin turned to Gina with a pout on her face, shook her head, and pointed upriver.

Gina motioned for her to get back onboard. When Robin pulled herself up onto the deck, Gina put the tug into reverse and backed out, again, to the middle of the river, turning to face the current. When she had things right, she pushed the power arm full ahead, and the tug started to gain speed and overcome the current.

She gave the tug's whistle a pull again, watching as Robin clapped her hands and grinned from ear to ear. Gina pointed to her own eyes and then to the shoreline, indicating to Robin to continue her watch for another marker.

They traveled for another hour before Robin began jumping up and down again. She pointed to a spot on the shore that was bare of other rocks and there it was: another three-stacked stone-marker. *Fwoop! Fwoop!* Again, Gina pulled the rope. Her hand went to shade the morning sun from her eyes as she scanned the shoreline. Robin was at the bow, looking into the river again. Her right arm went up and indicated a rock in the water.

Gina deftly slid the craft past it, and they again pushed gently against the shore. Robin jumped the five feet and walked to the marker. She looked a moment and walked around the marker. Seeing the footprints heading away from the water, she tilted her head and studied the area. When she turned back to the boat, she looked first upriver and then back to the wood line. She pursed her lips and then turned fully towards Gina. Robin shrugged and pointed into the woods.

Gina chewed on her lip for a long moment and thought about it. She knew that Toby and Jayne would have had to find shelter from the other night's storm.... But that was two days ago, and they should have returned to remake the marker.... Gina held her knee against the wheel and used two hands to indicate to Robin to tie up the boat. She cut off the power arm and just let the steam bypass the piston.

She watched Robin pull at the heavy rope and struggle with it until she had it wrapped around the base of a medium-sized tree. Gina was impressed with the way the child handled her duties and knew that she would soon be a fully "able-bodied" crew member.

Gina pulled at the rope again and fired two long *toots* into the woods, half expecting the others to appear. She waited and then hit the rope once more. When no one showed, she went down and checked the fire, moving some of the wood away to lower the heat. By now the steam had disappeared, and there wouldn't be enough to blow the whistle again.

Robin was pacing along the shoreline and found the traces of footprints that hadn't disappeared from the rain. She pointed to them and looked to the boat.

Gina was at the bow, looking between Robin and in the direction she was pointing. She paused, but finally called out, "Come here, Robin!" The puzzled Robin took one more look into the woods before returning to the boat. Gina offered a hand and pulled her onto the deck in one easy motion.

The dog licked at the water running off of Robin's legs. She giggled and pushed him away. "Feet go—there!" Robin announced, holding up a wet arm and looking at Gina. Gina smiled at her and then stared into the trees.

"We must WAIT," she said slowly and motioned with her hands, as though pushing down the air in front her.

This didn't please Robin, and she stomped a foot on the deck and pointed into the forest. "Jayne! TOBAY! There!" This time she stomped harder. Then she went to the rail and screamed as loudly as she could: "JAYNE! TOBAY!" She did this several more times over the next five minutes, stopping and listening to the quiet of the woods in between each shout.

Gina leaned on the railing and sighed with impatience. She, too, watched the forest and wondered how far they had gone. Couldn't they hear the shrill steam whistle? Gina tried calling a couple of times and started to get worried. It must have showed on her face, because before she realized it, Robin clicked her tongue at the dog and hopped the railing. The dog bounded once to the tug's rail and then again to the muddy shoreline.

"Robin! Just wait here, they'll come!" But that didn't deter the girl and her dog. They started into a trot and disappeared into the woods. "Robin!" Gina shouted, but she knew it was useless. She was nearly over the rail herself and furious with the little one for leaving. It suddenly dawned on her that she had done the same thing by running out on the others.

In that same instant, she realized the remorse she felt. She allowed her longing for Toby, and the jealousy she felt towards Jayne for being with him, to overshadow her responsibilities. *How could I leave without talking to the others? There's gonna be hell to pay for this!* She thought about how she even fell for that weird story Robin had told her. *How crazy was that!? Something about an old woman being inside Jayne! How will I explain this?*

She was nearly biting off her lower lip. *I can't leave the boat—that would be a major sin.... But I can't just stand here!* She kicked at the railing post and paced the deck. She whistled loudly, hoping to hear something, anything! She called the others' names again, even calling for the dog. She felt more lost and alone than she had for quite awhile.

She leaned stiff-armed against the railing and hung her head. She looked at the water and listened to the silence.... *There has to be something I can do.... And damn it, this WAS the right thing to do! We can't abandon our own....*

"Toby!" she screamed into the forest. This time it was loud enough to create an echo from the valley upriver. She hammered her fist on the rail and began to pace. She realized that they'd been on the river long enough that the sun was in the afternoon sky. The shadows on the deck shifted, and still she paced…

◊ ◊ ◊

2-24

~strawberries, chipmunks, and yellow custard~

Robin and the dog ran through the woods, first crossing a small stream and then following the deep muddy prints of her sister and Toby. There was no doubt about the tracks and the direction they traveled. She ran through a few open areas and stopped in the same strawberry patch the others had been in just days before. She stayed only for several moments; she squatted as she listened, watched, and pulled berries from the plants. The dog sniffed at the berries, and then proceeded to make a circle, checking for something else to eat.

Robin's sense of direction in the woods was as good as anyone's, and she knew exactly where the boat was behind her. Her eyes saw everything there was to see, and she noted a couple of ferns that had been trampled. She knew in her heart that Jayne and Toby weren't too far ahead.

Robin heard the chirping of a chipmunk stop and then a quick rustle of leaves. She didn't even have to turn her head to know that the dog had just caught its lunch. She rested a little more and ate several more handfuls of berries, waiting for the dog to finish its task. When things were quiet, she stood and whistled. The dog appeared with the rear legs and tail of the chipmunk hanging from his mouth.

She rubbed the dog's shoulder and started on the trail again. Ahead of her, she saw a rise in the forest and the trail leading uphill. Her short, stout legs carried her up it without much effort. The dog had made the summit and stood with its hackles up.

Robin stopped in mid-stride and surveyed the site. She saw the hovel first, and then slid her eyes along the other manmade things lying about. She approached the hut slowly and listened for any sound. The place was deathly silent. She noticed a tree further up the hill that was broken and lying on top of a mound of fresh turned dirt. She ignored it and continued to the shack.

She made the sound of a bird, the signal she and her sister used for each other. When there was no reply, she stepped closer to the shack. The dog smelled the air and stood beside her. Robin was five feet from the doorway when she saw Toby's boot. In the darkness, she could just make out the other boot and realized that he was lying on the floor—face down.

Robin turned quickly and looked behind her, carefully listening for the sound of anyone or anything. Softly, she repeated the bird whistle and stepped closer. Her heart was pounding in her ears, and she wanted to call Toby's name. Now at the edge of the doorway, she could see inside and saw her sister lying on the bed frame. With only a quick glance backward, Robin hurried inside and watched Toby as she went to her sister.

"Jaynee…. Jaynee!" Robin said in a hushed, hurried voice. The smell of the room hit her, and she wanted to throw up. As her eyes adjusted to the darkness that hung in the room, she saw a creamy, yellowish fluid oozing out of her sister's mouth. She put her hand on Jayne's shoulder and spoke a little louder. Her skin was clammy and cool, but Robin knew she was alive.

She shot another glance at Toby and saw the same yellowish goo on the mud floor near his mouth. Before she could do anything else, a wrenching cough erupted from Toby and more of the fluid came from his mouth. He gave another small cough and cleared his throat, only to cough again. He was barely conscious, but was able to keep his air passage clear and take shallow breaths.

Robin was now crying and pushing at Jayne's shoulder, trying to wake her. She glanced back and forth between the two and had no idea what to do next. She continued to rub her sister's shoulder. Robin knew that they were terribly sick and that neither would be able to move.

Now absorbed in panic, she pounded on Jayne's shoulder blade. After the fifth stroke, Robin saw a flutter beneath the other girl's eyelid and shook her harder. Jayne coughed and a huge glob of yellow, pudding-like phlegm spewed out of her mouth. She gasped for a deep breath and coughed again and again. She was breathing a little better now. Just the act of trying to wake her had helped. Robin pounded on Jayne's back again, and Jayne opened her eyes slightly. She recognized her sister and gave her a weak grin. Robin ran her fingers in Jayne's hair, and her tears stopped flowing.

Jayne spoke to Robin in their native tongue and asked where Toby and Gina were, before she coughed again and weakly spit out more of the thick fluid. Robin leaned back to avoid the mess and looked at Toby. She moved away from her sister, but answered her as she knelt beside Toby. She hammered him on the back and felt him stir. He coughed, gasped, and coughed again. Several more blows and he repeated the process.

Jayne's eyes were open fully now, and she was looking around. She seemed to be thinking about Robin's answer and how they could get word to Gina. Toby was now awake too, slack-jawed and staring at Robin. When he looked at Jayne and realized that she was awake, he asked her—in-between coughs—if she could move. She tried to shake her head, and he realized she couldn't. He whispered to her to explain to Robin what to do.

In a few minutes, Robin was sitting on the ground just outside the doorway, with the rifle pointed towards the sky. Toby wanted her to keep the butt of the rifle solidly on the ground and pull the trigger. She did and the gun fired. Toby and Jayne shared a weak smile, and Robin had a wide grin on her face as she reached for the next cartridge. She fired it and reached for the third.

Back at the boat, Gina's head shot up at the sound of gunfire. She looked at the sky for a moment and then realized the significance of the three shots: They were the universal signal for trouble! She leapt from the railing and landed on the bank. She stopped for a minute and thought of the boat. Her eyes traced the mooring line, she checked the knot Robin had tied, and then she quickly inventoried the boat. Nothing seemed to be needed, but she wondered if she should take something with her. Nothing came to mind, so she turned and dashed into the woods in the general direction of the gunshots…

◊ ◊ ◊

2-25

~crushed grapes and fwee-oop~

Gina and Robin helped Toby and Jayne by clapping them on the back with cupped hands. The two of them started to cough in earnest and were starting to draw deeper and deeper breaths. Toby was the first to take a few breaths in succession before coughing again. He was still only semi-awake, but he slowly raised his finger and pointed. "...Outside," he said in barely a whisper. Gina was puzzled for a moment and then she understood. She also felt the staleness and odd smell of the room.

Without hesitation, she rolled Toby over and tugged at him. She tried to drag him outside, but he was too heavy. "Robin, help me!" Robin looked at Gina and then back to Jayne. She was still clapping her sister on the back and didn't want to leave her.

"Robin!" Gina said in a calm, but commanding, voice. "We'll get Jaynee next!" Gina glared at her, still holding Toby half-up in her arms. Robin scrambled, crab-like, across the floor to Gina and Toby, lifted his arm, and helped to drag him outside. Gina looked back to the cabin, and her first instinct was to stay with Toby. It took Robin a bitter second to see Gina's thought, and she spun on her knee and hammered a fist onto Gina's forearm! "Jaynee!" she barked at Gina.

Gina's eyes darted to the hut, back to Toby, and then to the small girl's face. She quickly rose and followed Robin back inside. They grabbed Jayne under each arm and pulled her outside. Robin didn't lose a second and began hitting her sister's back again. Jayne was breathing better now, and her eyes were halfway opened.

Gina again grabbed Toby and pulled him a quarter turn so that his head was lower than his feet. Gravity would help to drain him as she continued pounding on his back to loosen the phlegm. When Robin looked at her, Gina saw the pleading in her eyes to help her and Jayne. Gina didn't even stand, but moved like a four-legged spider to the other girls. With a quick lift and jerk, she spun Jayne's head downhill, and then she stopped to think.

She looked around for something that she could use to elevate Toby's hips. The only thing she saw was a short log that looked like it had been used for chopping wood. The log was stuck in the dirt and grass, but Gina pushed it free. It was about four feet long and nearly twenty inches in diameter. Once loose, she pivoted it and started rolling it towards the others. Robin was still clapping Jayne's back and watched Gina, trying to figure out what was going on.

Gina placed the log between the semi-unconscious pair and lifted Toby's upper body to hang him over the log. By now she was exhausted, and her strength was nearly spent. She gasped several breaths and looked at Robin with wide eyes. She nodded at the girl, indicating she would help with Jayne in a moment. With one last effort, she rolled to her knees and stood.

Hovering over Jayne, Gina smiled at Robin and nodded for help. Together they hung Jayne over the log and started their beatings once more. It was now more than an hour since they'd begun their rescue mission, and both of the rescuers were barely holding on. Their energy was sapped, and they gave up the last of it by tapping on the others' backs.

Both Toby's and Jayne's breathing had steadied, but they still coughed up the putrid, yellow fluid. On several occasions, Gina pulled the slop away from Toby's face and mouth, as his head still lie in the dirt. She couldn't do anymore. Her last motion was to lay her face on his back and pass out. Little Robin didn't last much longer. Her small taps dwindled to nothing, and she rested her face on her sister's back, listening to her rattled breathing.

The four of them—two hanging over the log and the other two hanging over them—were motionless. The sun's rays kept them warm while they slept. Except for the iridescent-black flies that swarmed around the spittle and mucus on the ground, nothing in the forest moved or made a sound. Even the birds were silent.

◊ ◊ ◊

Gina woke when Toby moved. He gave a half-cough and turned his head, looking for Gina. She was awake in a split second and drew back so she could see him clearly.

His eyes were glassy and unfocused, but after several blinks he opened them wide. He grimaced as he tried to move but couldn't.

"Oh…Toby!" Gina hugged his arm and kissed it. "Toby…."

He gasped as he tried to move off the log.

"Toby, try to rest some…."

He pushed her arm slowly and tried to move again. "I—" He winced as he spoke, but continued: "I have to move, you've squashed my grapes!"

Gina was crying with joy as she helped her mate into a sitting position on the side of the log away from the mess. Sunlight was still seeping through the tree canopy as she held Toby's arm. He turned his head and began coughing again. He held his sides and felt the pain in his chest muscles.

When his coughing fit subsided, Toby let his head drop to rest on Gina's for awhile. Gina fell back into an exhausted sleep. Toby turned and looked at Jayne and Robin. Robin was also sound asleep, and Jayne was still hung over the log. He thought of how uncomfortable it was for her to lie that way. Her face was partially turned in his direction, and he noticed her eyelid flutter when a fly walked across it. He knew he had to move her, but he didn't think he could even move himself. Gina had stirred slightly when he moved, so he nudged her once, and then again. She woke up and looked at Toby.

"Let's turn her over and get her comfortable…." Toby tried to move, but that only brought on more painful coughing. Gina rolled to a wobbling stance and stepped over to Jayne and Robin. She used her foot to rake some leaves over the puddle of phlegm and gently moved Robin off of her sister's back. Then she pulled up on Jayne's shoulders.

Jayne was still in a fog and not fully conscious. When Gina had her half turned, Jayne broke into another fit of coughing. By the time Gina had Jayne rolled over the whole way, Robin woke up and slapped Gina hard on the arm. Gina drew back in surprise, wondering why Robin was angry.

Robin gave her a look of grim determination, and in one quick move she pulled the knife out of Jayne's belt and held it towards Gina's face. She gave several growls and made short jabs with the knife, motioning Gina to get back.

Gina leaned back from the knife, shocked. She held up her hands in surrender, and rose slowly, her eyes fixed on the knife. Once she was outside of Robin's reach, she looked at the little one's face. There was such hatred and loathing in her eyes. "Robin, I was going to help her...."

Robin jabbed the knife in the air towards Gina and spit, showing her clenched teeth. Gina looked at Toby and wasn't sure if he'd seen all of this. She backed away further, still looking at the girl and the knife. She sat on the ground near Toby, well away from Robin and Jayne.

Fwee-oop! Fwee-oop!

The sound cut through the silence of the moment. "It's the others!" Gina said before anyone else could realize what it was. "Toby, it's the others! They're here!" She was on her feet and walking in circles. "Toby...." She looked at him and saw him smiling a weak smile. She looked over at Jayne and met with Robin's protective glare. She went to them and knelt down, just out of Robin's reach. "Robin, Jaynee will be good! It will be good!" Gina nodded at Robin and smiled, but the little girl's look frightened her.

"Toby—tell her!" She watched as Toby tried to turn his head to see what was going on. But weakness was still his master, and he could only glance at them and say: "Gina, get the rifle and shoot it...." Cough. "...shoot it three times!" Toby finished the command with another series of coughs.

Before Gina understood what he meant or where the rifle was, Robin dashed to the hut and came back with it. Without prompting, she sat on the ground and pointed the rifle into the air. First one shot; a reload; another shot; and then.... Then Robin was looking for another bullet. There were none. The four of them sat in silence, sure that the rest of their crew on the tug wouldn't need the traditional three-shot call for help to come to their aid...

◊ ◊ ◊

2-26

~yellin' and stompin'~

Pete appeared through the trees, his rifle lowered and ready to shoot anything if need be. He looked in all directions and tried to figure out what the threat was. Slowly, he lowered the rifle and studied the others as he approached them.

"Afternoon...." He looked at each one of them to decide if anybody was hurt before focusing his attention on Gina and Toby. "How is everybody?" He came closer now and locked his eyes on Jayne and Robin before squatting in front of Toby.

Toby nodded, coughed, and cleared his throat to speak, but he was cut off by Gina's sudden stream of explanations. "They were both nearly dead. Toby was barely breathing, and Jayne was worse. But they're startin' to breathe and coughin' up all that slime. Pete, if I hadn't left...." She paused and reconsidered her words. "If I hadn't run off on you all, they'd be dead." She gave Pete a hopeful look, desperate for him to believe her. After losing Robin's trust, she didn't think she'd survive losing Pete's and the others', as well.

Toby nodded and labored to breathe, exhausted from trying to clear his lungs. He looked at Jayne, who still seemed to be in danger of not breathing on her own. Foamy, yellow fluid dripped from the corner of her mouth, and Robin was back to patting her sister's back with a cupped hand. She gripped the knife tightly in the other.

"How long you been this way, both of ya?" Pete asked, looking at Toby's face and neck and picking up a hand to study it for color.

"...Dunno. We got here.... Found the old lady and...." He held up a finger to pause, coughed, and wiped his mouth on the back of his hand before continuing. "...It was the day it started to storm when we burned the grass that was on her bed. And it was raining, and the smoke.... " He coughed again. "...The smoke wouldn't go out. It filled the house, the room. We both started coughing later that night...."

Pete stayed still as Toby spoke, and he waited for the whole story to unfold. He nodded and scanned the area around the cabin. His eyes landed on the dead chickens and he tilted his head. "Those chickens alive when you got here?" Pete asked.

Toby shook his head and gave a shallow cough.

"Two days since the rain, and today.... That makes four days and you been out for three days...." Pete was pondering something and looked at Gina before speaking again.

Gina was chewing a hangnail and waiting.

"We'll get back to the boats. Gina, you're going to have to get a fire started and build up steam. Eula is keeping ours hot. We'll take Toby and Jayne back with us."

Gina started to protest because she didn't want to be away from Toby any longer. But Pete shot her one of the hardest looks Toby had ever seen from him, and Gina stopped mid-sentence.

"Girl, you've got a mouthful comin' from Ernie *and* Ella! When you left, we was comin' with people for you—to bring upriver.... But all that you gonna hear from the bosses!" He stared at her longer than needed to reinforce what she was in for. "Tob', can you manage?"

"With help....somebody to lean on. Yeah, I'll make it. You gotta help Jayne!"

From the corner of his eye, he saw Gina stiffen at the mention of Jayne's shortened name. Something in it rang of a closeness between Toby and Jayne.

"Gina, you help Toby, and I'll carry Jayne. Let Robin carry the rifles and other things." Pete instructed.

When Pete moved towards Jayne, Robin quickly flashed the knife and glared at him. He brought his hand up slowly and curled his fingers around the blade of the knife. Robin gave him her meanest game face, knowing she could twist the knife in his fingers and cut him horribly. But she didn't. Pete gently pushed the knife back to her chest and slowly released it. Robin watched him carefully as he picked up her sister and carried her, leading the way back to the tugs.

Robin shouldered one of the rifles and picked up the second, pointing it at Gina for a moment longer than she needed to. Her face was still set in anger. Gina was taken aback. She looked at Toby and then back to Robin. "I was going to HELP her.... Oh Robin! I *was*...." With that Robin spun on her heel and followed Pete and her sister.

Toby half hung on Gina's shoulder and stumbled through the woods. They hadn't said much to each other so far. His coughing persisted, but he was able to draw deeper breaths now. The going was slow, and they nearly fell in the small creek as they tried to cross it. Toby bent to the water and cupped several handfuls to rinse out his mouth. Gina steadied him and waited as he drank the clear water.

Toby stopped when he saw Jayne's arm drop and hang limply from Pete's hold. "Pete!" Toby said in a hoarse voice. Pete had felt the arm drop and looked down at Jayne. Robin was there in a flash, peering into her sister's eyes.

Robin bounced on her toes and cried. She dropped some of the things she was carrying and grabbed her sister's hand. "Peed, Peed!" Robin said, begging Pete to do something. He stooped and sat Jayne onto the ground. Her head flopped to the side like a rag doll, and her eyes were half open and glazed. She wasn't coughing anymore, which meant she wasn't clearing her lungs. She wobbled, and Pete kept her from falling to the ground.

"It's ok! But she needs water to drink, too," Pete reassured Robin. He carried Jayne back to the edge of the water and knelt down. He dipped his hand into the water and brought it to her mouth, but she jerked away from the cold sensation. But when she licked her lips and tasted the water, she moved her head towards Pete's hand. He dripped handful after handful of water on her lips so she could drink that way.

Finally, she started to blink and focus her eyes, letting the rest of the water drip from her open mouth onto her chin. Her eyes immediately sought out Toby. When she found him, she smiled, closed her eyes, and rested her head against Pete's chest. He looked at the others and smiled. Then, drawing a deep breath, Pete scooped up the girl and continued back towards the river. Everyone continued on, but Gina hadn't missed how Jayne looked at Toby; it made her wince.

Pete whistled loudly, and the sound of the tug's whistle replied, giving them a bearing slightly to the left of their present course. They half slid, half walked down the bank.

This was the most welcome sight Toby had seen in over a week. The freshly painted tugs gleamed in the late afternoon sunlight. Pete smiled at Eula as she helped to haul Jayne on deck. Toby decided he had just enough energy to make it over the railing of the boat, but Pete and Eula had to help him over the second railing.

"All we need now is some big fire and a lot of steam, woman!" said Pete. Eula gave him a mock salute, went to the firebox, and returned in half a minute carrying a burning stick. She handed it to Pete, who took it and chuckled at her. Eula smiled and then went back to look after Jayne. Robin was on her knees beside her sister and watched closely as Eula covered her with a blanket.

"Toby, you're goin' back with us. Gina...." Pete spoke to her, but his eyes were still on Toby's. "Eula is gonna bring back the tug you took.... And I want Toby to tend the fire on this boat. You'll keep the fire on for Eula." When he didn't hear a reply, he slowly turned his head to her. "Since you have to get your fire goin', we'll run a little slower, and you should catch up in an hour...." Gina was nearly in tears, but she chewed at her lip and nodded, all while looking at the ground. Pete looked back at Toby and said with a wink, "Toby—you stink!"

◊ ◊ ◊

Gina knelt before the firebox, adding wood and poking at the burning fire. The steam was up and Eula had the tug backed out, turned, and heading downriver. Gina was still in a whimpering mood over all that had happened. The others were furious with her—right down to Robin. She wasn't sure that she could explain herself to the child, nor could she explain leaving the others and "stealing" the boat.

As time passed, her mood changed and she gained a new sense of the entire situation. *If I HADN'T gone, Toby and "Jayne" would have been dead by now. And, damn it! Part of this damn boat is MINE! I've lived through a hell of a lot, been saved and saved others, and NOW what the hell!?* She was getting madder and stoked the fire a little harder. *They can buy me out, I'll just leave! I can do a lot of things!* She suddenly realized she was poking the hell out of the fire when she heard Eula's call.

Gina was startled to realize that they weren't but a mile from the end of the Allegheny River and the start of the Ohio, where they would turn The Point and start up the Monongahela.

"Gina!" Eula called again. Gina went to the bottom of the ladder and looked up at Eula. She was smiling! "Come up and take your tug in, girl!" Gina hopped onto the ladder and bounded up each rung.

"What? Why do I get to take us in?" She took the wheel as she looked at Eula's smiling face.

"Gina, you were wrong to leave without tellin' us. But, as it turn' out, you were right, and we thought you were too young and stubborn to listen. Ernie was angrier than I've ever seen him! Mercy, I thought he was gonna *swim* after you and skin your backside!" They both laughed at that description. Tears streamed down Gina's cheeks, some from the earlier anger and some from the relief that she was going to be with her river family again—real soon!

"Just you mind to be respectful to Ernie when he does his manly yellin' and stompin'...." They laughed again. Eula hugged Gina's shoulder with one arm; with the other she waved to Ernie and Ella, who stood watching the lead tug pull into the dock...

◊ ◊ ◊

2-27

~a sigh and a shrug~

When the two tugs were tied up, the crews cut back on the fires, loosened the steam vents, and banked the fires. Gina busied herself and tried until the last minute to avoid what she knew was coming.

Ernie and Ella checked everybody out and wrapped Jayne in a blanket, despite the warm summer evening. She had begun the serious part of coughing on the journey back and looked better in the two hours it had taken to return. Ella gave some hot broth to Robin, Toby, Eula, and Pete. The dog, ever-present at meals, sat with his nose an inch from little Robin's bowl.

They all were spooning the soup into their mouths when Gina approached the group. Tentatively, she looked at Ella first, and then to Ernie. They watched her for a moment before Ernie spoke. "Get yourself some gruel. There's also some bread and jerky." He didn't say another word until he turned and followed up with, "We'll have a talk later...." What Gina didn't see was the wink he gave Ella.

Gina dabbed the warm bread into the bowl of hot gruel and ate slowly. She was sitting beside Toby and glanced at the others when they weren't looking at her. As much as she didn't want to listen to the "yellin' and stompin'" that Eula warned her about, more than that she didn't want to leave this bunch of people—no matter what. But she had made up her mind that she would stand her ground and *not* take any blame for leaving to rescue the others. She began to chew on another hangnail, holding her bowl of food in her lap.

Toby was breathing in short gasps, but seemed to be none the worse for all that had happened. He and Pete were sitting on some crates on the deck of the tug that Toby and Gina would captain. "Pete, do you know what that stuff was? What makes it come out of our lungs? And could we have died...?" Toby asked in a hoarse voice.

"Don't reckon I know, but I've seen it before, just once and it killt three family members in the winter's cold. Guess you both were plain lucky.... If Gina hadn't got there, I don't wanna think on what mighta happened."

Eula stepped up and added, "I've heard of it. Most just say it's a poison. You mighta got it from burning the bedding of the old lady. Did you see any of the yellow slime on her 'fore ya buried her?"

Toby just shook his head. "No, and sure don't want to see it again!"

The others smiled and stared at the fire.

Gina was the first to see the figure standing on the bank above and to the right of the boats. She caught Pete's eyes and jerked her head. Pete quickly turned his head and saw the man's silhouette. He spun around into an action stance and cursed.

"Damn it! One of those posse men lookin' for Toby and Jayne! Bastards!" With that he hopped to the rail and then onto the railing of the other tug to find Ernie and Ella. After a quick exchange of plans, Ernie and Pete jumped to the bank and pursued the man, who had started to run.

Ella was in the top steerage cabin of the tug and saw them disappear around the corner of the boatyard's buildings. She stepped from the cabin and then looked to the others on their boat. "Eula, better get the steam up. It won't hurt to have that boat ready to go—and maybe this one also.... There's just enough light left. Get yourself backed up to the loaded barge! Toby, you'll have to tie it off. Can you manage?"

Toby pulled himself up with one hand on the rail and waved to acknowledge her order. Gina was at his side, helping him with the heavy towropes. When they were in place, Eula steadied the tug against the mooring ropes that held them to the dock. She studied the arrangement of everything and knew what was likely to happen next. It they needed to get away quickly, Pete would jump onto the deck and pull the line loose—and they would be off!

Toby looked at Gina and gave her a sigh and a shrug that told her: *Here we go again!* She held his elbow and leaned her head against his upper arm. "I'm not afraid, Toby—as long as we're together." Toby was still weak, but he lifted a tired arm and hung it over her shoulder. Jayne was sleeping on the bed in the corner of the cabin-room with Robin curled against her.

The mood was tense as they waited for the men to arrive. Toby fell into an exhausted sleep in Gina's arms. She held him dearly, mindlessly stroking his hair. And then they heard the cries of Pete and Ernie as they raced down the bank to the docks…

◊ ◊ ◊

2-28

~slidin'down the rail~

Pete, Ernie, and Ella had a hurried conversation while Eula waited at the wheel. Pete hopped from the stern of his tug onto the deck of Eula's. Toby was just stirring from sleep and stood to hear what Pete was saying. Before he could join them, Pete had kissed his wife and was hopping over the rail.

Eula waved to the others as she pushed open the power-arm, and they started to pull away from their mooring. Toby and Gina had now climbed the ladder to the steering cabin and were firing questions at Eula. She answered curtly before she hushed them and sent them forward to watch each side of the bow. Darkness was setting in, and she didn't want to get hung up on any of the shallows. She leaned to either side of the cabin, her hands glued to the wheel, watching the water like a night owl.

Fires glowed at campsites all along each side of the river. The direction they were headed seemed to be clearly marked, but any number of things could cause them problems. They were just coming under the newly built bridge to the South Side and would be turning up the Allegheny at The Point in just a quarter of a mile. Toby watched both sides of the bow, even though Gina was watching her side. (Toby just felt safer doing it himself. It was a guy thing!) He pointed in one direction or the other to help Eula guide it along its path.

He heard Eula's voice: "Get a lamp. I'm losing you in the dark!"

Toby nodded to Gina, and she went to the cabin. She took the lantern from the wall, and lit it with a tender from the main fire. When she returned to the deck, she held it up in the air and Toby admonished her: "SET IT ON THE DECK!" He didn't mean to sound so gruff, but he was upset she didn't realize that everybody onshore would be able to see them. "Turn it down, and sit behind it, so you can motion to Eula...." he said a little more kindly.

"To the right...." Gina raised her right arm, and they felt the boat swing in that direction. It went on like that until they were well on their way north and the campfires were in the distance behind them. Eula slowed down and called Toby to the cabin.

"Get that gaff pole up and hang the lantern over the bow. You'll have to watch for the current and the sandbars.... Just remember, we don't wanna get hung up and have to wait for them to catch us here in the morning! We're goin' as far as we can. We're probably only a mile from The Point, and I wanna make it past the Kittanning town by daylight! When we get past there, we're supposed to turn up that small inlet river, get outta site and wait for the others. They should be there tomorrow...."

Toby nodded weakly. He was still tired and hungry; he'd only had time to eat a small portion of food before the man had appeared on the hillside. But he returned to the bow and relayed the messages to Gina. She was standing and leaning over the bow, but stepped back when Toby tied off the gaff. The lantern light shone through the river's clear water, and they could see the bottom. It couldn't be more than three feet deep where they hovered, and Toby was worried that a stray rock could break the propeller and leave them spinning helplessly in the river's current.

For another hour, they were mesmerized by the river bottom passing beneath them. Even just seeing a random river cat broke up the monotony and drowsiness of the watch. Finally, Toby and Gina needed a break and decided to take turns relieving each other. When it was Toby's turn for a break, he went to the cabin to look in on Jayne and Robin. While he was there, he gathered up three tin cups and filled them with hot water from the boiler. After putting some loose tea leaves into the cups, he carried one to Gina and then climbed up the ladder to the steerage house.

"Eula, somethin' to keep you awake! Are you ok?" He stopped to catch his breath and steadied himself against the small built-in table. He coughed several times and blinked away the tears. His insides ached from the several days of coughing, but it was getting better.

"Thanks, Tob'." Eula took the hot tea and set it on the window sill, her other hand still glued to the wheel. "This eats into my nerves, but we'll make it.... How's Jayne?"

Toby nodded as he spoke. "Seems ok, still asleep. She seems to be coughed out. I hope her insides don't hurt as bad as mine!" He started to laugh, but that started another round of coughing.

Eula's eyes didn't leave the bow of the boat or the back of Gina, watching for any motion of direction she might give. "Toby, you had better finish your tea and get to Gina. She hasn't had any sleep since she picked you and Jayne up—actually since a day *before* that! I'm worried about her." Her voice trailed off, but her eyes were still locked on the light from the bow. "I'm worried that the sickness could get her too, if she gets too tired.... She tries to do everything herself and doesn't let up on herself if she makes a mistake. I think she was 'bout as crazy as one can get, when you and Jayne were together."

"I don't understand," Toby said.

"An' you never will. Toby, it's the thing a woman does.... Now, hurry along and let her sleep. Just give her a kiss first!"

Toby nodded at her directions and turned as he stepped onto the ladder. "Are you rested enough to do this?"

"Yes, now git!"

Toby returned to the bow and nudged Gina's arm. She jolted awake! She had locked her arms on the railing and was asleep—standing up! Toby took her arms and set her onto the deck. "Sleep!" he said as she crumpled into a pile. Toby was grateful that it was another warm evening as he leaned on the railing and continued her watch.

A little while later, they had a close call when Toby saw a boulder a second too late. But the barge glanced off of it and the big rock just scraped along the side of the tug. It startled Gina, but she quickly fell back into another sound sleep.

"Toby, I'm losin' steam," Eula called down to him. "Let's pull up and take a break. There isn't anybody that's gonna come by this late, and Pete will catch us in the mornin'. We *all* need the rest. Besides, I don't think we're but about a couple o' miles from the river inlet."

Toby turned and slid down the railing into a seated position where he fell asleep in less than a minute. His head was still looking skyward when he woke and saw that the stars were gone. The predawn darkness hung like a black velvet cover over them. Except for the fading glow of the lantern, there was no light anywhere. It was so dark that he was afraid to move. He could hear Gina's light snoring and his stomach growling. He drew his knees up to his chest and hugged them to him, giving his head a place to rest before he fell back asleep.

The huge bang against the side of the tug knocked Toby onto the deck, and his eyes popped open. Gina was instantly awake too, and was scrambling to her hands and knees when the next bang hit. It was harder than the first, and it rocked the tug so hard that it threw Toby to the deck again. He landed against Gina, and they tried to stand up together. Gina had a grip on the railing and on Toby's arm. She provided a prop for him, and they slowly rose until they each had a hold on the railing.

But it proved to be the wrong thing to do! There came another loud crash. They hit the deck again, and this time the fall gave Toby a bloody nose…

◊ ◊ ◊

2-29

~you can truss 'em up, but you can't take 'em out~

Eula's scream could be heard above the loud ruckus. The tug was still being battered. Toby wasn't able to get to his feet, but he crawled towards the steering cabin. At the bottom of the ladder, Eula was wedged with her back against the cabin wall and her feet against the railing. She'd locked herself into that position and was clutching her upper right arm, her face contorted in severe pain. Toby was still five feet from her, but he knew in an instant that her arm was broken. He kept moving towards her when another crash hit the tug.

He lost his balance and landed on his back. He turned his head to see how Gina was making out when he heard the rippling of what sounded like a heavy chain being drawn across the tug's keel. Gina was ok, but she was lying face down on the deck and turned her head to look at Toby. Her eyes were wide with fear. The next loud bang hit the tug's side.

Toby realized that the tug had turned and was being dragged back downriver. The dawn's light was still only a few shades lighter than the blackness of night, but it was just enough to see by. Over the railing, Toby could see the trees on the shoreline turning and realized that the boat was moving in a slow circle.

Toby was coughing again from the exertion, and he spit out remnants of the yellowish fluid that clung inside his lungs. He pulled himself across the deck and finally reached Eula's side. Tears streaked down her cheeks as she held her arm against her. She gulped in breaths as the pain hit with each jolt of the tug. She barely whispered a hoarse groan and pushed her legs harder against the railing.

Jayne was lying in the doorway to the cabin and gripped the door's frame. The pounding stopped and she stood up. They were still slowly spinning, but Toby jumped to his feet. He looked over the rail now and wasn't able to speak when he saw it: There were probably a hundred gigantic logs floating on the river's surface, and they had completely surrounded the tug.

Toby cursed and looked from Jayne to Robin, and then at the dog, and finally to Gina. When he was satisfied they were all ok, he took one last look at the sea of logs and squatted beside Eula. "What…is…it?" she asked through clenched teeth.

"Logs! There must be a hundred! They're chained together, and we got tied up in them. They have wrapped themselves around us—completely. We're trapped in them and floating back down the river!"

"See if you can't get us free. Ahhh!" Eula was doing her best to remain captain of the tug and ignore the pain in her arm. "Try to shoot the chains off o' them…. Isn't there anybody with the logs?"

Toby stood and looked upriver. He saw a small boat that seemed to be chained to the floating mass of logs. He looked at Jayne and barked, "Get the rifle!" When she handed it to him, he spun around and started back to the bow, then stopped and told Jayne to help Eula.

Gina was looking at the boat and yelled loudly: "TEND YOUR LOGS!"

Toby fired a shot into the air, reloaded another shell, and waited for a response. When none came, he fired again. This time a head popped above the side of the two-man boat. The man bent over, and Toby could tell he was attempting to wake somebody else. Finally, two men were standing in the boat and putting on their hats. The first man studied the situation as the other pulled out a long pole and handed it to the first.

Then they both stepped from the boat and started across the logs, hopping from one to another, balancing as they went. The first man crossed the forty or so feet of logs and stood on one that was pinned to the tug's side. His eyes darted past the tug's other passengers and paused on Eula. He spoke in broken English through some of the greenest teeth Toby had ever seen: "She… iz…ok?"

"No, she's NOT OK! NONE of us are OK! You damaged our boat! AND some of the goods on the barge!" Toby pointed with the muzzle of the rifle towards the barge, now jammed against the stern of the tug, its ropes straining at the tie-offs.

The man eyed the muzzle of the rifle warily and glanced back to the barge situation. "I have you loost—in minoots!" he said. He hopped along the logs until he reached the back of the barge. With several attempts using his gaff, he popped one of the chains loose, and several logs parted from their grip on the barge.

In something that Toby thought was Dutch, the two men argued back and forth as they hopped along the logs, deciding which to cut loose. Toby's anger was subsiding as he watched the men manage the tangled, floating mass that had snared them. He admired their deftness and agility. It was hard to blame them for what had happened. After all, they were handling their own "challenge of life," and Toby realized that it was just an unblessed event to meet them this way....

When the bow of the tug was clear, Toby tossed the anchor and waited until it snagged something firm on the river bottom. Jayne and Gina had worked on getting the work shirt off of Eula's shoulders to expose the compound fracture in her arm.

Toby instantly thought of the man in the mining accident at Hattie's farm. It seemed like lifetimes ago.... He squatted before Eula as her eyes drifted away from her arm and to his face. He studied the long sliver of bone poking out from her skin and was afraid it was one of those "spiral" break patterns he'd heard of. Those were the hardest kinds of breaks to set and the most painful.

He heard the sound of feet hitting the deck and turned to look. The tall Dutch man stepped behind him and leaned over the top of Toby's head, looking at Eula. "I fix this...goot!" he said. "Get roop for me." He traded places with Toby and knelt before Eula. "It vill be goot!" Toby turned to get the "roop," but from the corner of his eye he caught the swift motion as the man slugged Eula. Her head drooped to one side, and the man rubbed his knuckles.

Toby was half ready to jump on the man when he saw that Eula was no longer awake—or in pain. Unsure of what to do next, he fetched a piece of rope and handed it to the man. Toby watched as he tied it around Eula's wrist and then pulled the rope's other end through one of the higher rungs of the ladder. The man pulled up the slack and, when he felt the resistance, shuffled his stance. Pulling slowly, he tugged until Eula's backside was just about two inches above the deck. She hung limply, and the man watched intently as her arm stretched and the bone slid back into her skin. He held her like this for another couple of minutes until Toby stepped forward and wrapped the end of the rope around the railing to lessen the pull the man had to bear. They held the position for several more minutes until they heard the click of the bone finding its proper position. The man nodded and whispered, "Goot." He gently released the tension on the rope until Gina helped to lower Eula's arm.

"Not to move it...." he said in a soft voice. Then he stood and turned to the other man, who was still guiding logs past the boat and barge. They uttered more Dutch words, and Toby watched as the log jumper headed towards the shore. The man jumped on a log and used his pole to pry the "chain dogs" loose. He guided it the rest of the way till he could hop off, and then he disappeared into the woods.

He returned in five minutes, carrying several stout sticks. These he stuck into his belt, like swords. Using the gaff, he pushed himself back to the tug. He climbed aboard and nodded a greeting to everyone. Then, without a single word, he passed the sticks to his partner and turned back to his log work.

An hour later, they had a splint for Eula's arm. They trussed up her arm and got her on the bunk in the cabin.

"You can noot take her out...." The man said as he climbed over the rail and pried the last log loose from the tug. Toby nodded his understanding and waved as the men departed on their undulating mass of wood.

Toby tapped his finger on the paper with the names of the men and the company they worked for. He had asked them for this information so Ernie and Pete would know who caused the damage—*and* who helped them! He spent some time looking at the areas that were damaged. Next, he retied the ropes to the barge as Gina stoked the fire and built up steam…

◊ ◊ ◊

2-30

~a consuming feeling~

Jayne, Robin, and the dog took up position on the front deck, sitting in the sunshine. Jayne's breathing had improved immensely, and she was awake, but looked weak. Gina was showing Toby some of the things that he'd missed in the training of how to operate the tug, such as how to use the steam system to its full advantage. Toby caught on quickly and only lacked the experience of actually piloting the craft in the water. They stood at the wheel, and Toby felt he could handle the tug in the daylight and get them to the inlet.

Gina's lecturing was beginning to grate on Toby's nerves, and he was getting antsy to move on. For whatever reasons, Ella, Pete, and Ernie wanted them to be hidden up the inlet river, and that was *all* that was on Toby's mind. He kept glancing at Jayne and Robin. They seemed to be in a quiet conversation that captivated little Robin. Jayne absentmindedly curled her finger around the dog's ear as she spoke, stopping every so often to cough.

Gina took several trips down the ladder to look in on Eula. She was awake, but gazed blankly out the door in horrible pain. At each visit, Gina gave her "two fingers" of whiskey from the jug they had onboard. Now Eula was drunk and suffering in a stupor, but still coughed as soon as the fumes of the "nips" of whisky reached her nostrils.

Light water vapor hissed from the boiler as they waited for the head of steam to build. When the gauge registered the right pressure, Gina went to the bow to pull up the anchor. When she approached the girls, they quit talking and looked at her. Gina paused. Even though the conversation was in Indian and she didn't understand a word, she felt like they were excluding her on purpose. Gina and Jayne nodded curtly to each other as Gina stepped around them and pulled on the anchor line.

The current wasn't very strong, but it was enough to hold the line tight, making it impossible for Gina to pull the tug ahead and loosen the line. She looked at Jayne, not expecting her to be able to help, and then looked at Robin. The little one showed no inclination to help her, either. Then Gina looked at Toby and noticed that he was watching her. She turned and leaned on the railing. She looked down at Jayne and saw her smiling to Toby. Gina was furious! She stepped over the group on the deck and stomped her way to the ladder. Once in the pilothouse she nudged Toby away from the wheel and said, "Why don't you go down and haul that anchor outta the water?" He shrugged, still looking at her, and went to the ladder. "And you can say hello to the girls while you're there!"

Toby's eyebrows narrowed and he felt puzzled and angry at Gina. He didn't like the fact that she was back in her bossy mood. He blew out a sharp breath and climbed down the ladder. Before he went forward, he looked in on Eula. She gave him a little finger wave and a wink, but he knew she was in pain.

At the bow, he stepped past the girls and grabbed the anchor line. He pulled stiffly at the line and felt the tug move. He realized that he had only one good pull in him, which meant one chance to free the tug and pull up the anchor before his strength gave out. With a mighty effort, he managed it in one long, steady pull. Gina put power to the boat, taking up the slack and loosening the anchor. Hand over hand, Toby lifted the anchor, but almost lost his balance and nearly wound up sitting on Jayne's head. She quickly put her hand on his butt and pushed him back into a stand at the rail.

Toby wiggled his backside, and Robin let out a gleeful squeal of laughter, which all got a weak smile from Jayne. There was another surge forward, and Jayne had her hand on his thigh, holding him up. Toby looked up at Gina and smiled. But what he couldn't see was her white-knuckled grip on the wheel. He continued to look at Gina, but the "captain's" eyes were glued to the water directly ahead of them. After a couple more minutes of waiting for Gina to look back at him, he shook his head and turned to watch the river bottom and depth.

Every so often, he bent down to listen to something Jayne was saying or to tease Robin. They were all smiling and chatting away while Gina's grip tightened on the wheel. Jealously ate away at her, but she steered the tug determinedly. When no one was looking, she would quickly brush away the tears that burned their way down her cheeks.

Toby made the rounds, checking on the barge tied behind them; on Eula, who was sleeping soundly now (or passed out!); and back along both sides of the boat. He looked closely at some of the damaged areas on the tug and watched for any signs of leaks, but saw none. He tried not to think about what could have happened if the tug had sunk! They would have all been killed. They were weak and sick and wouldn't have stood a chance of coming up under the large floating mat of logs....

Toby spent another few minutes with the girls on the bow. When he gave Gina a quick glance, he saw her pushing her palm across one eye and realized that she was crying. He walked over to the ladder, stopped just long enough to check on the fire and add some wood, and then climbed up. Once he reached the pilothouse floor, he stuck his head just inside the room and spoke to Gina. "Why don't we take short turns at the wheel? We're all beat. We've lost some time, but we'll get there...."

Gina finally loosened her grip on the wheel. She wiggled her fingers and rolled her head from side to side to help ease the tension in her neck and shoulders. She was quiet for a moment and then said, "That would be ok with me." She stepped back from the wheel, but still held it with one hand. She wouldn't look directly at him and made it a point to appear to look around as if to check on the river. When Toby took the wheel, she quickly went to the ladder and disappeared down it.

Toby had no idea what she was upset about, but his concern dissipated as his focus on steering the tug consumed him...

◊ ◊ ◊

2-31

~a face of rock~

A few hours after noon, Robin was standing at the bow and began jumping up and down, pointing to their right. Toby looked and saw the river inlet. He wondered how she knew that was where they were heading. He gave her a thumbs-up when she looked up at him. She mimicked the signal and started gabbing to Jayne. Jayne was just waking up and nodded as a mother would to a jubilant child. She didn't attempt to stand, but her eyes went to Toby and they shared another smile.

Toby's attention went back to the inlet, and he slowed the craft and judged the proper approach. Mindful of the barge behind them, he swung wide and began to power up against the cross currents he felt moving them. When he had the opportunity, he glanced down at Gina. She had taken up a spot on the rear deck and was sleeping.

The smaller river was beautiful, and the shoreline looked like a miniature of the Allegheny River Valley. It was less than half a mile across, and the banks on each side were also small, but lush with green trees. The breeze reached them as they traveled with the wind at their backs. The place was so pristine that Toby wondered if anyone had ever been here before. The more he thought of it, the surer he was that Ernie and Pete must have come here before. Otherwise, how would they know of it?

He was coming to the first bend in the river and made another wide turn. He had been watching both sides of the river and saw something curious hidden in the trees on shore: a large wall of rock. He knew he was in the general area of where they were supposed to stop, so he kept his eyes on the rock formation and steered to it.

When they came to a thinning in the woods along the shore, he sidled up and whistled for Gina. She stirred but didn't wake. He tried again, but she still didn't move. He knew that Jayne probably couldn't drop the anchor since he'd just seen her in a coughing spell, so he pictured the movement he needed and went further upriver. He made a U-turn and then pulled back the power arm and let the tug drift to the shore.

He stood on the deck and went to the bow, watching the tug and the barge. He was right in all his guesses. As he tossed the anchor, the boat drifted close to the bank. They weren't fifteen feet from the shore when he felt the boat and barge turn softly and stop as the anchor found a hold on the bottom.

The barge swung closer to the bank and then bumped it sharply, jolting the tug. Toby heard Eula's scream of pain, and it dawned on him that she hadn't had any whiskey for a couple of hours. He rushed to the cabin and helped her roll off of her splinted arm. He soothed her as best he could and waited for her to drift off again. She patted his arm and gave him a weak smile. He watched as Eula drifted back into a stupor before taking the cup from her hand.

Toby then went and used the poker to rake back any unburned wood in the boiler to save for later. He saw the temperature needle on the steam gauge drop, and he closed the door. He was hungry and realized that no one had prepared the midday meal. He knew that Robin would be starving—and so would the dog, of course! He guessed that Jayne wouldn't want to eat and that it was best to just let Gina sleep. *Maybe,* he hoped, *she'll wake up in a better mood....*

Toby gave a soft whistle to Robin and motioned her towards him. She and her shadow (the dog) crossed the deck, and soon the two of them were carving dried beef and bread and tossing loose pieces to the dog. There was a hushed quiet around them in the warm sun, and they drifted off to sleep. Robin's head was on Toby's lap, and he leaned against the rail support. Toby kept thinking about the rock face he'd seen earlier, and then it would be a dream, and then when he would wake and realize it was just on the other side of the cabin, which he couldn't see.

He needed to relieve himself and lifted Robin's head from his lap. She woke and sat up, looking at him as if something was wrong. As always, she checked her surroundings for danger. Once she was satisfied of their safety, she looked to Toby for an indication of what he was doing. "Tobay?"

He took her small hand and pointed into the water. "Let's swim!" he said in a quiet, encouraging voice. Robin beamed with her trademark enthusiasm and went to the side of the boat.

Of course, the dog was the first to make it to shore, and stood shaking the water from its body just as Toby and Robin walked out of the water. When Toby wiped his eyes dry, he looked towards the cliff and marveled at what he saw…

◊ ◊ ◊

2-32

~a black idea~

Toby made his way through the trees and walked towards the rock face. It had to be fifty feet tall. Straight ahead of him, at ground level, was a seam of black coal about six feet thick. Above that was a twelve-foot thick "roof" of limestone, with thirty-some feet of dirt and rock covering that. He walked closer and placed his hands on the smooth face of coal.

At ground level, the seam was exposed horizontally for about a hundred feet. He recalled Mad Hattie's descriptions of her husband's coal mine and how valuable it was. He touched the seam again and pried off a piece of coal. It didn't seem to be very hard to work loose. Toby took off his hat and began filling it with coal pieces. He wanted to take them to the tug and see how they burned in the boiler. He wished he had a large sack to carry more of it.

He studied the surroundings and thought of how easy it would be to start a mine shaft here and slide the coal down a chute onto a barge. In his mind, he could see a ramp built from the wood that would be cleared from the site. *You wouldn't have to move it but once—straight onto the barges! It wouldn't have to be hauled by wagons—and that would give us an edge over the other people mining closer to Pittsburgh.*

If the coal works better for keeping a hotter and longer fire in the tugs, we wouldn't have to rely on wood. And coal could stand up to the dampness on the river better than wood. Toby's excitement grew as he looked around the site. *It wouldn't take much to build a camp here—even a house!*

When he looked at how many hemlocks surrounded the site, he realized it was possible that no one had ever seen this coal wall before. The only reason he could see it was because of the height of the tug's wheelhouse, which enabled him to see over the trees. You wouldn't see it otherwise.

Toby would have to ask Ernie if he owned this part of the valley, and then see if he could buy it from him. He thought about retrieving the old cart from its place in the river. The gold would be plenty to set up an operation and start mining.

His head was swimming with ideas, excitement, and more ideas as he carried the hat full of coal back to the tug. Both Robin and the dog came over to him, obviously interested in the hat. Robin pulled at Toby's hands so she could peer inside. She made a disappointed face and walked away when she saw the black rock. Toby figured that she and the dog must have thought it was something to eat.

Back at the shoreline, Toby hopped onto the barge, crossed it, and stepped onto the back deck of the tug. He put down the hat and opened the door of the fire box. The fire was "banked," but still had some small burning pieces going. He picked them up with a small shovel, pushed them to the center, and then placed the coal lumps around them. In less than a minute the coal was burning, and in less than five, there was a HOT fire going.

Toby stared at the fire and smiled to himself. Mad Hattie had also told him about the different types of the coal. If it had the yellow sulfur stink to it, it would burn poorly and not provide much heat. But this must be the very good coal!

He wanted to tell everybody. Well, maybe not Gina—unless she was awake! He looked up at the smoke stack and saw black smoke pouring out of it. He looked inside again and saw the steam gauge climbing. Since he didn't want steam at the moment, he pulled the poker off the wall hook and separated the coal lumps. It was a nice try, but unlike the wood, coal didn't quit burning when separated.

He didn't want to overheat the boiler; he'd been warned several times about the damage it could do—even to the point of exploding! Toby stirred the coals again, which seemed to lessen the fire in them somewhat. The smoke diminished a little, and Toby realized that the smoke of the city would now follow him into the clean air of his river valley. He didn't like that idea very much, but he thought of how things would develop upriver as new immigrants settled the area. Maybe it was only a matter of time before the city moved into the river valley.

He continued to puzzle over the situation. Gina woke and walked past him without speaking. He crossed the deck and looked at Robin and the dog sitting in shallow water. The girl wiggled her toes in the mud and the dog sat with its butt square in the mud. Toby grinned. As he turned, he saw the bow of the other tug heading towards them.

At the sound of the whistle, Toby saw Gina's head peer out the wheelhouse doorway and he caught the sound of Jayne coughing behind him. When he looked at Gina, she didn't look back. Instead, she just watched the others arrive.

Jayne was now standing on the deck and leaning against the rail, looking happy and healthier. Toby gave her a smile and she returned it, much stronger than before.

Toby could make out a man's shape at the wheel, and he guessed it was Pete running the other tug. He could tell there was at least one barge with him. As the boat approached, he saw others standing on the barge. It seemed to be a family; there was a man, a woman, and some children, along with what looked like their belongings.

Pete cut back on the power and drifted the tug alongside Toby's. When they were matched side-by-side, he tossed some ropes to Toby to secure the two tugs together. Pete was down the ladder and made the leap across both railings without any effort. He clasped Toby's hand and gave it a hearty shake. His eyes went to Gina in the wheelhouse, then to Jayne, and then continued the search for his wife.

Before Pete could ask, Toby described what had happened with the logjam and what they had to do for Eula. Instantly, Pete was kneeling at her bedside, listening carefully as Toby finished the story. Pete gently lifted the wrappings and looked at the gash in Eula's arm. It hadn't closed yet, and still seeped the yellow, red, and clear liquid the wound needed to heal. When Eula heard her husband's voice, she woke and held him with her uninjured arm. Toby backed out of the cabin and waited just outside.

Pete came out of the cabin a few minutes later and looked at the position of the sun before speaking. "Toby, I'm going to take her back to Pittsburgh and get her to a doctor. I can't take a chance of her arm festering.... Ernie and Ella aren't too far behind me, maybe three hours. I'll stop and fill 'em in. They'll meet up with ya all...." His eyes wandered aimlessly across the water as he thought of everything that needed to be done to move Eula and unhook the barge.

Within half an hour, they had tied Pete's barge to the rear of Toby's, moved Eula to the other tug, and were making final preparations. As Pete climbed over the railing, Gina appeared with her blanket roll and a canvas bag of her belongings. She followed him over the railing, and without looking at Toby's surprised face, she stated, "I'll go and help with Eula...." She shot Toby a glance over her shoulder (and it was colder than the water at the bottom of the river!).

Toby stood motionless, watching the tug nearly to its last turn out of sight. Suddenly he realized that the barge passengers were now on his tug deck and staring at him.

"I'm Oliver Murphy and that's my wife, Luwellen. I calls her Lu for short...." Toby's skin puckered into goose bumps when he heard the name "Lu." He didn't want to think of who else he'd know with a sound-alike name. "And dem's the kids: Paddy's the oldest, and Quinn, then there's Annette, and little Mary." Each nodded or curtsied as required, but they didn't say a word. Little Mary was looking at the dog and Robin, obviously wanting to play.

It was clear that Oliver ran a very tight "ship" with *his* "crew." It seemed that they weren't going to move without Toby's directions, so he turned and introduced Jayne and then pointed to Robin and the dog onshore.

"Uh, we'll probably be here tonight, waiting to...waiting for Ernie and Ella to arrive." He noticed that Luwellen was looking warily at Jayne and saw that the Indian girl had a fiercer look than normal. The mother had an arm over each of her girls, but the boys were staring at Jayne's tanned legs. Even Papa Oliver seemed to be taking her in.

"We should put together something to eat," Toby said. "We'll get the brazier started...." Without a word from Toby, Jayne stepped past him, gathered some wood from the woodpile, and carried it to the cooking platform. Toby was proud of her, and soon the others brought some of their supplies forward for cooking.

Oliver asked about fishing. Toby handed him a long pole and walked him forward to the bow. He made a couple of hand gestures to Robin and she began turning over rocks and gathering bait...

◊ ◊ ◊

2-33

~talk about planning~

The men fished for two hours and brought up seven huge fish. Oliver and the Murphy boys had never imagined fish so large from a river! Oliver had talked the entire time, and Toby knew more about them than he cared to. But he did learn a lot of very useful information. Oliver mentioned in passing that he had once worked for a coal mining company back in Ireland, and then in the shipbuilding business as a framer, constructing heavy timber frames for ships.

Toby's mind raced; here was a man with all the essentials needed to pull that coal out of the hillside and build a loading barge site! Oliver was probably just under thirty, and had an amicable personality that Toby liked. The youngest kids were all swimming while Jayne and Lu cooked. They seemed to be getting along well, too. Toby could tell that Jayne hadn't told Mrs. Murphy that she understood much English, and he smiled at her coyness.

Gina would have talked the woman's ears off—and drove away the fish by now! Toby smiled at the thought and felt bad that she'd left the way she had. In the back of his mind, he had a cold feeling that there was a possibility that she might have gone for good. But he pushed away that thought....

The sunshine was slipping away from the water and making its way up the other side of the valley. The kids were out of the water and dry, and the tempting aroma of the evening meal wafted across the deck. Everyone migrated in that general direction.

Toby and the Murphy family talked at length. Everyone was full of questions, answers, and stories. Jayne of course, sat quietly and took it all in. This went on until the last of the daylight clung to the sky.

That's when Ernie's tug rounded The Point and headed their way. Two short *Fwoops* on the whistle announced their arrival. Everybody was watching and waving as Ella and Ernie arrived smiling.

Several hours—and nearly a jug of moonshine—later, and Toby was finally able to casually ask Ernie if he owned this valley.

"You BET, Toby…. Why? You wanna buy it!?"

When Toby nodded, Ernie's surprised response was, "OK, it's yours!" But Toby was uncomfortable when he saw Ella looking at him with some suspicion….

"We'll sleep on it…." Ella added as everyone started moving towards their sleeping blankets. Both Ella and Lu helped their husbands off to bed.

Toby went to the bow of the boat and looked again in the direction of the rock face hidden in the forest. He felt two hands slide around his waist and turned to see Jayne, looking better than ever. In the sickle moon's light he kissed her, and they sank down on the blanket she had laid out earlier. (*Talk about planning!*, Toby thought…)

◊ ◊ ◊

2-34

~breakfast and big bidness~

The narrow river ran east and west, which meant that the morning light came in quicker here than on the main river. The sun lit the entire length of river, making the water glitter for a mile. Toby woke up alone under the blanket. He sat up and felt the effects of the whiskey he'd been allowed to drink. He briskly rubbed his hair and dressed. His legs were a little stiff, and his eyes tender to the bright morning sun.

Only Jayne was up. She was heating water in a kettle on the brazier. She smiled without looking at him as she made a cup of strong tea, added honey, and then handed it to him. He took the hot metal cup in his hands and went to perch on the railing.

Ella smiled as she came out of the cabin. She hopped to the barge and then to the shoreline, disappearing into the wood to relieve herself. In a few minutes, she returned and accepted the next cup of hot tea from Jayne. She joined Toby at the rail and sat with one butt cheek hooked over the top wood railing. She let her leg dangle as she stared into the reflection of the sunlight on the water. Halfway through the tea, Toby was awake enough to speak.

"When do you think Pete and Gina will be back?"

She looked at him for a moment and seemed to be choosing her words carefully. "He'll be back probably early evening." She looked away, seemingly disinterested in his question.

"Just wondering, what will Eula do now?"

"She's gonna stay in Pittsburgh for a few weeks, maybe as long as six. The doctors usually want two months for a bone to heal. An' that ain't for those spiral breaks—them take longer...." She sipped on the hot tea again, slyly waiting to pick Toby's brain on why he'd asked Ernie about this particular place on the river.

It didn't take as long as she thought, though. Toby tried to sound casual in his next question: "Ernie said—last night—that you both own this part of the river?"

"Mmmmn, I suppose," she said in a dreamy voice, glancing upriver and then into the sky. "It's kinda nice here...." she continued. "I always liked the peacefulness.... BUT, I suppose it will all change—as more folks like the Murphys arrive and start to settle it." She wiped her mouth on the back of her hand and looked at the tea leaves in the bottom of her cup. "I suppose with the loss of the house, and our business losses with the fire, we'll have to sell it sooner than we planned." She swirled the tea leaves and watched them resettle in the bottom of the cup.

"I think we could do something that could make a big difference," Toby said. She looked at him and noticed the Murphy man climbing over the rail. Toby continued in a quieter voice, "Let's go to the bow...." Toby led Ella past Jayne, who filled their cups with more tea. He gave her a squeeze on the shoulder to show his appreciation.

As the rest of the passengers woke, Jayne handed out portions of cooked oats, warm bread with honey, and more tea. She looked around the cabin and watched Toby and Ella discussing something in earnest. Toby was pointing at the forest and using his arms to describe something to her. Jayne wished she could be part of the conversation, but she continued playing hostess. She looked radiant in the morning light and smiled a lot. Mrs. Murphy didn't seem as bothered by Jayne's "Indian heritage" today.

Jayne had to suppress a laugh when she saw Lu slap her oldest son for giving Jayne leering looks. She was flattered, but knew the boy could never compete with the feelings she had for Toby.

Ernie was on his way back from "nature's call" among the trees. He was about to throw his leg over the tug railing when he stopped, cupped water into his hands, and rubbed them on his face and in his hair.

He was using his fingers as a comb as he approached the breakfast crowd. He raked at his hair and gave them all a broad smile and a hearty "Mornin'!" He stepped up behind Annette, the oldest Murphy girl, and shook his head over her, splashing water on the back of her neck. She jumped and the others laughed. Ernie had everybody awake and merrily enjoying their meal.

He gave Ella a brief, meaningful look as she and Toby joined them. He seemed relieved when she returned the smile and kissed him on the cheek. Ella spoke to the adult Murphys and invited them to the front of the tug. Ernie looked puzzled. Toby interrupted Ernie's thoughts by inviting him to go to the other tug and get the fire going. Toby knew they were going to be leaving shortly and desperately wanted to ask him about the property.

With a last glimpse at Ella, Ernie and Toby stepped over to the other tug and started a fire. They weren't in a hurry and lingered over their cups of tea. "Ernie? Ella said you own both sides of the river for two miles upstream...."

"I reckon she'd know better than me." He turned and looked up and down the narrow river.

"I wondered.... Well...if you both would sell me some of it. It would make a good place to build a trading post. And it's not on the main river, so if it flooded...." He was adding thoughts and arguments faster than Ernie could consider it all. Toby's throat was hoarse from talking it out. He knew he was trying too hard, but he just couldn't stop himself.

Ernie studied the valley from one end to the other, and started with slow nodding.".... I reckon it'd make a right smart thing to do, Tob'."

Ella appeared then and climbed over the two tugs' railings. "You men look like you jus' figgur'd somethin' out...." She smiled and winked at Toby. Ernie was once again studying the tree lined valley. Toby followed Ella's lead, and together they led Ernie into thinking he'd just come up with a great plan. Ernie blathered on about "his" new idea, repeating everything that Toby had said about the property. Ella suppressed her grin and nodded as her husband told her of Toby's request to buy the property.

After some dickering on a fair price, they agreed that Toby was to be the new owner. He would rescue the cart and its gold and use the money to build a place here. They shook hands, and the deal was final. Then Toby and Ella let out their laughs and offered to lead Ernie to the future building site. The three of them walked into the woods and slowly approached the black wall of coal. As they did, Toby and Ella really started to laugh when they saw the stupid look on Ernie's face: his jaw hung open and his wide eyes were locked on the wall in front of him.

Oliver ran up behind them carrying a rifle and slowed his pace to staggering steps when he saw the wall of coal. "...Heard the squeals o' you, thought there was trouble...." he murmured, his eyes never leaving the cliff. "Sweet LORD!" He paced along the wall, trying to go in two directions at once. "Sweet LORD!"

They spent the rest of the morning and the better part of the afternoon talking about how they would mine the coal, transport it, and build a place for the Murphys to live. Once all the arrangements were covered, Ella made one last loving tease at Ernie, put her arm around him, and pulled him into a kiss. "He don't miss much—that man of mine!" she said with a laugh.

The rest of "the Murf's" family seemed to like the idea, too. The kid's had disappeared to explore the valley (after being sternly warned about snakes!), and Oliver and Lu were deciding where to build a cabin. It was an opportunity they couldn't have imagined. They'd survived famine in Ireland, crossing the ocean, and traveling across land to Pittsburgh. They had planned to work their way onward, but when they ran into Ella and Ernie, they all knew it was a great and fortunate event.

Toby could hardly wait to tell Gina about everything, so he hung out on the rear of the tug and waited for Pete's boat to appear.

Jayne brought him some bread and stew that the others were eating for the evening meal, and she seemed to know something that Toby didn't...

◊ ◊ ◊

2-35

~when eyes rain~

After the evening meal and a prayer by Oliver for success and a blessing on the site, Toby excused himself from the gathering and climbed to the wheelhouse of the tug. He watched until dark and then saw Pete's boat turning into their river.

Toby looked closely, but he couldn't make out anybody on the deck. It wasn't until the tug was very close that he noticed Pete was alone. *She's in the cabin—sleeping!*, Toby thought as he leaned over the side of his tug and grabbed the mooring rope that hung along the other boat's side. Pete cut the power to his tug, bounced onto the deck from the ladder, and tied off the rear of the boat.

"Mister Toby!" Pete greeted him with a weary smile and pulled out a handkerchief. He dipped it into the river and used it to wipe the dirt and sweat from his face.

"Hi, Pete." Toby's eyes peered into the cabin doorway, "Uh, is Gina sleeping?"

Pete had expected Toby's questions, and it appeared he had practiced answering it in advance. Pete waved to the others and banked the fire. "She's gonna stay with Eula—to help her. Eula's gonna need all the help she can get...."

By then, Ella and Ernie had hopped the rails and were listening to Pete's news of the trip. "Doctor says her arm was gettin' some putrid to it, but he thinks he got it cleaned out, and made one of them casts for her arm. And she's gonna be there at least six weeks.... How's everything here goin'?"

The three of them headed across the tugs. Toby knew that Ernie and Ella would tell Pete all about what the Murphy clan was going to be doing for the company. Toby stayed behind and looked into the darkness back down the river. He stood there for a long while before he headed back to join the others.

The adults were just about finishing up with the tale of finding the coal seam and how they were planning to mine it. Oliver excitedly interjected bits on his expertise with mining and timber handling. Pete gave Ernie and Oliver cigars and passed around a burning stick from the brazier to light them.

Pete looked at Toby and smiled. "Another masterful stroke there, Tob'...." He offered him a cigar. Toby looked at it and remembered the choking and puking on Ella's porch. He shook his head to decline, thinking about how long ago the chewing tobacco incident seemed.... Still, the memory was so clear—as was the memory of how Gina had disappeared that night! He instantly tasted bile in his throat and felt anger rise in his chest.

Toby turned, walked to the bow of his tug, and propped himself against the rail, leaning forward into his stiff-armed grip. Jayne had put Robin on the bunk in their cabin and then came to him. Mrs. Murphy and her brood had gone to sleep, and the others were still seated around the fire of the brazier. In a soft whisper, Jayne said, "We must sleep inside the cabin tonight."

Toby quickly spun in her direction and then softened his demeanor. "Uh, why?"

"It will rain in middle of the night." She looked into the starlit sky and then continued. "No lightning, thunder that way...." Her arm pointed east. "Light rain, but into morning." She wiped her nose with a finger, almost scrubbing it.

He knew not to question her weather forecasting. He realized how tired he was and followed her into the cabin. She had laid their two blankets on the deck beside the cot, and a dimly lit lantern sat beside them. Toby undressed as she did, lie down on the blanket, turned onto his side, and quickly fell asleep. Careful not to wake him, Jayne lie down beside him. She soon fell asleep, too, as the tears dried on her cheeks.

Sometime during the night, when the rain started pelting the roof of the cabin, Toby turned to her and placed his arm across her stomach. He whispered to her with a softness she'd never heard from him. "Jayne, we are going to be a *very* strong pair. We are going to enjoy a good life on this river. You and me—and Robin!"

Jayne turned to him and buried her face into his chest. He drew back and asked, "Are you crying?" He was shocked; apart from her anger, he'd only ever known her to check her emotions.

She brushed the tears across her cheeks with the back of her hand and answered him. "My eyes—rain!" She snorted a soft laugh and buried her face in his chest again…

◊ ◊ ◊

2-36

~wheelhouse tootin'~

Toby and Jayne were the first ones up and moving in the morning. With an oilskin covering the rear deck, Jayne had a fire going and water boiling. Toby sat on the rail and smiled when she turned and looked at him. *She will be the perfect one to help ferry passengers on the boats,* he thought. *And also to help with the hard work that will be required.* Something came to his mind that he hadn't thought about before: *She should be paid! Gina had been—and so should Jayne!* He decided to mention it to the others before they all started north. He leaned out and let the rain dripping off the oilskin wash over the back of his neck.

The activities started as the others woke. Everyone seemed to know that the day held a lot of hard work, and they ate heartily. Toby thought of the food they had brought and wondered if there would be enough for the whole trip.

A couple of hours passed as everyone went about their tasks, and soon Toby found himself alone with Jayne, Robin, and the dog. He climbed the ladder and went to the wheel. As each tug's mate tossed their mooring lines free, the boats began to drift apart. Pete spun his tug around in the river as Ernie's followed. Toby gave them each a wide berth and followed at a safe distance.

The rain had passed—just as Jayne had predicted—and the day became very hot and humid. Toby brought up two small crates: one for Jayne to sit on and the other for Robin to stand on at the wheel and steer. The dog sat at the bottom of the ladder and whined, but nobody paid attention.

Little Robin was thrilled about steering the tug, and kept pushing Toby's hands away whenever he tried to correct her course. Soon, Robin was seeing things that the others didn't. She could spot a submerged tree limb or ripples that indicated a rock too close to the surface.

When it was time to check on the fire, Toby didn't have any problems with leaving Jayne to watch over Robin. Something in the way the girls had been raised had taught them to see everything around them—and that made for a good pilot.

The tugs soon created a check signal for themselves, from boat to boat. The leader tooted first, the second boat tooted twice, and Toby answered with three short blasts. So much of the river looked new to Toby. He'd missed a lot of it coming downstream, what with all the storm travel, the walking, and the other problems they'd suffered. Jayne and Robin were pointing to areas on the shore and speaking in Indian. They seemed to have some familiar stories themselves.

Toby had taken off his shirt and was on the lower deck when he called to Jayne. "What's a man gotta do around here to get fed!?" They traded places and Toby held the wheel as the girls worked on a meal. After he'd eaten, Toby leaned over the wheel to look ahead. They were at West Monterey, and Toby looked deep into the water, as if he could see Bea, the mule. He smiled sadly at his own foolishness and slowed the tug as he followed the others into the dock.

Within a couple of hours, they had transferred cargo in and out of the warehouse and were back on the river, heading for Parker's Landing. The trip was so fast that in just another hour, Toby could see the warehouse docks at the Landing. This was their destination for the night, and Toby knew that the morning would bring a lot of heavy lifting.

Ernie, Pete, and Ella stayed on the docks and took inventory. They "shooed" Toby and his crew to go along and take in the sights of Parker's Landing.

The irony was that *they* had become the local sight. People watched them warily; they weren't used to seeing a white boy and two Indian girls walking around town. When the girls or Toby waved, nearly every one of them turned away. On a couple of occasions, Toby wanted to pull out his whip and correct their bad manners.

But as always, there was someone who didn't hold the same backwards attitude towards Indians and spoke to them. "You kids is famous! Vy, you're the ones that the story is 'bout!" The man stepped forward and offered a hand to Toby. "Name's Braun, Helmut Braun." His eyes shifted to Jayne and he looked her up and down. "She's a, how they say? A looker!" He grinned at Toby, but Toby's face drew into a stern gaze as he sized up the other man.

"She's part of my crew!" Toby said in a low, level tone. "And she is quite able to handle herself...."

"Most of them Indians are, I heard...." He looked at Toby and then realized that he wasn't gaining much favor with him.

Jayne stepped forward and spoke in perfect English: "Thank you for your compliment, and I won't cut your tongue out for making a remark like that!" Robin had sensed the tone of the moment and was at her sister's side. Her hand was on her knife handle, and she had her game face on.

Helmut raised his hands very slowly and spoke in an apologetic voice. "No offense meant.... Sorry if it sounded like that. I—uh—vee all heard about vhat happened downriver, and maybe the story's all true...." He looked at Toby as if seeking his help. Toby scratched at his chin and seemed not to hear the apology. Helmut looked to Jayne and said, "I'm very sorry that I said something wrong."

Jayne motioned for Robin to put the knife away. "You are excused, and we'll overlook your rudeness," she said.

Helmut smiled and offered them a place to sit. "Been here for about a veek, and nobody is offerin' verk. I can't offer you much, just got some stale beer."

They declined it, and Toby studied Helmut's size and obvious strength. "... You lookin' for work, then?"

Helmut's eyes widened and he nodded eagerly. "Yah, verk! I must verk. Find somethin'—and soonly!"

Toby laughed at Helmut's English, held up an apologetic hand, and corrected him: "Soon. Find something soon." Helmut gave him an appreciative smile.

"You seen that Channel Cat Trading Warehouse?" Toby nodded back over his shoulder. Helmut screwed up his face trying to translate and remember the location. "It's on the river. The large red building...of brick?" Toby added and saw Helmut begin to put the descriptions together. Helmut nodded. "Yah, yah I been there two days this veek, and nobody was beside.... No, sorry,. In–side?"

"Yes, inside...." Toby smiled. "Be there tomorrow evening, say five? If you can lift your own weight. We're gonna need help unloading some barges." He watched closely to make sure Helmut understood everything he'd just said.

Helmut reached for Toby's hand and pumped it with gratitude. "Ich kann. Sorry, I can! I can lift more than that! An' I beside there early evening?"

"*Be* there. It's 'I'll *be* there.'" Toby corrected him again as they shook hands.

Toby stood up and the girls followed suit. He said goodnight to Helmut with a silent nod and turned to go. They made a circle of the small town and then headed back towards the tugs. "He'll make a good coal miner," Toby said in a low voice. When he turned to Jayne, she was watching him with quiet admiration…

◊ ◊ ◊

2-37

~an old traveling friend~

The crew and their dog took their time walking back to the docks. It was a beautiful, warm evening, with a slight breeze dropping over the west hill of the river. They ignored the staring of others and walked slowly. Finally, Toby was disgusted with the whispered comments. He turned to Jayne and planted a kiss on her mouth. Surprised, she broke from the kiss and pulled back, blinking and smiling.

Robin was asleep, riding piggyback on Jayne, and woke just as the kissing ended. She gave an embarrassed giggle and turned her head away. Toby also planted a kiss on her head and rubbed her back. When they continued walking, · they simply nodded to the people who gaped at them.

As they passed a small storefront window, Toby caught sight of a girl's face before it disappeared. She was nobody he'd ever seen before, but he saw her looking at the whip hanging on his belt. He let it pass until he heard the snuffling of a horse. He turned to look and went rigid for a split second.

Jayne noticed it. "What is it, Tobay?"

"I know that horse! Go over and wait by that rain barrel, and stay outta the light…. I'll be back!" Toby walked towards the horse and clicked his tongue softly.

He circled around the flank of the critter as it turned its head to him. The horse shuffled in short steps, trying to turn and fully face Toby.

It was the same horse! Lew's horse! Toby petted its long nose and talked softly to it. The horse nuzzled against his arm, whickered, and seemed to be happy to see him. It had been a good horse, and Toby had treated it well. His first instinct was to look around for Lew or Lucca! But that was ridiculous. *We buried both of them*, he thought. Still, Toby was creeped out and kept a watch over his shoulder as he continued talking to the animal.

The horse wore a saddle, but not the one that Toby had gotten from Lew. Puzzled, Toby gave his old friend one more pat and stepped back. He looked around for the owner and realized that no one was near. Toby had the impression that someone inside the small store would claim ownership. He hesitated; maybe it wasn't a good idea to ask questions. But curiosity got the better of him, and he went to the doorway to look inside.

There she stood again; Toby was outside of her field of vision. She was talking to two lumbering twenty-somethings. They were half whispering, and the one's eyes were glued to the front of her peasant blouse. Another was standing at the window looking at Jayne and Robin across the street. The men turned and followed the girl to the back of the shop, where she let them out the side door.

Toby went in and looked at the other men seated at several tables and benches. They were putting away mugs of beer and calling the girl to the tables. "Rosa, c'mere me-gal. My gills are gettin' crispy!" The others laughed and called for her to get them fresh beers, too. She still hadn't see Toby at the door and was schlepping mugs to a nearby table.

She put down the mugs, waited on one to empty, suffered some nasty comments, and twisted away from a groping hand. She wore a fake smile that dissolved the second she looked at Toby. Quickly, she turned and went behind the counter to avoid him.

He decided to confront her, ask about the horse, and mention that it belonged to someone that he knew. He walked past the other table of men and innocently cut her off from the rest of the room. She was pouring two more mugs of beer and watching him from the corner of her eye. In order not to face him, she rapped her knuckles on the large wooden keg and acted like it was empty. Without turning, she went through a doorway and out of sight.

Toby chewed on the inside of his cheek as he watched the doorway for her return. "ROSA, ROSA!" The men called her name in a sing-song manner. Another minute went by and she poked her head out, telling them to be quiet. This time she looked straight at Toby, since she really couldn't ignore him again. She wiped her hands on her apron and picked up the mugs. She wordlessly waited for him to move out of her way. He did and then waited for her to return.

"Can you tell me who owns the short steed outside?" he asked.

Without any hint of coldness, she asked the color of the horse. When he described it, one of the men at the nearby table barked out that it was Rosa's nag. Rosa gave him that quick-flash smile that didn't quite reach her eyes. Toby could see that she'd practiced that smile often, like any good politician. Her voice was cautious as she answered him: "It's mine...."

Toby knew there was no point in pressing the issue and quickly added, "Sorry, it looked much like one a man I knew rode...."

She had the upper hand and then knew the truth of who he was. A flash of red crossed her eyes, and Toby wondered what she knew of that night at West Monterey. She gave him a level, cross look as she waved for him to back up and let her pass.

Toby and a couple of the other men heard the horses outside neigh. He wondered what had fussed them up and walked to the doorway. As he stepped into the darkness, it took a moment for his eyes to adjust. He walked back to the horse and petted its long nose again. He looked to the rain barrel across the street and couldn't make out Jayne or Robin anywhere in sight!

He gave the two note whistle that was their signal, but didn't hear a reply. *Strange*, he thought as he slowly crossed the road and swung his head around, looking for them. Even in the dim light, he spotted her foot sticking out from behind the barrel...

◊ ◊ ◊

2-38

~a hundred lifetimes~

Toby raised Jayne's head tenderly and felt the warm blood on his hands. The dog lie nearby and didn't move. Toby knew without checking that it was dead. He could feel Jayne's breathing against his throat, but she was completely out. He looked everywhere he could and even gave a soft whistle to find Robin. She had disappeared completely.

Toby took several minutes to analyze the scene and looked for someone to give him a hand. As he scanned the darkened street, he glimpsed Rosa standing at the window again. She looked directly at him and then stepped back out of view.

Toby was furious and realized that she was involved. *It must have been the two men she let out the side door!* He wanted to take the whip to her and get her to confess in front of the other men in the tavern.

But for now, he had to get Jayne back to the docks. He knew that Ella would be there and could help. He would deal with Rosa later; he would make her pay, and the men would be nothing but cold flesh by the time he was done with them!

Toby didn't like leaving the dead dog there to be eaten by rats or thrown in the river, but he couldn't carry both the dog and Jayne. And more importantly, *where was Robin?*

He carried Jayne like a baby and felt more warm blood on his chest and arm. Under the light from a street lantern, he saw the gash in her head and was nearly blinded by anger. *Oh, what would they do to Robin?* Jayne started to slip from his hold, but he gently hoisted her back up.

He was so bloody furious! Everyone connected with that damned Lew was poison. Toby was certain that Rosa was Luke's wife, and she wanted revenge! He carried Jayne until his arms were rubbery and he couldn't go any further. He was panting from the exertion and could no longer whistle for Robin. He was about to erupt into tears from sheer frustration when he realized he had reached the wharf. He yelled to Ella, Ernie, and Pete. The light in the warehouse was still on, and Toby cried out again. The door to the building burst open, and the lantern light framed Ernie's silhouette in the doorway.

He saw Toby staggering towards him and hollered for Ella before pulling Jayne into his arms to carry her inside. They put her on the temporary table that they'd made from some empty crates.

"MY GOD!" Ella exploded as she parted Jayne's bloody hair and examined the wound. The bleeding had slowed a little, but in less than a moment, the top of the crate had a dinner-plate-sized stain on it. Ella grabbed a clean cloth and held it to the wound as Toby tried to catch his breath and ramble off what had happened, including his suspicion about Rosa and her pals, and how he thought they had Robin.

Even after his breath was back to normal, he was still shaking from anger. "Ernie, I'm going back and whip the skin off that woman...."

"NO YOU WON'T! Listen to me when I tell you this...." He paused to make sure Toby was listening before he continued. "I remember how Luke was almost afraid of her, even thought she was the devil. NO! I'm not kiddin', Toby. She is *foul-tempered*, that woman. Maybe she heard what happened in Monterey and is mad at you.... I don't know, but what I do know is she wants blood."

"Mor'n likely money...." Pete added, holding Jayne's head up for Ella to work on.

"Money!?!" Toby acted like he was going to laugh. How could Luke's wife possibly know about the money that Toby and Gina got from delivering the whiskey still to Mad Hattie? Then it dawned on him that Gina could have told Luke they were planning to make the delivery and collect the gold. And Luke must have told Lucca. That's right! Lucca *had* mentioned the gold, just before they killed him and Luke at West Monterey! So Luke's wife *must* know about the gold, too! *Damn that Gina!* "We've got to go after them. Robin's in trouble...."

"Not likely, Tob'," Ernie said. "My guess is that Rosa wants the gold, and she *won't* hurt Robin...unless...." His voice trailed off and he looked at Pete.

"We can't just sit here!" Toby said.

"That's *jus'* what we have to do!" Ernie gently pushed Toby back onto a crate, trying to get him to stop and think.

"Ernie's right, Tob'," Pete explained. "She wants the gold. And, I bet she threatens to cut up Robin if that's what it takes to get it...."

Toby was drawing deep breaths of total rage. He wanted to strike back—hard and now! He felt the reason of Pete's and Ernie's thinking, but he didn't like any of it!

"I've got to stitch this up!" Ella said as she threw down the blood-soaked cloth. Toby could see the exasperation on her face. "Get me a piece of horse hair and a needle, Ernie." Pete still held the unconscious Jayne's head, and his hands were soaked red.

"Also some water—and scissors, Ern!" Ella called out. "Toby, I'm going to have to cut her hair. I really hate.... Thanks, Ernie."

Toby shrugged and nodded, still shaking. He got another lantern from its bracket and used a piece of straw to light it from the other lantern. He stood shoulder to shoulder with Ella, holding the lantern up for more light and watching her cut Jayne's beautiful hair.

Nearly an hour had passed when Toby finally put down the lantern and saw the terrible swelling under the stitches—all twenty six of them. Ella had done a very neat job of the work, but it still looked horrible. Stiff and sore, she slumped onto a crate behind her.

"I need a walk...." Toby said as he stood up.

"Tob'! I don't need to tell you how bad it could be for Robin if you go near them now." Ernie said quietly, holding Toby's arm.

"I'm going after the dog.... And YES! I understand how bad it could be!" He pulled his arm loose from Ernie's grasp and went to the door.

"Toby!" Ella's voice was firm, but quiet. "You can take your walk soon enough. Stay here for now so we can think through a plan to get Robin back. You need to *try* to stay calm. It might help us to barter...." She nodded solemnly.

Toby pounded his fist on the doorframe, but turned around and came back into the warehouse. He tried to sit down while they talked, but he had too much angry energy. He paced around, so agitated that Ella finally snapped at him: "Tob'! For God's sake, sit down or at least stand still! We've almost got everything figgur'd out. You can get outta here in a minute."

Toby nodded and stood in one spot while Ella, Ernie, and Pete finished discussing the details of the plan. Finally, Ernie looked at Toby, who was kicking his boot against a crate, and said: "Okay, Toby. You got all that?" Toby nodded, chewing the inside of his cheek. "All right then. Go. Walk off some of that steam and take care of the dog!"

Toby turned and walked through the door, back into the darkness. He retraced the path to the shop. As he walked, his mind cleared a little bit. He hadn't once considered his appearance. Now he realized there were smears of blood on his face, his shirt was soaked with it, and his pants were streaked, as well. But none of that mattered now. Jayne's blood was just a reminder of the rage that boiled in his own blood.

As he approached the corner and the rain barrel, he saw the lights still on in the tavern. Laughter rang from inside, further adding insult to the hatred that burned in his heart. He weighed the words of caution that the others had given him, and resisted bursting into the place and settling the score. But as he picked up the dog and carried it, he turned and was drawn to the light like a moth to the flame.

He stood at the front window, watching Rosa and the two men laughing and toasting each other with mugs of beer. Toby stepped closer to the window so that he could be seen in the light, and waited. His desire to kill them all, right then, was paramount. He could smell the death of the dog on him, which reinforced his desire to get even for yet another death.

He was patting the dog slowly, with a grim stare at Rosa. After several long moments, she looked up and saw him. She screamed, dropped her mug, and backed into a corner, finally sliding down the wall. The sight she saw was something she would never forget—not in a hundred lifetimes…

◊ ◊ ◊

2-39

~holding hands in the dark~

Robin had cried herself out and was now seething with anger. She had quit pulling on her arm, realizing it was tied and that she wasn't going to get it loose. Her wrist was bleeding where the rawhide strap cut into it, and she was sitting on the dirt floor of a shed. It wasn't dirt so much as mud, since she'd had to relieve herself twice in the eight hours that she sat in the darkness. She tugged once more at the arm that was stuck through a hole in the wall, but she couldn't reach in to untie it.

Robin listened to the men in the other room as they slept. She didn't remember much of the attack because she'd fallen asleep in Jayne's arms. She woke when she heard a solid thud and was dropped on the ground. Jayne fell on top of her, but someone pulled her off, stuffed Robin into a bag, and carried her away. They roughly pulled her into this shed and then yanked her arm through a hole in the wall. She struggled the whole time, but they were just too big and strong for her. They took her knife, tied her wrist to something in the other room, and then one of the men ripped the claw necklace from her neck.

Robin was past caring about her own predicament or even being afraid of the situation; she was more worried about Jayne. And being caged like an animal made something inside her boil! If she could, she would cut off her own arm to escape!

Earlier, she'd screamed and screamed, but soon realized that nobody could hear her. She figured she must be quite a distance from anybody who might help. Where was Toby? And Jayne? Why hadn't they come to save her? All she wanted was to be freed—and to get at those men WITH HER KNIFE!

She used her free hand to cover herself with the sack she'd been carried in. She was cold, hungry, and ached all over. Her hand was tied in such a way that the back of it was up against whatever held it in place. She couldn't tell what it was, but guessed that it was the leg of a table or bed. She could hear the men snoring in the next room, probably sleeping off the alcohol she had smelled on them.

She'd heard rats scurrying during the night and had even felt one brush past her leg, but they were now gone. She could tell that the night was nearly over because an owl had stopped hooting and she heard the stirrings of some animals nearby. It would be light soon.

She almost screamed when she felt two taps on the back of her hand. It was a light touch; someone's fingers gently letting her know that he or she was there! She turned her head, but couldn't see anything in the other room. But she had acute hearing, and she heard someone's slow, raspy breath. She felt a slow sawing motion against the rawhide strap and then felt the strap drop from her wrist. Slowly, carefully, and as silently as she could, she pulled her arm through the hole.

So softly that she barely heard the voice, someone said "Stay." Her heart leapt and she wanted to squeal in delight, but held the silence. She put her hands over her mouth to quiet her joy!

It took nearly ten minutes for her rescuer to slip out of the other room and get to her. It took another five for them to make it outside and into the woods. She was led nearly a quarter of a mile through the forest, tightly holding to the hand, before she turned and jumped into his arms. She kissed his cheek and whispered something in her native tongue.

Robin's grandfather held her as tightly as he could, but he was weak and frail. Robin climbed out of his arms and walked beside him. When they were a mile down the hillside and nearly back into the town, they decided it was safe to talk. Robin poured out story after story of what had happened to her and Jayne, giving him all the details about what they'd lived through in the past months.

Grandfather had to pull her to a stop several times so he could hold onto a tree and catch his breath. Finally, they sat together and talked until the morning was ready to break. They decided to get to the warehouse before any workers were up and moving around the town.

But Robin kept looking back to study the path to the house. It was her intent to go back and get her knife and claw necklace—and some revenge! Maybe she *and* Jayne would go together. *That* would be the way of the warrior, and the thought of it pleased her. But for now, it pleased her to once again hold the old man's hand…

◊ ◊ ◊

2-40

~nuthin' to do but sweat~

When they reached the warehouse, the door was ajar. Inside, Robin first saw Toby with his head resting on his arm, and then her sister lying on the tabletop! She ran to them, and he turned and lifted her onto his lap. They exchanged several quick kisses and firm hugs as she turned to look at Jayne.

Robin began to cry when she saw the bloody bandages wrapped around Jayne's head. She searched Toby's face for an answer. Her eyes pierced deeply into his, and without a word he knew the answers she sought. He whispered to her that everything was "ok," but he looked tired and worried, and Robin realized that he was afraid, too.

Toby's gaze passed Robin and landed on the old man, who was standing at a distance, waiting quietly for permission to approach. Toby nodded to the Indian, and the man came quickly to his other granddaughter's side. He picked up her hand and stared at the bandages on her head. He could tell by the blood soaked cloth that it was a serious wound. When his rheumy eyes floated back to Toby, Toby gave him a small smile and nodded.

The old man, whom Toby knew as Yeah-no, chanted a song, and Robin fell asleep. She smelled a bit repulsive from sitting in pee and mud all night, and Toby soon carried her to a bundle of sheep's wool that they had been using as a bed. As Toby watched the old man keep vigil over Jayne, he felt that his watch was over and decided to get some sleep. He slumped down beside Robin and fell into a deep slumber.

Toby had been asleep for less than two hours when Ella popped in through the door. She hadn't expected to see anybody but Toby and Jayne there, and caught up short when she saw the old man.

Her eyes moved to the bed and she spied Toby—and Robin! She went to their side and smiled as she tried to wake Toby with a gentle shake of his shoulder. He didn't stir or even mumble. His world was somewhere else at this moment. At that point, Ella sat back on a chair and watched the old man continue his trance-like chanting.

Ella hadn't slept since yesterday. She and the men had spent the entire night making plans for the now unnecessary exchange to get Robin back. But the worry was over, and everybody was safe. All her children were home.... Her head drooped ever so slightly until she was slumped over the wool bale and snoring softly.

The sunlight started to heat up the warehouse, but still no one stirred. Things were exactly the same six hours later—except the temperature was thirty degrees hotter. The old man was still chanting, and the others were still sleeping. It was near three in the afternoon.

Earlier in the day, Pete and Ernie had left a note on the front of the tavern telling the culprits to meet them at the warehouse at five. They would have made the meeting earlier in the day, but they wanted the kidnappers to think they needed the entire day to go and get the gold.

So in the meantime, Pete and Ernie had been on the tug. They made a trip upriver to Foxburg and to Ernie's cabin, and had even loaded two barges. Now it was nearly time for the meet-up, and they headed back to the warehouse to make sure everyone was ready. When they walked in, they were shocked—and relieved—to find Robin and her grandfather there. They decided that the original plan would still work; they'd just hide Robin and play out the scene as it afforded.

Ernie checked his pocket watch again and saw that the exchange was to take place in less than an hour. He wanted nothing more than to find a place to lie down and sleep. He was exhausted—and so was Pete! They were soaked in sweat. Wet dirt clung to them where rivulets of sweat had made clean streaks down their arms and faces. But there was no time for rest now.

"Can you do anything with him?" Ernie nodded to the old man.

"I think so...." Pete replied in a weary voice. He went to Yeah-no and spoke to him in the Indian's language. The old man was still chanting as Pete held him steady and walked him to the other end of the building. Pete got

Yeah-no settled into some soft fur bundles, where he sat silently.

Ernie woke Ella, first with a nuzzle and then with a kiss. Finally, she right-ed herself and sat blinking at him. "It's near time," Ernie said. He pulled at Toby's arm and had him sitting up, too. "We need to put everything together. Toby, just as we planned...."

Ella and Toby got up quickly and took turns drinking water from a dipper in the water bucket. Pete stood in the loft, looking out one of the high windows that faced the street. He wiped away some of his sweat with a kerchief. Toby thought of how hot it must be up there and was thankful he wasn't in the loft. "What are we going to do with Robin, and how are we going to get her to ap-pear at the right moment?" Toby asked Ella.

"We just need for her to keep quiet and out of sight." They both looked at Robin's sleeping figure. "I reckon you'd better wake her and get her back to her grandfather, though...."

Toby gently touched Robin's arm and said her name. Once she stirred, she was fully awake in just a few seconds. She sat up and hopped off of the make-shift bed, quickly blinking to focus her eyes. She instantly returned to Jayne's side and looked around for her grandfather. Pete called down to Robin and explained what was going to happen, and that her job was to stay out of sight. Robin smiled up at Pete and gave a firm nod, indicating that she understood.

Toby watched Pete cross the loft and look out another window. "Where the hell is he?" Pete murmured. He took a white cloth out of his pocket and waved it near the window. A moment passed, and he called down to Ernie, "He's here. We'll get him inside before the others arrive—I hope!" Pete returned to the original window-lookout and continued his watch.

A large piece of sackcloth hung over Jayne's body and reached down to the floor. Robin sat under the table, and everyone else wondered if she clearly understood what was going to happen. The other man had entered the building, and Ernie ushered him to his spot behind the door. They each took a turn at a drink of water and passed the dipper up to Pete. There was nothing else to do but wait and drip sweat...

◊ ◊ ◊

2-41

~watered down sweaty stew~

Ernie used the wait to tell each of them what to expect. "Remember, WE don't have to do anything! We have Robin, AND we have the gold. They probably don't know that Robin is with us—if they even know she's gone.... They'll try to bluff us and demand the gold, then give us a story that she's in a safe place, waitin' for us."

He looked to the loft and checked on Pete, who kept looking between Ernie and out the window. Ernie glanced at each of the others and continued. "We'll let them explain. I'll try to ask all the right questions, and if they answer them all—we'll have them."

The large man stood partway behind the entrance door, but still in sight of Ernie, listening to his directions. His job was to hide behind the door and trap the others inside the room so they couldn't escape. He checked his pistol and slid it back into the holster, wiggling it loose so he could draw it quickly if needed.

Ella leaned back against a crate and folded her arms across her chest. Toby had seen that stance before, and he knew it was her "I'm-not-buyin'-it!" look. Even in such stressful conditions and what was about to happen, she was the calmest looking woman he'd ever seen. Her face didn't even have a glow from sweating in all this heat! Toby could feel the sweat trickle down his back and stop at his already soaked waistband. They waited....

Jayne must be hot under that cloth, Toby thought. He picked up the dipper of water and stepped towards her. He thought he'd dab some water on her forehead to cool her down. Ella shook her head at him and said, "Toby, we don't want her to wake up, 'specially now. She has to appear dead. I've been watchin' her breathing and she's doin' ok. Ernie, do you think they'll notice her breathing?"

"Not if we keep them talkin' and make them nervous...." he replied.

"They're makin' *me* nervous!" Toby added and everyone smiled at him.

"Ern, I'm thinkin' they know the little one is missin' and they're tryin' to figure out what they're gonna do about it," Ella said.

Ernie drew a long breath and nodded. "We'll wait. Jus' don't miss them comin', Pete."

When Ernie turned, he saw the old Indian walking back to Jayne's side. Yeah-no sat down and started chanting again. It was a soft but repetitious sound that started to grate on Toby's already raw nerves. Pete yelled something down to Yeah-no, and the Indian finally got up and went back to his spot on the fur bundles. But ten minutes later, Toby was turning in a circle, trying to break the chanting that had entered his brain and wouldn't leave....

After another half hour of sweating and waiting, Pete called down from above: "Ella, better water down the sweaty-stew. Company's comin'!"

Everybody took their positions, including Pete, who ducked behind a barrel in the loft...

◊ ◊ ◊

2-42

~dancin' chin to shin~

"Toby!?!" the voice from outside called. The young man approached the warehouse. "Mr. Toby! Wo bist du?"

Toby was the first to recognize the voice and told everyone to relax. He went to the door and saw Helmut. Toby forgot that he'd told him to come to the warehouse! Toby motioned for him to get inside quickly.

Helmut looked confused, but did as he was beckoned to do. "I come to verk, like you said, Mr. Toby." He stopped talking when he entered the building and saw the others staring at him. He nodded hello to each one before he saw the covered body of Jayne. He wasn't sure what was going on and started to mumble something, but Toby cut him off. "Helmut, I'm sorry, I forgot you were coming today. Uh, can you wait for me down at the boats? I'll be along as quickly as I can."

"No time, Tob'," Pete announced from the loft. "Our real company is just turning the corner!" When Helmut saw him and his rifle, he gave Toby a wary look.

"Helmut, it's just a little matter we have to clear up," Toby said hurriedly. "Hide behind those sacks piled there!" Helmut was quick to follow the instructions and was out of sight in several seconds.

Everyone re-positioned themselves and watched the doorway.

The first young man stopped outside the entrance; he stepped aside to let Rosa step around him and walk through the door. Once her eyes adjusted to the light, she slowly glanced across each of the faces staring at her.

Ella's eyes were half-lidded, and she gave Rosa a stoic look. They had met several times before; even eaten together when Luke had worked for her and Ernie! Rosa nodded, but when she didn't receive a response, she looked to Ernie and said, "Well, we're here, and it's time for you and YOU," here she looked at Toby, "to pay me some money for killing my Luke!"

Ernie didn't let a split second pass. "And why would we do that? Your husband tied a woman to a post—to BURN HER! And he tried to kill all of us while we were on the barges. Or didn't you know THAT?"

"Yeah, I KNEW that, but that's...."

"Him AND that no good daddy of his!" Toby added quickly. "They jumped us downriver. _And killed my mule!_"

Rosa gave Toby a cocky smile and looked at Ernie and Ella again. "I know. I saw it all. I was hid in the woods when it all took place.... I held the horses and was ready to ride out with them—_with_ the gold, o'course!"

Ella interrupted her: "We treated Luke like a son when he worked for us...."

"You treated him like a slave!" Rosa shot back viciously. "You promised him—us—better pay and a share of the profit—"

Ernie interrupted her: "But he just didn't work out! He could barely count, and he was stealing from our warehouse!" Ella looked to Ernie and saw that he was barely keeping his temper.

Rosa held her ground and pointed at Toby. "When _you_ showed up again with that....that hussy—_and_ the gold—we figured it was a good time for us to take it!" Rosa mimicked Ella and folded her arms across her chest. She looked smug. "So, you have that gold for me?" She suddenly turned red and looked back to her partner who hadn't entered the building. "For _us_, I mean!" She smiled at her companion and then cocked her head, motioning for him to enter the warehouse. He strode to her side and gave Toby a half-toothed grin. It looked to Toby that his teeth had been broken off, probably during a fight. Toby suddenly had the desire to punch the rest of them out.

Ernie fired a question at Rosa before she had the chance to continue her act of brazen boasting. "Where's the girl?"

"Oh, the Indian tramp's little sister?" Rosa said and her sidekick gave a stupid laugh.

Toby clenched his fist tighter. He was only one step away from that tooth-less goober and tense enough to leap and fire off a punch in one quick movement.

"She's with a friend," Rosa said airily. "And when we get the gold, we'll send her to you...."

Toby noticed the sweat on Rosa's upper lip. He knew she was lying, but he noticed how good she was at it.

"You think we're gonna give you the gold without the girl?" Ella asked, beating Ernie to it.

Rosa leaned forward and jutted her jaw in Ella's direction. "I don't care what *any* of you think."

"Goober" and Rosa spun around when they heard the door to the warehouse squeak shut. Both jolted at the sight of Archibald, the sheriff, and realized that he had been there the whole time and heard it all. The bravado quickly melted from their faces. They looked up when they heard the rifle cock and saw Pete standing in the loft above them.

"You got everything you need there, Arch?" Pete asked.

Arch nodded and raised his pistol to make sure the two saw it. "Reckon I do," he said as he stepped forward and handed some locking chains to Ernie.

"I DON'T!" Toby said in a louder than necessary voice. "I want the knife you stole from the girl—and THIS!" He reached to the man's throat and curled his fingers around the claw necklace. He gave it a sharp pull, but it didn't come loose!

He saw the knife out of the corner of his eye, but before it moved another inch he jerked the leather strap again and head-butted Goober, causing him to drop the knife and stagger back.

Robin burst out from under the table and grabbed Goober's leg. She opened her mouth and buried her teeth in his calf! Goober screamed curses at her and tried to kick her off, but Toby drew back and punched him—harder than he realized. As Goober fell, Toby grabbed his hand and said, "THAT one is for the dog!"

Ten minutes later, Arch had Goober hanging over his shoulder and was pointing the pistol in the center of Rosa's back as Ernie cuffed her. They were headed for the jailhouse.

Robin had uncovered Jayne's head, and she was awake now, but still dreamy. Toby sat beside her, holding her hand and smiling. Robin beamed with happiness and pride as she put the claw necklace back on. Grandpa—who had finally finished chanting some time during the episode—watched silently with a grin on his face, as well. He held a longing gaze at the claw necklace.

Helmut stood off to the side and sheepishly stepped forward. "...Jus' some business to finish?" He repeated Toby's earlier words.

Ella smiled at him and said, "I think I like him...." She nodded towards Helmut as she looked at Ernie.

"Well you can't have him!" Toby interjected. "He's gonna work with the Murphys, mining coal...if he wants to."

Helmut shrugged and said with a grin, "As long as I don't have to do business with you bunch!"

$$\Diamond \ \Diamond \ \Diamond$$

Early the next day, smiling and pleased with themselves from the previous night's festivities, they all went in different directions, loading, sorting, and preparing for the trip downriver. Toby was working as hard as anyone when Ernie came to him and said, "You're forgettin' somethin'...." He pulled Toby out of earshot of the others and spoke again. "You're gonna be working while the others are resting. *You're* gonna be steering the tug and barges, and I want you rested to do that. Also, you have to have the ledgers ready. So let these guys do their work—and you do yours."

Toby was tired and wiped his brow. He thought he should be helping to load the barges, but realized that Ernie was right. He knew he had a different role to fill now. He nodded in agreement and walked with Ernie back into the warehouse.

$$\Diamond \ \Diamond \ \Diamond$$

A crowd had gathered to see them off; but what they really wanted to see were how the new steamboats operated. There was a lot of fanfare and waving, and the steam whistles blew. Ella was staying behind to take care of Jayne. She gave a sorrowful wave to Ernie. She knew he'd be back in two days, but she hated to not go with him. Smoke poured from the tug's stacks as the crew members turned their backs on the onlookers and prepared to leave.

Inside the warehouse, Toby talked quietly to Jayne and protested her decision. She told him that her grandfather wanted her and Robin to go back with him to the woods where he'd grown up. He was sick, and wanted to die there. Toby looked disappointed, but Jayne whispered in a weak voice: "I will go with him, and wait. When it's over, I will come back to you. Robin and I will miss you very much."

The whistles blew again, and Toby looked to the boats. He knew there was no argument: He would have to make the trip (and how many more?) before they would be back together. He picked up Robin and kissed her. She squeezed his neck, and her tears dampened his cheek. He held Jayne's hand, kissed her softly on the lips, and then turned to go. With one backward glance, he turned and trotted to his tug.

Helmut tossed the line off the cleat and watched as Toby slowly curled his fingers around the steering wheel. Toby spun the wheel and opened the power arm. Something new welled up in Toby's chest, an emotion he couldn't explain. Then he realized that he was alone—again—but that he was part of something new and exciting on the river…

◊ ◊ ◊

2-43

~the social climber~

Toby held a course directly behind Ernie's tug and its two barges. Behind him, Pete followed, also pulling two. He and Helmut pulled a pair, as well, but they weren't as heavy, since Toby wanted his tug to make better speed.

Helmut was as social as anyone could get. He talked for most of the trip, telling Toby about his home in Austria, some place in the Alps. He told stories of how he'd never seen lightning until he came to the United States because his home was so deep in the mountains that they never had lightning there. Toby couldn't imagine being so high up in the mountains that you were above the clouds.

Toby was still dwelling on the fact that Jayne was gone (for now), and so was Gina. His mind drifted between the two women, and also back to his mother and sisters. He was feeling homesick for the first time in over a month....

"Oh, you vould *love* the food, Toby. And the maidens, and the beer gardens on a summer afternoon like this one! They have bands and every...-one dances! It is much fun...."

Ernie's whistle gave a *fwee-oop* and Toby returned it. Like Ernie, he'd also been watching the shoreline and agreed that they were close to the place where they had lost the cart in the storm. Toby guided his tug towards the shore and reduced the speed to its slowest, barely more than the current itself.

Helmut was still babbling about the Austrian countryside, and Toby was thinking how well the young man and Gina could have gotten along. It would have been interesting to see who would last longer talking and telling tales!

Toby thought he saw what he was looking for....

"...You could feel the ice cold air coming down the mountains, even on the summer days...."

Toby nodded absentmindedly. He spotted what he wanted. There it was, just as they had left it. Only now, part of it that had been hidden by the high flood water from the storm was exposed. Helmut finally stopped talking and followed Toby's gaze to the cart that was wedged among some rocks and a dead tree.

"Was ist das?" Catching his mistake, Helmut switched from German to English: "Uh, that? Vhat is that?"

"Our—*my* cart." Toby smiled, but his eyes never strayed from the target. "We lost it in a storm, and now I'll have it back."

Helmut climbed down the ladder and looked over the railing at the mud-covered cart. The single-tree on the front of it had broken off, and Toby sadly remembered the times he'd hooked Bea up to that harness.

"Go back and drop the anchor," he told Helmut.

Helmut jumped from the tug, across one barge and then to the last one, and swung the heavy anchor, watching for it to tighten the line. After it caught, he tied the line off to a cleat and returned to Toby on the tug.

The only sound they could hear was some unused steam bypassing the opened valves. Toby's mind began playing the events of the evening that it had happened. He could almost feel the cold, wet rain again. The memory of being trapped underwater, the darkness and the feeling of helplessness, still sent a chill through him. He remembered being trapped, his sleeve caught on the axle as he tried to stop the cart from sliding off the barge, and how he'd been pulled overboard with it all. He shivered, remembering how he was a minute from dying and how Jayne had reached him and used her knife to cut him free....

"Toby, are you all right? You look like you've seen a...a—vhat is the vord you say?"

"A ghost," Toby replied and stepped back from the rail. He looked up and saw a large tree limb directly above the cart. *It might be close enough*, Toby thought. He visualized how he could use it. *With a rope...to lift the four hundred pounds....*

"Helmut, how good are you at climbing?" Toby was looking at the tree and thinking of how much rope it might take.

"Clim-bing? For *that*?" Helmut nodded towards the tree limb. "It's—how you say? A walk in the cake!"

Toby looked at him for a second before he erupted into a laugh and said, "That's a 'walk in the *park*,' Helmut! Now, if we could get a line over that limb…it would give us a chance to pull her up...."

"I'll get there and you toss me a rope." Helmut pulled off his shirt and studied the water beside the boat. Once he felt sure he wasn't going to land on a large rock, he jumped in and went to the cart. He was standing in water up to his chest, and it appeared that the rock he was on was slippery. Doing his best to keep from slipping, Helmut pushed hard at the cart and it seemed to loosen. He moved past it and made his way to the shore.

It was another five minutes before he made it out on the limb and sat just a short distance from the cart. "See, I am your 'minkey.'" He gave Toby a broad grin and pounded his chest.

Close enough, Toby thought. *Some things are the same in all languages.* He laughed loudly, readied his footing, and tossed the rope.

"Give to me some more," Helmut said. He tied off the line and pulled in enough to make a loop. In another ten minutes, they had rigged a "snatch block," along with a block and tackle. Technically, the rope was held tight by the limb, and only when Helmut was back in the water by the cart did Toby relaxed.

It was time! Toby pulled on the rope and was amazed how easy it was for him to lift the cart—by himself! He wasn't sure what Helmut was about to do, or how they would get the cart onto the tug's small deck, but Helmut seemed so sure of himself. The cart was now hanging about eight feet away from the railing.

"Toby, tie off the line and toss me another...."

Another five minutes, and the muddy cart was lowered onto the deck. Toby quickly went to it and looked at his muddy coat—still tangled in the axle! Without saying anything, he worked it loose and secretly felt the collar. The coins were still there! He hung the coat on the ladder. "That coat was nearly my death," he said. He told Helmut the whole story as the Austrian shook his head in awe. Toby continued talking as he casually rubbed mud from the floorboard, checking to see if the secret hiding place was intact. It was!

After they retrieved the ropes and rigging, they prepared to haul anchor and try to catch the others. "I do not understand. Why you want to take the cart, the wheel is broken, the 'tree' is gone, and its deck is war-ped pretty good," Helmut said.

Toby was standing beside the ladder, the coat in his free arm, ready to climb up to the steering cabin. "It's pretty special to me," he said. Helmut just frowned at that answer, shook his head, and continued to haul anchor.

With the current in their favor, they were nearing the "Murphy Mine" in the narrow river inlet by late afternoon. The other tugs had indeed made good time, and they never caught them. Toby and Helmut waved a hearty greeting to the Murphys as they came into view on the shoreline.

Once they tied up the tug and made the necessary introductions, Toby explained that Helmut needed a job and went on to praise him for his help so far. Mrs. Murphy was thrilled to find someone who knew German, as she hadn't spoken it much ever since she left Germany for Ireland as a young woman. It wasn't long until she was chatting away in German with Helmut, her hand on his arm. They both were in heaven (or whatever it's called in German) as they gabbed heartily and she literally dragged him to the campfire cooking area.

Toby tried his best to beg off from mealtime and start downriver, but he could see *that just wasn't gonna happen*! He was led to the mine site and was shocked at what the Murphy boys had accomplished in just a few days. They had framed a shaft opening with heavy timbers and started a rough wooden ramp towards the river's edge. As Oliver Murphy rattled on about the plans and the agenda, Toby couldn't be happier with his choice to employ this man and his family.

Over a great thrown-together meal, Toby noticed how Mr. Murphy continued to size up Helmut, and how Mrs. Murphy and the oldest girl Annette fawned over him. Toby figured that he'd be attending a wedding here in "Narrow River" in the not-too-distant future.

The guttural German conversation seemingly had no end, but the daylight did. Toby knew it would be a lack of serious judgment to start downriver into the coming darkness, but he wanted to see Gina as soon as possible. He stirred in his seat on the halved-log bench and kept looking back at the tug to see if there was still smoke issuing from the stack.

Finally, he couldn't wait any longer and stood as he announced his departure. It came as a surprise to the others, who had assumed he would leave in the morning. But Toby's brain was somewhere else.

Mr. Oliver followed Toby to the tug and showed no signs of ending their conversation. While they watched the fire's heat build up steam, Mr. Murphy asked, "Toby, you have the list I gave you?" Toby nodded and poked the last piece of firewood into the firebox. The Murphy boys had stacked coal onto the deck of the barge, and it was almost time for Toby to crank up the steam to the engine.

Finally, Toby shook hands with the older man and tried to indicate that he needed to leave, so he went to the ladder and pointed to the rear barge. "I'll be back in several days. And I'll have the tools and supplies you listed. If you can, would you mind pulling up the anchor for me?" With that, Toby turned and climbed the ladder to the steering house. He wondered if Oliver might not be so hungry for conversation after listening to Helmut for a few days…

◊ ◊ ◊

2-44

~runnin' on vapors~

Toby swung the tug and two barges into a U-turn and cleared the far shore easily. He waved (for the third time) to everyone on shore and headed to the main river. Once he made the left turn and was in the deep channel, he stood looking ahead. He stepped from one foot to the other and finally realized what his impatience was all about. He wanted to see Gina—desperately! He wanted to know what she planed to do with her future. He tried to push the power lever to its full-on position and realized it was already there! He was disappointed; he wanted more speed. In his head he had already figured out that he wasn't going to make the twenty-or-so miles before total darkness fell, so he drew a deep breath again and judged the distance that he could make.

It also dawned on him that he wanted to check on the gold, and he rethought the trip. It would be best for him to pull up soon and use the last of the daylight to tear apart the floorboard of the cart. Toby looked at the smokestack and saw sparks shooting out. He bit his lip at the thought that he was just now getting to a full head of steam and would be making his best time.

Two miles downriver, he saw the flats. He pulled up and decreased his speed until he was drifting in the current. He put the "stay rope" loops onto the handles of the steering wheel and let the tug drift towards shore. He left the steering cabin and went down to the deck. Quickly, he jumped to the first barge and then to the second, where he dropped anchor. *There has to be a better way to do this,* he thought as he retraced his path back to the tug's deck. He felt the soft slowing of the trio as each of the towropes tightened and the barges finally came to a halt, causing the tug to stop, too.

In the last of the twilight, he looked around and studied everything. It all seemed good. He went to the cabin's toolbox and came back with a pry bar. In less than a minute he had the floorboard loose. In another minute he had the cover pried off and saw the glimmer of the gold pieces through the bee's wax that held them in place. One by one, he picked them out of the muddy wax and used his thumbnail to clean them.

All five of the twenty-dollar gold pieces were cleaned and in his pocket. He stepped to the cabin and took out the jug of "firewater" that all of them carried "for medicinal purposes." He went to the firebox, opened the door, and sat on the deck, watching the fire for quite a while. The evening was quiet, warm, and getting a little fuzzy from the firewater.

The soft lapping of water on the side of the boat, the smell of the air in the valley, and the nice breeze filled him with a quiet sense of pleasure. The moon rose in the channel over the river to the south, towards Pittsburgh *and* Gina! Toby wished she was here on the boat with him; they would spend the night under the stars that had begun to appear in the sky. He could then ask *her* questions for a change; there were so many things he should have asked her before.

Toby kept sipping from the jug and looking into the night sky as his thoughts skipped across the people currently in his life. After a little while, he thought about the fact that *none* of them were with him at the moment. His thoughts slowed and then came to a complete stop. All around him was a quiet stillness and an overwhelming sense of aloneness. It didn't bother him at first, nor did it seem like a permanent condition. But the more he thought about it, the lonelier he felt. When he looked at the sky, the vastness of it made him feel more insignificant.

The constant sipping of the moonshine had fuddled him, and he decided to get some sleep. He tried to shake the lonely feeling, but it nagged at him. His mother and sisters seemed like they were part of another lifetime, yet he missed them very badly at the moment. Jayne also crossed his mind, and he wondered if she and Robin were watching the same sky. Did they miss him also? He lowered his head as if he were looking at his shoes and nodded asleep.

When the loud noise of something hitting the deck woke him, he realized that he had dropped the jug and that its contents were spilling out onto the deck. He watched in a stupor as the liquid glittered in the light of the fire from the firebox....

Slow to realize the potential of the situation, Toby watched the jug roll across the deck and continue to spill its liquid. Now moonshine was splashed across the deck. Only then did Toby remember how the fumes could explode when they got near a fire! He pushed himself up, lost his balance, and fell into a firewater puddle. Again, he tried to stand. He finally made it to a full standing position and wobbled. He was afraid now, and THAT instantly sobered up his mind, if not his body.

He lurched towards the canvas bucket hanging on the wall of the cabin. He went to the railing and quickly leaned over. Gripping tightly, he swung his arm and the bucket into the river and pulled up a bucketful of water. With one fluid move, he splashed the water across the deck towards the firebox. But that only pushed the moonshine closer to the fire!

There was a loud *"foom"* as the vapors contacted the fire. Instantly, a flash of fire covered the deck and backtracked to Toby! He couldn't move in the split second it took to reach him. His clothing flashed, and he was covered in the fire! He turned quickly and dove over the railing into the water…

◊ ◊ ◊

2-45

~the stand-in-line reunion~

Toby rose in the dark water and slipped his head out slowly. He fully expected to see the flames engulfing the rear deck of the tug, but there was nothing! He swam to the first barge and pulled himself up onto its deck. His knee ached from hitting it on a rock submerged in the water. He sat there in relief, even smiling at the foolishness of the event.

Can I be any more stupid?, he thought as he stood and felt his knee's weakness. He swung his leg over the railing of the tug and pulled himself across to sit a moment and look things over. The deck appeared to be singed, and the varnish seemed to have lost its shine, but there wasn't enough light from the firebox to see clearly.

He ran his hands down his arms and squeezed the water out of his shirt. When he went to squeeze the water from his hair, he felt something wrong! Since he didn't believe his first impression, he felt around the rest of his head until he realized that a good portion of his hair was burned off! He swore and pulled at it to determine its length. He swore again and groped at both sides of his head. There was a great difference in the length. This time he stood up and swore three times. He tried to imagine what it must look like. He limped in circles around the deck, still swearing. His pirate imitation didn't last long as his knee really started to hurt, so he sat on the railing and looked up into the night sky again.

Soon he started laughing and hopped to the doorway to the cabin, hopped again, and made it to the bunk. Once he stripped off the wet clothing and lay on the bunk, he fell into a deep sleep.

Morning came, and Toby woke feeling drowsy and lazy. His knee felt thick and stiff. It was all he could do to get dressed. It took him an extra half an hour to get the fire up and try to climb the ladder to the wheelhouse. His one boot was unlaced because he couldn't bend over to tie it.

He was burning some of the coal with the wood, and black smoke poured out of the stack, layering along behind him as the tug started ahead. When the cold, morning air hit the stack, it made the smoke's temperature about even with the air temperature. This allowed the solid black trail of smoke to widen, but kept it from drifting upwards. When Toby turned to look back, he saw that the stack acted as a paintbrush, smearing the heavy black smoke in the sky. It hung motionless about twenty feet above the river. He felt some remorse that he was probably the first person to bring the soot of the city into the pristine valley, but he figured it was just a price to pay for progress....

The tug and its cargo made the next twenty miles in just over three hours. Toby checked the temperature gauge; he still had plenty of heat and steam to go further! He was beginning to think that a single load of coal in the firebox would get him from the warehouse in Pittsburgh to the Murphy Mine. He thought to make a test of it when he started back north.

He was at his destination before he realized it. He quickly backed off of the power arm and steered the tug towards the shoreline. The other tugs were there, and he was starting to get antsy to see Gina. The current on the "Mon" River was against him, and he had to power up to make any gains against it. "Must have been some rains up that river," he said out loud just as he spotted Ernie standing at the railing, watching him approach.

Toby waved to him just as Pete stepped to Ernie's side and said something. They both turned and entered the door into the warehouse's "counting room." Another man that Toby had never seen before waited at the dock to tie up the tug. Toby steered in, shut off the steam valves, and stepped to the ladder to look down. That's when he felt how stiff his leg had become. He wasn't sure how this was going to work, but he hopped onto the ladder and had to mostly use his arms to lower himself, one rung at a time.

He crossed to the railing, spoke to the deck hand, and approached the long wooden stairs that ran up the side of the building. He had to hop up them, relying heavily on the handrail. It was exhausting work, and Toby took a break on a three-foot landing halfway up the stairs. He looked up at the next twenty-or-so steps to the top, sweating as the day's temperature started its climb, as well.

He guessed it was going to be another day in the mid-nineties. Near the top, he said, "Five more to go" through clenched teeth and hopped along.

Once at the top, he stopped to catch his breath. Several men stepped onto the porch from the ground level and gave him a funny look as they passed and entered the door ahead of him. Toby wondered what that was all about, but hopped around the edge of the doorway and then inside.

It took a moment for his eyes to adjust to the light, and when they did he was looking at Gina. She was standing behind the counter and had looked at him briefly as he acclimated to the room. But before he could smile and say hello, she looked back to the men ahead of him and began talking to them.

Toby used his hand to brush his hair flat and remembered: He was missing some of it! He suddenly realized how terrible he must look, and his eyes searched the other parts of the room. Ernie was leaning stiff-armed over Eula's desk, his knuckles buried in the leather desktop, with Pete looking over her shoulder. Her arm was wrapped in heavy bandages and tied in a sling. She looked pale and in need of rest, but Toby knew her and how tireless she was at any task. When he looked at Gina again, she had been looking at him, but quickly glanced back to the men that stood talking to her.

Toby knew he needed to sit down—and soon! He hopped forward and stood at the railing just across from Eula's desk. The railing was the only thing that stood between him and the chair just on the other side of it. He swung his swollen leg over the rail and then his other leg, and slid into the chair before the others looked up and saw him.

The three of them studied him for a moment without saying a word. Then Ernie smiled slowly, followed by Pete and Eula. "Long trip, there, Toby?"

Toby knew the ribbing was going to start, so he put his elbow on the arm of the chair and rested his head in his hand. "Not too bad, all in all," he said. He felt his singed hair again and attempted to sit up straight, his stiff leg sticking out towards them.

"Good," Pete said with a wry smile. "We've got a lot of stuff that needs carried up from the warehouse...."

Toby responded with a heavy moan and put his hand up to hide his face. "Uh, sure, but I jus' need to talk to Gina first...."

Ernie started laughing, and Eula asked him, "WHAT in God's earth have you done NOW?"

Pete looked at Ernie and added, "Maybe the kid can jus' haul stuff DOWN stairs. It'd be easier for him!"

The three laughed and Ernie pressed on: "Tob', you don't look so good. I think Eula might be able to carry more than you!"

Eula slapped Ernie's arm and gave Toby a more caring look. "Toby, Gina should be finished with them shortly. And I think you both should go to an early lunch!" She shot the others a glance to see if there was any opposition.

Toby groaned and nodded, still half smiling at Pete, waiting for another jab.... "Everything is just great!" he said sarcastically, shifting his eyes first to Ernie and then to Eula.

In a serious tone, Ernie said, "As soon as I get some of that coal onto my tug, I'm headin' north. I've got one barge of passengers and one of goods to get back to the Landin'. Pete will leave next, and we'll get to the flats to camp by dark. How's the river?"

"Gettin' low.... We're gonna be in trouble if it doesn't rain some." Toby said, feeling for the first time like he was helping.

Ernie gave him a nod and an appraising look and then looked over at Gina. "I figgur you ought to stay the night." He winked at Eula. "...An' you can leave in the morning—not too early...." This time he winked at Pete. The men stood up. Pete kissed Eula's hair and followed Ernie to the door.

Eula's eyes followed them, switched over to Gina, and then back to Toby before she asked, "Are you ok?"

He nodded.

"Why don't you go into the loft area and clean up some? I'll let Gina know." She returned to the bookkeeping as Toby struggled to his feet.

"How's the arm feelin'?"

She shrugged and nodded without looking up...

$$\Diamond \, \Diamond \, \Diamond$$

2-46

~two new looks!~

Toby took one last look at Gina as he rose from the chair and started towards the door with the "private" sign on it. There was something—what was it? Something about the way Gina looked. Her hair was pulled up and brushed, and she had a "pinched" look about her as her half-lidded eyes looked at the man speaking to her.

It held his attention, and there was something, something he'd seen somewhere. *Where?!* Gina still avoided looking at him, so he hopped to the door and entered the rooms that Eula and Pete used as their "winter home."

As Toby closed the door and looked around the room, it dawned on him what he had just seen. It was kind of haunting. He wanted to turn, open the door, and look again, to see if he could shake this feeling....

He had two visions in his mind: one of Anna, that clerk in Callensburg so long ago, and the other just seconds ago! They were almost interchangeable. Except for the age difference, both of the women had the same look about them! *What was it? A sternness? A no-nonsense look?* Toby pondered the likeness as he sat in a soft chair and pushed off his unlaced boot.

It was a little unsettling as he leaned back and considered it. Just months ago, Gina was a scrawny-looking girl, shy and backward. Now, she seemed to be doing something that she was made to do.... (Or *made* to do?)

Toby's eyes drifted across the room and its furnishings as he continued to muse on the change in Gina. He saw a mirror hanging on the wall and levered himself out of the chair to go get a look at the fire damage to his hair.

At first, he couldn't believe what he saw. One eyebrow was gone! Half of the hair on his right side was singed away, and his un-tanned skin showed the whiteness of his scalp! His sun-streaked, brown, wavy hair was GONE! What was left was matted down against his head and looked dirty.

"NO!" he repeated several times as he used his fingers to lift and separate the remaining locks. There was nothing to be done. He felt more ashamed than he had ever been. He didn't want Gina to see him like this…. But she already had! He thought of his hat, but realized that it wouldn't hide everything.

He returned to the chair and fell into it. He propped each of his arms onto the arms of the chair, buried his head in his hands, and sulked. Logic told him that it shouldn't matter, not after all he and Gina had gone through. But there was something in the way she'd looked at him when he entered the building. It was a kind of distance he'd never felt….

But at the moment, all he could do was sit and wait. (And mope…)

◊ ◊ ◊

2-47

~back on the river~

After about twenty minutes of waiting for Gina, Toby was pacing the floor, despite his stiff knee. There were three windows in the room. One faced the main street. The middle one looked across the holding area where they stored items that had just been brought downriver to sell. This holding pen was also used for goods they were going to take up north to sell at the Parker Landing warehouse.

On his last two trips to the middle window, he saw some immigrants camped in the holding area, waiting for passage. It seemed like there were more people than supplies today. Toby watched the families as they mingled and shared stories. The men gathered in one spot and the women in another near the area dedicated for cooking. After some time studying the passengers, Toby went to the third window, which overlooked the river. He leaned through the open window and looked upstream, wondering what was in that direction, as he'd never been there....

He returned to the first window and looked at some of the people passing on the street. They seemed to have a different level of activity since the great fire and set about with purpose, rather than with the hang-dog look from before.

Toby turned his head and saw an older kid—talking to Gina! She was standing with her back to Toby, but close to the tall kid. Toby guessed he was seventeen or so. The guy was listening to Gina, and then looked at the window where Toby was standing. Gina's thumb pointed over her shoulder towards the warehouse as she spoke, but then it seemed to disappear into her mouth as she chewed on her thumbnail. The older boy divided his glances between her and

Toby without any show of emotion. Finally, he dropped his hand against his thigh, turned away from Gina, and started walking away. He turned once and said something that Toby could only guess at. Gina turned and looked at the window, but Toby ducked out of sight.

Through the curtains, he watched Gina start back across the street. She wove her way around a passing wagon and waved at the men who had jeered at her. Toby studied the scene for another moment before moving to the window overlooking the holding pen.

He didn't turn around when he heard the door open behind him and heard her approaching. He stayed with his head out the window, leaning his elbows on the sill. He was waiting for her to say something and pretending to be occupied looking at the river and his tug being loaded. It took a moment for her to speak, and he withdrew from the opening and turned to face her.

She saw the condition of his face and head and said, "Oh, Toby, what happened?" He saw the slight curl of her mouth suppressing a grin. "Are you ok?"

She seemed concerned about him, but in his mind he could still see her and that boy across the street. "Sure, just a stupid…thing I did…." he said.

She reached up to the side of his head, her eyebrows pinched together in concern, but she was still smiling.

"It was a flash fire, spilled some of the whiskey, too near the firebox," he said, studying her. Something was missing in the look she gave him. The months they'd spent together had given him a second sense about her—and her moods.

She seemed to want to hug him, but resisted, as did he. They spoke at the same time as he sat back onto the window sill. They both stopped, and he smiled for her to continue.

"I was, uh…thinking I could put some food together and we could eat here?" He noted that it was a question, not a statement, but decided to ignore it and try to get a sense for who the guy across the street was.

"I'd like to go somewhere," he said casually. "Maybe that place Ella described once?" He motioned to the ribbon in her hair and told her how nice it looked. She backed up a step.

She glanced away, past him to the river, and tried to divert the situation. "How was the trip down? And how is Robin? …and Jay-nee?"

"How's Gina?" he asked her pointedly. She leaned back from him very slightly, but it gave him the answer he was seeking.

He dropped his arm and turned to look at the river again before speaking, "Jayne and Robin went to help their grandfather to...to die!"

"What?"

"We ran into him, and the ol' bugger SAVED Robin! We didn't know where she had been taken...." He started to recount the story, but she stopped him.

"Ernie tol' it to us last night. Said you helped both of them, and..." She used this opportunity to back up from standing so close to him. "He said that you and—is it Helmut?—went after the cart...."

So that's what this is about, thought Toby. *She's lookin' for the gold!* He paused in answering her to see what else she was hiding. When she was quiet, he turned and said in a burst, "So, what about this place to eat? You'll be needin' to get back here, and make *us* money!" He gave her one of the "wide arm swings" they used to share, purposefully missing her. He could tell she was put off by his vagueness, and he decided to watch her reactions more closely. He headed for the door, opened it, and turned, offering the opened door to her.

"Toby, I'm not sure that there's enough time...."

But he was already walking past Eula, who looked up and said to Gina, "Honey, you two just go eat and take your time. I'll keep the store runnin'."

Toby smiled and continued to the doorway, where he stopped and waited for her to exit first. He turned and saw her making a face at Eula. "Toby, I could get us some fresh fruit...and bread...." He held out an arm, guiding her towards the street. She gave a strained sigh, knowing he would persist until she gave in.

As they walked along the street, people stared at him and his missing hair. He glanced at the side of Gina's face and noticed that she was trying to avoid looking at anyone. *She IS embarrassed!*, he thought, wondering who she was trying to impress. She nodded to several people, but didn't stop to speak to them, actually turning to look at the path as if she'd stumbled along it.

When they had traveled about a hundred yards, they reached a small building that was sort of a store and restaurant combined. The neighborhood hadn't developed much yet, but there were houses and shacks with vacant spots of land in between. Toby made a little spin in his path and had a flash of a thought:

need to buy a piece of land here.... But his thoughts were interrupted when they crossed the threshold into the building. It was filled with loiterers and locals, and along the walls in a separate room were tables, mostly filled with workers from the nearby businesses.

When Gina walked in, the heads turned, and several of the men smiled and spoke to her. Several others acted as if she were going to join them, moving in their seats to make room. As she passed them, Toby smiled and nodded, following her to a table in a quiet corner.

"This will be quieter, and we can talk. You can tell me how everything is going—with the mine, an' at the Landin'," she said as she allowed him to push in her chair. He felt some of the laughter and snickering behind him as he sat down. She was turned away from the others and facing the wall.

"We have cold and hot tea...." the small girl said as she approached the table, nodding to Gina and staring at Toby's singed hair. She rattled off a list of the food that was cooking.

When they had ordered and had the cold teas in front of them, Toby smiled and sipped his drink. It wasn't actually cold, but it was tasty. He also looked around the room and nodded at several of the people looking at him. He started to enjoy watching people quickly look away when he caught them staring.

His eyes returned to Gina, and he decided to let her talk. As flustered as she was, she proceeded haltingly. "So, tell me what, uh...how things went."

"Which things?"

"Well, the trip. And Yeah-no. He was so evil, how could they *go* with him!?!"

"Family...." Toby offered the word as if it should be understood without discussion. He nodded again at another gaping couple.

Gina brushed a fly away from her arm. Toby thought she was acting prissy. In the corner on the other side of the room, he saw the older boy that Gina had been talking to earlier, and Toby caught him watching them.

"...Besides," Toby continued. "He was going to die with *his* family, and wanted them to be with him."

"Will she be back soon?"

Toby sipped some more tea and then sucked in a breath. "I...don't know. She said she and Robin would return before the snow."

"Well that's good...." Gina said as she leaned back and allowed the kitchen helper to set down a couple of bowls of what she'd just called "a soup." Toby noted the insincere tone of her answer. Gina sat bolt upright as she scooped up the soup and lifted each spoonful to her mouth. Likewise, Toby imitated her and put on his "propers," making fun of her attempts to act so dignified. He was enjoying himself at her expense.

"So, you've been gettin' used to the city?" he asked between slurps of soup. She nodded and seemed intent on not spilling the liquid during each spoonful's long trip. "Makin' any friends?" He looked again to the man in the opposite corner.

"I see some of the people, on the street, time an' again. They seem nice...."

Toby sliced a piece of bread and offered it to her, still stuck on the end of the knife. She frowned, as if he had just broken all the rules! He shrugged and dragged the bread off the knife onto his plate.

"So you didn't have any trouble gettin'...."

He cut across her question, "So Eula's arm is gonna be good? She'll be able to use it ok?" The older boy was still watching them.

Gina nodded, her mouth full of soup. When she swallowed it she continued, "Doctor sez—SAID!—that she'll be good. He said that she was so strong and fit, an' that she should heal quickly."

Toby nodded politely and cut another piece of bread. (He was still chewing the last!)

They danced around with more conversation, as Gina looked for the right time to ask again about the gold, and Toby threw in another tidbit about the time they had been apart.

Toby turned his head when he saw the older kid finally stand and start for the door. Toby figured he must work in the area and had to get back. "Hey! You should say goodbye...." He nodded at the older boy and Gina turned to see who he meant. She quickly saw him and turned back to face Toby.

"Oh.... He works...." She paused, and Toby realized that she probably didn't even know where he worked. Gina's face blushed a deep red, and she lowered her eyes to her soup bowl. Her hand trembled as she attempted to load the spoon again.

"I think he works, somewhere nearby." Toby simply looked at her and didn't respond. "OK! I've talked to him several times!" she said in a loud whisper.

"Talked...?" Toby said with one eyebrow raised.

"His name is Geoff, and he came here with his family—from England. They seem to be very nice!" She stopped when she realized that she had said too much.

"Met the folks?" Toby said in a quizzical voice. He was pulling at a hard piece of crust from the bread and studying her face.

"Uh, met them in church!" She said, becoming bolder with the seem-ingly innocent answer. "They had a very miserable trip across the ocean. Seems they all got sick and stayed that way for a couple of weeks on the boat. His mum nearly lost her baby from the sickness."

Toby shook his head and sucked butter from his finger. He saw the disgust in her eyes when she looked at him.

"What church!?!" Toby suddenly was glaring at her.

"What?"

"What church did you meet them in?"

"Oh. ...The Catholic one, uh, towards town." She pointed in some direction behind Toby and then glanced at the floor in a nearby corner.

"Nice church?" He pretended to believe her as he unbuttoned his shirt pocket and pulled out the leather pouch with the coins. He opened the pouch's drawstrings and poured the gold coins into his hand. He selected two of the better ones and placed them on the table in front of her, but her eyes were still looking at the other coins sitting in his hand.

"Those are yours for helping with the trip." He started putting the others away when he looked at her and saw that she was on the verge of tears. He paused and looked again at the coins. He picked up another and carelessly tossed it on the table with the first two. "And 'cause I want you to be happy...." He looked at her, pausing only long enough to reload the pouch and tug on the drawstring. He looked at her some more and realized that she wasn't going to say anything. He slid back the chair and began to stand. His knee throbbed, but he managed to stand upright.

Gina's eyes welled up with tears and she looked to her lap. In a quiet voice, she said, "Toby, I CAN'T go back. That life's too hard! *You* know you said so *yourself*. I just want to be in the city! I sort of like the activity here. I want to...."

The one that could talk for hours was speechless. She was out of stories. Or was she? He waited. Finally, she picked up the coins and stood up. This time he didn't help her with the chair, but he did take her arm and steadied her.

They were halfway back to the boatyard and neither one of them had spoken. Finally, Toby said, "I understand."

"YOU DON'T UNDERSTAND!" Gina shot at him. Several people nearby turned and looked at her before continuing on their way.

Her voice became vicious, and she glared at him. He remembered that look, and the last time she had a knife in her hand. He looked down at her dress to see if there was a bulge where she carried the knife. In a quieter voice, but still with malice, she continued, "You don't know! I had to watch you and Jayne, and watch her 'manage' you.... You were like a puppy dog, HER puppy dog! I loved you, and you just went with HER!" She wiped her nose on the back of her sleeve and pushed the tears away. "You have NO Idea! NO!" She back away as he reached for her. "Don't touch me! EVER!" With that she spun on her heel and marched towards the counting office, which was now just across the street.

Toby was aghast and watched her walking away. He continued walking for a short distance, thinking of several defenses to what she'd said, but he turned and went back to the warehouse.

He stepped up and into the "office and receiving room," as the sign on the door said, and noticed that Gina wasn't inside. When he looked at door to the apartment, Eula called to him. He saw that she knew what was going on. She motioned him to her and said, "Leave her for a while—she'll think things out." Eula nodded assurance to go with the advice and held Toby's puzzled eyes with her own.

Without thinking, or looking at Eula again, he asked her for the manifest for his next trip. He took it from her with his eyes fixed on the door across the room....

"Hey, Tob'!" It was Pete's voice. "We're gonna give you two families to take north...."

"Get 'em loaded," Toby said. "I wanna get back on the river..." Without looking at Pete, Toby marched past him. Pete looked at Eula. She shrugged and they both looked at the closed door...

$$\Diamond \Diamond \Diamond$$

2-48

~what lie ahead~

In less than two hours, Toby was turning the tug in the middle of the river, pulling two barges of people along with their belongings and some cargo. He was still having the argument in his head with Gina; still defending all that had happened. He tried to remember how many times each of their lives had depended on the other. He gave one last rueful glance towards a window in the counting room before he felt the tug pull out and begin to gain speed.

It wasn't ten minutes and they were turning north onto the Allegheny River. For the next couple of hours, Toby poured on the steam, almost punishing the tug's abilities. But he was so mad that he was passing more steam than that little tug!

The tug was fighting a strong current against it, but Toby still felt that they would make good time. He looked back at the passengers and then to the sun. Everything looked good. In six hours, they would reach the area known to them as "Moss Grove," where there was ample water and a nice place to make camp.

Toby re-fought the same argument in his mind for the next six hours. With each repeat, he seemed to lose a little more interest in the outcome of who was right or wrong. He felt that she had had a notion, all along, of living like a "city lady," not seeing the years of toil and hardship that Ernie and Ella had sacrificed to get where they were in life. She wanted it all and she wanted it now! He shook his head (for the fifteenth time), not understanding how she could miss something so basic. *This is best*, he said to himself. *I want to put everything back into the mine. Get the production going. Live on this tug, and make A LOT of money!*

In his mind, he saw the corner property where the Narrow River joined the Allegheny. It would make a great trading post. A place to drop off the immigrants, feed them in tavern fashion, give them a place to sleep. He could also check on the mine that was just a mile away. It wouldn't be too much to do. He thought of how long it might take to get started and wondered how much money he would need to build a suitable tavern. With all the new people heading upriver, surely there would be someone to run it, maybe even be a partner....

Since it was part of the property Toby had purchased from Ernie, it was his to do with what he could. Maybe Ernie and Ella would have some good ideas, or even want to be part of it....

"Mr. Toby?" Toby looked back just as a man's head appeared over the top of the deck. He pulled himself up the ladder and stood holding on to the railing. He didn't seem to be comfortable on the uppermost deck.

"Yes...." Toby smiled at him and tried to think of his name and which family he belonged to.

"I wanted to ask you some questions about the areas north of here. Me and the family won't have much of an idea of our next step, 'cept that we heard there was a lot of good land this way...."

Toby kept his eyes on the river, but glanced at the man from time to time as they talked. "What kinda work you do?" he asked.

"Done a lot: farmin', minin', house and barn constructin'. Guess I should make a list...." The man smiled. Toby liked his smile and gave him one of his own. "...Shoot, I guess me and the family can get along pretty well with a small place. Maybe build an orchard, make 'jack.'" Toby smiled and nodded. "Reckon that'd sell?"

Toby nodded again and asked, "What ya gonna do till the trees get big enough to pick the apples?"

"Oh that's the future, maybe just a dream. Anyway, thought you could tell me what you haul in from north?"

He and Toby talked a full hour about all the different things Toby had heard Ernie and Pete say they thought would be needed as the area grew. Something in the man's ability to see the ideas as Toby described them showed Toby how shrewd he was. He didn't seem to be a man with formal education, but he was very smart.

Toby caught a whiff of some food cooking in the brazier that the man's wife was tending to, and it made his stomach ache from hunger. "That's some fresh lamb that we got in Pittsburgh, as we planned to have a big meal tonight. I hope you will join us and the other family for dinner?" the man asked. Toby liked the idea. He looked forward to the food and to talking some more with the man about different ideas.

Moss Grove was in sight now, about a mile upriver. Toby mentioned it to the man, telling him that it was the night's campsite. Another several hours into the darkness and the youngsters were asleep, while the women and men sat around the fire. Toby told them frankly how hard his trip had been and about the perils of living in the wilds. As he spoke, the women glanced nervously over their shoulders and then to their sleeping children. The men stared into the fire's light and nodded with solemn understanding about what lie ahead....

Later that night, Toby was back aboard the tug, pacing the deck. He was thinking of something he'd just heard. He was so excited that he forgot the "Gina fight" episode completely. He tended the fire and watched it awhile before he went to his bunk in the sleeping cabin...

◊ ◊ ◊

2-49

~at the mouth of Narrow River~

The tug, two barges, two families, and Toby stood just off the northeast corner of the Allegheny River and the mouth of the Narrow River. Once ashore, they started up the wild slope and found that it leveled off about sixty feet above some high-water marks on the trees. After several passes along the ground facing each river, they agreed on two sites.

When the men told the women and children to start clearing the area to set up a campsite, there were murmurs and groans from the older children. Toby counted the kids for the first time and realized that there were fourteen! Two of them were not much younger than he was, and they seemed to resent his authority. They also seemed to be disappointed in the fact that the location was so desolate.

Toby, the two men, and the oldest boys scouted out the other side of the river across from the Murphy Mining Area. They walked two miles and could see the clearing, a wooden house, and part of the mine's cartway where two barges waited at the river's edge for Toby to pick up. One was fully loaded and the other nearly so.

Toby and the others climbed over rocks, passed through the large ferns, and stood in awe at a towering waterfall of blooming flowers that ran up the hillside for several hundred feet. It was mountain laurel in bloom. The flowers were about the size of a man's fist and covered each bush fully. They were hard to pass through, clustered as they were, so the men skirted them on the downside and pressed on.

They stopped about every hundred feet, squatted on top of a rock, and surveyed the area around them. Toby had a sharper eye and kept a watch out for snakes, his whip coiled at his side. He thought to tell the others to be careful, but he didn't want to spook them. Besides, the heat of the day had the snakes down deep in the rock crevices to stay cool. Toby decided to warn the men and their entire families at dinner.

Almost directly across the river from the coal mine, they found another outcrop of coal. Toby remembered what Jayne had told him: that she had seen many of these outcrops in her travels. He also seemed to recall Mad Hattie saying something about them, as well. Toby wondered how many other coal crops he might be able to find along the river.

Using a short-handled axe, they marked the trees in a path back towards the campsite and arrived as the women had a fire going and food cooking. Over the next hour, Toby and the others talked and seemed to reach mutual understanding of the scope of work that would be done. Toby replenished the fire on the boat so it would be ready to leave and then shook hands all around.

Everyone thanked him profusely and gave him some "vittles" to go. After the final waves goodbye, Toby was cut loose from the shoreline. In the dual flow of the two rivers, he backed his tug and barges into the center of the river. He put the power on and headed to trade the empty barges for the loaded ones.

During the brief off-loading, Toby told the Murphys about their new neighbors and described the project they were going to be doing. Oliver scratched his head and looked at the mountain across the river. He said, "Then they got them a whole lotta rocks to move." He shook his head and wandered back towards the mine, carrying his ledger book.

On the trip back to the city, Toby worked the figures in his head several times. He came up with the same numbers each time, and they were better than he'd hoped. Mr. Murphy had mentioned that they could up the production of the mine with more people, and Toby promised he could find them easily. Many of the immigrants were weary when they reached Pittsburgh and just wanted to stay there and work. But Toby knew that with some selection, he could find the right people and everything would come together.

◊ ◊ ◊

Weeks passed as he and the others raced up and down the river. Except for a week when the water got very low and the travel was a bit more risky, they were making money hand over fist. The tugs rarely shut down, and soon, each of them had a helper to tend the fire, shovel coal, and mind the barges. This left Toby rested enough to take on longer hours at the wheel.

Toby often ran into Ernie and Pete along the river, and they always shared information. With the speed of the new boats, they were running short on goods to take to the city. But the crops were starting to come in now and soon they would be busy with grain, lumber, leather, salted meats, and whiskey hauling. Their cargo trips north were always filled with people and their belongings, cattle, and items needed for farming, building, and now—bottling!

The Trading Company flourished and developed a good reputation among immigrants looking for safe passage. Toby was amassing a small fortune with each load of coal he hauled. Soon he had a lockbox on the tug to carry his gold. Even though he "plowed" a lot of the profits back into the mine, it just came back to him faster.

He always asked the others about Jayne and Robin, and even made several trips to Parker's Landing to see if they had shown up. It had been over a month, and he was disappointed each time there was no sign of them. So he buried himself in work, making himself efficient in every aspect of shipping and making the customers happy, right down to the smallest child on his trips.

At nights though, his longing reminded him of the happiness he missed. He had written to his mother and sisters, but hadn't received any word from them. Jayne and Robin weren't around, and Gina had become a "distant acquaintance…"

$$\Diamond \; \Diamond \; \Diamond$$

2-50

~a new mail lady~

Early morning: The tug creaked in the water, straining at the rope cleats and gently moving up and down in the river's waves. A soft wind came up the river valley; it held a chill that foretold the season's coming change. Some of the trees' leaves were tinted red, and shades of yellow tipped the others, making the shoreline a different sight these days.

Toby was on his second helper in a month, as the younger man didn't seem to like the long hours of watching the shoreline pass by. Anyway, Toby had an older man now who was as quiet as a man could be, and he was working out well. It seemed that the man had left something on shore that he didn't ever want to see again, and Toby never asked him about it. Toby wondered if he was wanted by the law, but then decided not to ask. He too had been down that "river" and knew the law could be as confused as any man could.

They ran the last of the Allegheny and turned up the Monongahela, where they would soon start unloading goods from the north. Toby made a mental list of what he wanted to do and the things he needed to get while he was on shore. With his eyes glued to the docking area, he steamed along and judged the current and his approach.

"Toby!" Ernie's voice hollered from his tug, "Stop over...." He motioned to Toby as he turned and carried some bags to his cabin.

When the tug was tied and straining at its own cleats, Toby turned to his deckhand and said, "Altman, cut down the heat, and we'll start swap-loading. Looks like there are several families to haul, but better wait until I talk to Ernie—see what he wants." Toby saw the disappointment in the man's eyes, so he dug into his pocket and then handed him a dollar. "Why don't you go and get something to drink—maybe a couple—and rest up first!"

Altman nodded agreement and hopped across the railing onto the dock. He limped along and started up the long wooden staircase. Toby hoped he would come back in decent enough shape to work, but knew that the man needed what was in a bottle at the moment. He hopped across the railing too and went to Ernie's tug.

He waited as Ernie finished talking with one of the new passengers. They were always so full of doubt: *What would they need? How long would they be on the water? When would they eat next?*

Ernie finally turned to Toby and rolled his eyes as he sucked in a deep breath. He was smiling and clapped his hand onto Toby's shoulder. "Good trip?" he asked.

"Guess so. Not much changes on the river," Toby said.

"Don't be too sure!" Ernie pulled Toby into the cabin and sat at the small table. Toby sat on the edge of the bed, looking at the sparse furnishings in the cabin.

Toby leaned forward and asked, "Too sure of what?"

"Looks like we're gonna get some competition. Been 'spectin' it, to tell you the truth. There's a bunch from down near Wheeling that are expandin' up this way...."

"Why would they want to start runnin' the Allegheny?" Toby asked. His thoughts were racing at what this could mean to his business. "There's a lot more headin' west...."

Ernie held up a hand and nodded. "I know. It seems funny, like they know somethin'...." He cleared his throat to speak again when another passenger shadowed the doorway.

"Captain, kin I have a word?"

Ernie stepped outside and listened for several minutes. Toby couldn't hear the conversation, but he could guess. It would be the same old story: *I'm a little short on money, and I wondered if I could do some work to help pay the passage for me and the family.* They'd all heard it so many times. But on several occasions, it had worked out nicely.

Ernie poked his head into the cabin, winked at Toby, and asked, "You got any work available for this fella? He wants to work off his passage." Again, Ernie rolled his eyes as Toby rose off the bunk and went to the door.

Toby looked at the man, who had the weary face of someone who was out of his element and afraid for his family. His face was pocked, and his pores were filled with tiny black spots. He looked like so many others who worked in dirty places. Toby felt sorry for the man and looked at Ernie. Toby shook the man's heavily calloused hand and asked, "And what sort of work do you do?"

"Stone mason, er, Sir? Captain?" He was slow to add the last title as he wasn't sure that a man so young could be a captain. He pulled at the handmade cap he held in his hands, squeezing it between his fingers as he waited.

Toby considered him for a moment and looked at Ernie before speaking again. "Your family's all in good health?" The man gave a series of quick nods and looked at them on the barge. They were all too young to do any really hard work, but they looked to be in good shape. "Put your stuff on this barge." Toby pointed at the one behind his tug and said, "There's a brazier you can cook on, and better set them poles up and cover yourselves—from the sun, and maybe rain...."

The man was still offering help when Toby turned and pulled Ernie along. "I can put him to work at the Narrows. They aren't gonna finish without some more help. The weather is setting in, and if it starts raining...." He shrugged and left Ernie to finish with the others as he bounded the steps to the counting office.

Toby stepped through the open door and right away saw that Eula had the cast off her arm. She looked up, gave him a broad smile, and waved him over. "Toby! What do you think of my white arm?" Her previously tanned arm was faded to a pale pink now, and a lot of the muscle had withered.

"Nice!" Toby smiled and touched it.

She recoiled and laughed, holding out her arm to show him the goose bumps. "You gave me chicken skin!" She laughed again and sat back into the chair.

Gina stood nearby and watched the exchange. She held a slight smile on her face, but it wasn't the same as she used to share with him. Toby nodded to her with a polite smile also and handed over the loading sheets on the coal he'd brought. When Gina entered it into the log, Toby noticed how much her writing had improved. Eula had done well teaching her to write, but he didn't want to say it! Even if he meant it as a compliment, Gina would take it otherwise....

He took the receipt and handed it to Eula, who looked it over and asked: "How you want it this time?"

"Half in gold and half in silver—this time...." Toby said as he noticed Gina looking at him from the corner of his eye. Toby watched as Eula counted out the coins and stacked them on the counter. Toby took them and slid them into his leather pouch.

"Oh! Wait, I'm gonna need some shovels, and picks, stone chisels—maybe four—and a hand sledge." Toby stepped back in front of Gina and waited for her to tally up the amount. She was still slow with the writing, but it was always neat. She copied the prices from a list on the wall, painstakingly avoiding errors as she added it up.

"Toby, you should congratulate Gina. She got us the mail to haul!"

Toby gave her an impressed look, but she didn't look at him. "Nice!" he said and started to ask what that meant.

Eula waited for Gina to speak, but then quickly added to her statement, "We're gonna get the mail, to haul north! And it means a good amount of money to the company!"

She waited for Toby to respond, but he sighed and asked, "Up the frozen rivers?" He glanced at Gina. "Uh, that's great! It is!"

Toby noticed the two vertical creases that framed each side of her mouth and that were beginning to make her look dowdy. "Here you go." Toby placed the money on the counter, as he'd already added up the prices in his head. She gave him a severe frown, but he smiled and ignored her.

"Give Pete a good kick, if I don't see him first!" He said to Eula. "An' I hope you get over that chicken skin!" He and Eula laughed while Gina pretended to study her ledger.

When he stepped out of the room, he stopped to tie his boot and heard Gina ask, "What do ya suppose he does with all that gold?"

"I reckon he's got to pay all the people that are doin' the mining, and the ones building that tradin' post...."

"What post?"

"He agreed to put some of the passengers into workin' in a tradin' post, and they're building it in exchange."

Toby heard what he thought was a fist pound on the counter before he tiptoed down the wooden stairs…

◊ ◊ ◊

2-51

~pass the hand and cheek~

They were all pulling three barges a piece now rather than the normal two. With each trip, they added more settlers. Ernie, Pete, and Toby had their choice of workers heading upriver, as most of the immigrants were looking for work in an area that they could settle in.

They had found a wheelwright who could make the steel-lined wooden wheels for wagons, as well as a woodjoiner/carpenter who could build carts and wagons from scratch. In the last several weeks, the mouth of the Narrows had changed dramatically! A portion of the ground had been cleared, and the trees were being used to frame-in the trading post.

A ramp was being carved into the side of the mountain to serve a dual function. The stone that was cut for the foundation of the trading posts was trimmed on the spot, and the "spaltings" were raked across the rampway to make a base for the road that would eventually crest the top of the hill.

They planned to create a "gateway" on the hilltop to enable the immigrants to find areas to settle. Timber, wild game, fresh water springs, and good ground for farming were all plentiful. Some of the passengers brought plants and shrubs from their native lands that they would plant once they got settled.

Toby remembered one passenger, an elderly woman, who had a small, clay pot of shamrocks that never left her side. She told Toby that it was all she had of her heritage of many generations in Scotland. Toby could still see her face in his mind, but had forgotten her name. He had transported so many families in the past months that he was losing track.

◊ ◊ ◊

They had postponed the celebration of the opening of the Trading Post until Toby arrived. Ernie and Ella had made the trip from Parker's Landing, and Pete and Eula came from West Monterey. The four were standing on the shore when Toby's tug appeared. Toby knew the Post was set to open, but he didn't expect the gathering to be so large! There seemed to be nearly thirty people gathered there, all watching his boat arrive.

He saw that a good portion of the folks were the Murphys and their helpers. He began to realize just how many people's lives he had helped and got a lump in his throat. Children pumped their fists into the air, seeking the steam whistle's scream. Toby obliged them. He laid on the horn's rope and steered towards the partially built stone dock. The other tugs were parked upriver and left the honored spot for him.

Altman stood on the front deck, holding the rope to toss to a man on the dock. He glanced back at Toby to watch his expression. At the last three bellows of the steam whistle, everyone clapped and tossed their hats into the air.

Toby blinked in rapid succession to keep his eyes dry as he stepped onto the dock and looked at all the smiling faces. Ernie was the first to shake his hand and Ella was the first lady to kiss him. Then his hand and cheeks were passed around to everyone in the camp.

Inside the Post, the fireplace was burning brightly and two long tables were set with an assortment of plates, silverware, and goblets. Many dishes of food sat on the tables, waiting to be devoured. And children with perpetually empty stomachs glared at the food, waiting to devour it!

After prayers were said and all were seated, silently waiting for the go-ahead to eat, Ernie stood at the head of the adult table and thumped his beer stein on the table. When complete silence fell on the room, he lifted his stein towards Toby. "We're all here to toast and celebrate a special occasion. We, and I mean *us all*, have opened this wilderness for settlement.... *You youngsters* will tell your children of this day! And your grandchildren!" There were knowing smiles and nods from the parents as they beamed and watched the children, who were still bored and hungry!

"BUT, there is much to do—and it will be hard. There's a winter soon to come upon us, and many of you don't have your homes built. That will be the shared work we will do next. We'll all help until everyone is sheltered, including the animals. If the winter holds off, we have several months to go, and we can do it.

"But! For tonight, we honor Toby, here. He had the wisdom to see all this as we now see it. He took a chance, and used all of his pay to make it happen...." Many of the folks were lifting their goblets to Toby. "Don't, for a moment, think that a man's age has limits. TO TOBY!"

"TO TOBY!" everyone chimed in.

Before Ernie could say another word, Ella jumped up and—her voice louder than Ernie's had been—said: "And before anybody starves, pass the food!" There were hoots and laughter as Ernie shrugged, smiled, and sat down.

Later, Toby sat with the fullest stomach he'd had in a long time and a permanent smile glued to his face. He nodded at people who spoke and held a goblet aloft to him. He studied everyone who filled the great room and noted the arrangement of people. Looking across the tables to the children's table, he noticed Annette Murphy smiling at him. Even at this distance, he could see her blush. And despite Helmut's hovering, Toby seemed to feel a special connection with her. But the last thing Toby wanted was another crush on him. Even though he smiled at Annette, he felt sorry that Gina wasn't here. She had made significant contributions to all of this and deserved recognition.

Toby touched his singed hair and the nearly-bald spot that now sprouted fine hairs, and he wondered what the young girl could possibly see to attract her. The bald spot reminded him of Jayne and her partially shaved head. Where was she now? Was Robin safe, and was the grandfather still alive?

For the remainder of the evening and then later, alone in his bunk on the tug, all Toby could think about was that *one female* that made his heart ache. His dreams that night varied, and yet each came back to one central theme: He was back on the cart, pulled by Bea as they traveled across a vast land...

◊ ◊ ◊

2-52

~nice to meet—Oh Hell!~

" I think it's a great idea! And I can't imagine a better time to do it, Tob'. You've been through more than anybody in the last five months, and .... that deserves a break."

"But I don't want to run out on things here. It's just that I really want to see my mother and sisters...."

"Exactly," Ernie added to Ella and Toby's conversation. "You've done nothin' but work—everyday, and many nights, too. You've created everything at the Narrows, and things are slowing down. A lot of things will pick up when the crops come in. But Toby, as fast as we are turning the river trips, we've outgrown things for a bit.... Besides, Pete and I can manage with what's coming in. Go! And don't look back till you're ready to come back."

Toby nodded, his elbows resting on his knees as he stared at the floor. "I just wish I knew where Jayne and Robin were, and when they'll be back...."

"Toby, you know we'll take them in till you return. That shouldn't be a worry, so I also vote you go," Ella said.

Ernie clasped him on the shoulder and said, "You have got people workin' at the Narrows and they know Pete and I will act in your stead. Besides, if you're worried that they'll be mad at you if you go, remember this: You'll make enemies no matter what you do in this life. Think Ella and I don't have any?"

Ella gave a snorting laugh and nodded her head. "Got a list, *we* do!" Ernie smiled back and rolled his eyes.

"Hell, Toby, if I were you, I'd be steamin' south this day. And you could maybe see if you can find a need for anything we can take that direction."

Toby nodded and chewed on the inside of his cheek as he thought of everything they'd said.

Pete rocked forward onto all four legs of the chair he'd been leaning back in and added, "Get—and quit stinkin' up the place!" They all laughed.

Ernie was the first to stand. "Why don't we go through the warehouse and get you some supplies...." He looked up and saw Altman standing in the shadows. It was obvious that the man had taken it all in. The others turned to look at him also.

"Altman?" Toby asked, "You need anything?"

Altman hesitated, and then spoke. "No, sir. I just wanted to tell you that we are nearly loaded and should be able to leave in half an hour." He seemed nervous and his voice faltered. He turned and started down an aisle in the warehouse.

"Altman!" Toby addressed him in a loud voice. "Pete and Ernie will be a day behind us, and they're lookin' for you to help them on their barges while I'm gone."

The old man just nodded and walked off.

"Odd one, that Altman," Pete said as he rose and followed Ernie.

Toby gave Ella a hug. "We'll miss you, and be safe!" She said as she held his face in her rough hands. "Now go!"

After loading some extras for Toby's trip, they stood on the dock and shook hands. Toby waved from the wheelhouse and guided the "Allegheny Bea" back from her berth and into the main current of the river. He was empty and not pulling a barge, as he planned to pick up two barges of coal from the Narrows on his way through.

Altman was standing at the aft rail and seemed to be talking to himself. Toby puzzled at it for a moment and then pulled the steam whistle three times. He waved to people on the shoreline and they waved back.

Toby was as headed up with steam as the "Bea" was and charged with adrenaline. He thought of the new name plates on all the boats and wondered if Gina would be angry that he hadn't named the tug after her. Oh well, she would have to just live with it....

Two miles downriver, he saw the sand bar that had been his home for several days so long ago. As he watched it approach, he saw it! Three stacked stones! He couldn't believe it! He cut off the tug's steam and cut the wheel hard. Altman was nearly knocked off his feet and looked at him sharply.

"Get an anchor ready!" Toby yelled at him. He put a tie rope on the steering wheel to hold its course, yanked the power arm, and then yanked the steam whistle rope three times. Without delay, he dropped down the ladder and went to the bow, stooped over, and began to untie his boots. Hurriedly he kicked each one off and yelled to Altman to drop anchor.

There she was! Standing on the sandbar and smiling at him.

He dove into the river and began swimming towards the shore about thirty feet away. She also ran into the water and began swimming. When they met, he threw his arms around her and kissed her with a passion he'd nearly forgotten. They sank into the water, still locked in a kiss. As Toby's feet landed on the bottom of the river, he pushed up and they broke the surface of the water before they broke the kiss. They took a long minute to catch a breath before they began talking.

"I thought...you weren't going...to make it back...."

"I'm here!" She smiled and brushed her wet lips across his, still trying to catch her breath.

"I mean before I left...." Toby gasped.

"I missed you...." she started to say.

"I missed you, too!" Toby laughed.

"No! I mean I missed you the last time you were here! Two days ago!"

"Why didn't you go to the Landin'?"

She smiled and touched the short hair on her wounded head "They don't seem to like me much there!" She threw her head back and laughed.

"But Ella was there. She would—"

Jayne just cut him off with another kiss and they started swimming to the tug.

Toby swung around in a circle and faced the shoreline. "Where's Robin?"

"She's ok. She is going to stay with my half-sister." She saw the disappointment in his face.

They were just getting to the tug, and Toby reached up to grab the rail. He pulled himself onto the deck and reached down to pull her up. *She is so beautiful*, he thought as he helped her over the rail.

When her feet landed on the deck, she looked up and saw the face of Altman, and her face froze. Toby saw it and turned to look at him, thinking to introduce Jayne, when he saw the pistol pointed at the two of them...

◊ ◊ ◊

2-53

~how do you like me now~

"Altman?" Toby asked softly.

With the muzzle of the gun, Altman motioned Toby to sit on the deck away from Jayne. "Don't get funny on me boy."

"What is this about?"

"'What is this about?' he sez," Altman mimicked Toby and motioned Jayne to sit down also, as he stared at the wet tunic snug against her figure. "I'll tell you! I'm here for the gold you two stole from my girl!" He stepped behind Jayne and wrapped his fingers into her hair. She grimaced and gritted her teeth, but said nothing.

"An' I intend to have it!" Altman jerked Jayne's head, testing the grip. "You left me and my missus with two kids to care for when they arrested Rosa! Me an' the missus had only the money Rosa could bring in, and NOW! Now we don't got the money, but we got KIDS! We're too old to have kids to raise!" He was raving and spittle sprayed on Jayne as he ranted.

"What GOLD?" Toby asked. He was quickly trying to gain an upper hand and make up a story.

"Don't tell me ya got nothin'. I see an' I watch. Each time you leave the countin' office you got gold in your pocket. An' I figgur it belongs to me."

"But I pay the people at the mine for the coal we haul! And buy the food, and pay for the others at the Trading Post." Jayne was looking at him and seemed to be in awe at the news of the mine and post.

"I see. I watch! You're hidin' as much as half!"

"You're crazy, Altman! Just as crazy as that daughter o' yours...."

Altman kicked Jayne in the thigh, causing her to wince and Toby to quiet down. Under normal circumstances, he'd certainly be able to outthink Altman, but at the moment he was too stunned to do anything.

"So you tell me where it is afor' I shoot this worthless squaw. Was tol' she was dead anyway!" He pulled her hair and spit on her. Toby could see the muscle in her jaw start to flex.

"You're right! You're right...." Toby lowered his voice. "I'll tell you where it is." He was looking at Jayne and hoped she knew that he was lying. "You'll need me to show ya, and I'll take you there.... Let her go, she can swim back and we'll leave."

"Ain't gonna happen! She's gonna be right here, tied to my hand—and dead if she tries to move!"

Toby reached for his boots and started to put them on, but was stopped when Altman pointed the pistol at him and said, "Just put them on and tie the laces together."

"But I can't climb the ladder to the wheelhouse that way."

"You'll make it!" Altman wheezed and stayed on the opposite side of Jayne as Toby short-stepped his way to the ladder.

"You gonna haul in the anchor?" Toby asked as he pulled himself up one rung at a time.

"NOPE. She is!" With that he pulled Jayne to her feet by her hair.

Toby backed up the Bea and loosened the line to the anchor. He watched as Jayne pulled up the heavy anchor and swung it over the rail. For a second she seemed to be trying to add some extra swing to hit Altman, but she tossed it to the deck.

They were heading downriver, and Toby's mind raced; he had to think of something and quick. With the next turn in the river, he had it! He pointed to the building hidden in the trees at West Monterey! "It's there! In the cistern!"

Ten tense seconds later, they approached the stone dock, and Toby wished that Eula was there, holding her rifle. But this time she wasn't; she had gone up to the Landing with Pete.

They shut down and tied off the tug, and Toby lowered himself, one rung at a time, to the deck. He stood there waiting for Altman to lead, but he gave Toby a crooked, toothless smile and said, "Why don't you lead?"

Toby did, and they walked up the grade towards the red-sided building. He saw the doorway and knew it was locked. He got the skeleton key from its hiding place first and then opened the door.

"What the hell are you pullin' at, boy!?!" Altman wheezed again.

"Haf' to use the crank-winch to raise the stone lid." Toby pointed to the huge, flat stone that lie on top of the cistern. When Altman leaned around Jayne, Toby gave her a pointed look to be ready.

From inside, Toby pushed out a piece of rope and continued to feed it out of the small window until there was enough to reach the heavy rock. He returned to them and tied the rope to a wrought iron loop that had been inserted into a hole in the rock. "I have to go in and crank it up. It weighs over two hundred pounds!" Toby explained. Altman nodded and rewrapped his fingers into Jayne's hair. He motioned with the pistol for Toby to go.

At the winch, Toby could just reach the handle and see over the sill of the small window at the same time. He turned the crank with some moderate force and felt the rope tighten. At each one-eighth of a turn, a latch clicked to prevent the wheel from spinning backward from the stone's weight.

Click, click, click. The lid rose and the clicking continued. Toby was watching closely and tried to gauge the right height of the lid....

"Where IS it?!" Altman demanded. He was looking inside the cistern, kneeling beside Jayne, who stood bent over, her hair still tangled in his fingers. She was making a fist in each hand and was ready to strike!

"Out here, boy!" Altman said in a commanding tone.

"Can't. I gotta hold the lever 'cause the latch needs fixin'. You can reach it. It's under the lid in the back."

Altman studied the situation and didn't like it at all. "Squaw here will get it!"

Toby hadn't counted on this, and his whole plan came to a halt! He bit on the inside of his lip as Altman lowered Jayne down and forced her to reach under the precariously-tied stone. Toby shook his head ever so softly to Jayne as she looked at him and knelt down.

He hoped she could think of something. He was ready to give up when she made attempts to fuss with something under the water. "I... I can't... I can't get my fingers on the handle...." She grunted, and even Toby believed her act. He was beginning to think something was in there!

"Get the hell out of the way!" Altman pulled her back and stuck his arm into the cold water. "Where is it?"

With Altman's one hand in the cistern, his other glued to Jayne's head, and the pistol lying beside him, Toby saw his chance. Just as Altman turned his head to ask Toby a question, Toby grabbed the rope, pulled himself up, and with his boots still tied together, used both feet to kick the latch. The rope jerked him upwards and he let go just as his fingers reached the pulley. Outside he heard the sickening crunch of Altman's arm being crushed and the rock finally finding its former resting place. Altman screamed. Toby tried to get to his feet, but lost his balance. The second time he tried to get up he pulled off one boot and freed his foot.

That's when he heard the gunshot and Jayne's scream…

◊ ◊ ◊

2-54

~size does matter~

Toby fell twice getting to the doorway. He had one boot on and one off, and they were still tied together. He finally pulled off the second boot and tossed them aside. He shot through the doorway and grabbed the corner of the building to help him make the quick curve to Jayne.

He stopped short and looked at the situation. Jayne was on her knees, her back to Toby. She seemed to be holding her stomach, but Toby wasn't sure. Altman was pawing at the ground in the direction of the pistol. His wrist and hand were crushed flat between the stone lid and the cistern. Each time he groped at the ground beside the pistol, he recoiled from the pain in his other hand. When he saw Toby, he stopped and reached to the mangled hand. His face contorted as the pain began to consume him. Toby knew Altman would soon pass out as he went into shock.

"Jayne?" Toby said in a quiet voice as he stepped closer. "Jayne…?" He could see her shoulders heave as she tried to catch her breath. The next sight he saw was her hands covered with blood. "Jayne!"

She was hanging over Altman now and glaring at him. He looked like a whipped dog. His eyes darted to her and away, and then back again. Jayne reached over and tangled her bloody fingers into Altman's hair. When she turned his head towards her, she spit into his face.

Toby touched her shoulder and tried to determine how badly she was hurt, but he didn't want to pull her away from what she needed to do at the moment. Jayne jerked the man's head back and forth, causing him to moan in the agony the movement caused his crushed hand. Toby took the moment to look Jayne over for injuries. There was no hole in her tunic, and although the blood was there, it seemed to be from Altman. Toby began to realize that they had fought for the pistol; the blood was all over Altman's good hand, too.

Jayne spat on him several more times. The man was so terrified he couldn't take his eyes from hers. He whimpered and sobbed, "Get her away from me.... *She's cursed!* Please get her away from me...." he begged Toby.

Again in a soft voice, Toby said, "Jayne?" This time he pulled steadily on her arm, and she began to loosen her grip on Altman's hair. The wounded man sighed, dropped his head onto the ground, and began crying.

Toby coaxed Jayne to pull herself back onto her heels and stand. He saw her knife in the other hand, but it was clean and not used—yet! Jayne's fingers were white with the grip she had on the knife, and Toby knew not to try to take it from her until she had lost the blood lust.

It took two more minutes before her eyes focused on Altman and her breathing settled down. She looked at Toby and then backed away, turning to find a clean spot on the ground to sit. When she was settled, Toby stepped in front of her and squatted down. Again, he searched for wounds and was finally satisfied there weren't any.

"I want to kill him...."

"No!" Toby said in protest.

"I WANT to kill him.... HE was going to kill us! YOU can go back to the boat.... I will kill him! It is the way of my people."

"NO." Toby said firmly. "He's already dead. He won't survive the trip back anyway—even if we took him back.... Maybe a doctor could help him, if we took him to Pittsburgh."

"I won't go! With him *or* you! Tobay, you leave too many enemies standing behind you. One of them will live to kill you!" Jayne started to lean forward, and it seemed to Toby that she really was going to go for Altman.

Toby put his hands on either side of her head and said in complete conviction, "You ARE right, but we don't have to kill him. I don't WANT to kill him.... But I will give him a chance; I will leave a knife here for him to cut his own hand off. You're right. He was going to kill us, and STEAL. It's the way of MY people—OUR people—Jayne! A thief gets his ear cut off.... Well *this* thief will have to cut his own hand off! Everyone will know—IF he survives!"

Jayne's glare slowly dissolved, and she let Toby help her to her feet. She took one last look at Altman, and then cocked her head at an idea that came to her. Without a word, she left Toby, entered the building, and returned with an old skinning knife. She took it to the rock lid and drew it across the stone a few times. Several swipes later, she tested the knife and was satisfied that it was dull enough. She stuck it into the ground beside the unconscious Altman.

She didn't want Toby to second guess the situation, so she pointed to his feet and said, "Boots?" Toby took one last look at Altman and sighed with resignation as he turned to go inside to get the boots and lock the door.

They washed themselves off near the river's edge and sat silently for a little while. Toby took one long, last look up the river as he realized that it would be some weeks—maybe months—before he would see it again. And even then, it would be changed. The bright colors of fall would blaze and fade, and the snow of winter was certain to follow. In the quiet time that passed, Toby thought of the amputation Longy had done at the Hattenfelt farm. It all seemed so long ago....

It didn't take long for them to get the steam up and get underway. They both stood in the wheelhouse, and Toby was glad that the space was slightly small. It was good to be near Jayne again…

◊ ◊ ◊

2-55

~farewell or...~

The tug entered the mouth of the Narrow River valley and made its way to the barges filled with coal and waiting for their trip to Pittsburgh. Even though it was nearly seven in the evening, Toby declined the offer to stay—but not the offer to take some of the food Mrs. Murphy had prepared.

Once the two coal barges were hooked to the tug and they were back on the Allegheny River, he and Jayne delved into the food. There was smoked wild turkey meat, fresh bread, and some leeks. Toby held a drumstick in one hand and the tug's piloting wheel in the other.

He chewed and smiled as he made the most of the last hour and a half of daylight. Jayne looked at him and asked, "Why do you smile, Tobay? This was a hard day."

"I was smiling at the surprised look on Mrs. Murphy's face when she saw you and not Gina."

Jayne didn't seem to share the humor, and fell silent for a bit. Toby bit into the turkey leg and pulled off some more meat. It took him a moment to notice her silence. He said, "I only meant that she didn't expect to see an Indian girl... with me...." (*This isn't going well, at all!*) Toby thought about asking her why it should matter, but decided to shift the subject. "So what did you think about the Trading Post?"

She seemed surprised by the question at first, but went with it. "It's beautiful, and it will do very well. I think the road over the mountain will make it, uh, make it important?" She wasn't sure if that was the word she wanted.

"It will be important," Toby agreed. "And you and I will be there. I wanted it for you. The people there will run it for two years and then it goes back to me... To us!" He smiled at her and waited for a response.

She was puzzled. She mulled over what he had just said and studied his face. "You want me there?"

"Yes, but it would be your decision...." Toby saw the confusion on her face. "YES! I want you there!"

Jayne leaned against his arm and looked at the sky. "Then I will be there.... But, why? Where is Gina? She does not want to stay with you and me?"

"No, she, uh, wants to be in the city. She likes the safer life, and she didn't like the struggle out here in the wilds." Toby kept his eyes on the river ahead and didn't look at Jayne.

"She wants to stay in the city, without you?"

"Guess so...." Toby thought of the young man he'd seen talking to Gina, but didn't mention it. "It would be better, besides. She's doing the business part at the Pittsburgh Warehouse. And Eula says she's great at it."

"She is a fool, Tobay. She won't find what she wants in the city." With that, Jayne went to the ladder and climbed down to the main deck. A short while passed, and Toby looked to the rear deck where she was squatting down beside a bucket of water. She had her deerskin tunic off and was bathing herself. Toby watched the beautiful girl in silence, glancing back and forth between her and the river ahead.

They reached the flat landing on the west side of the river where, so long ago, they had all camped. They dropped anchor and decided to stay onboard for the night. Toby went ashore and gathered some dry wood to burn in the brazier. He didn't want to use the coal, as the smoke and the smell would be a little disturbing.

He sat on a small bench, and Jayne sat on the deck with her back against his legs. He stroked her hair, and they sat in silence, listening to the sounds of the river and the wildlife starting their nightly search for food.

Later, in the bunk, they began to catch their breath and knew that sleep would part them till morning....

When Toby woke, Jayne was near the brazier, holding some meat on a stick. It smelled wonderful, and after he returned from the front deck to relieve himself, they ate breakfast and enjoyed the sunrise. Each morning the dawn came later, and it wouldn't be long before the air was frigid. Toby used some of the burning wood to get the boiler's fire going. When they finished breakfast and the steam was hissing, it was time to head downriver.

Jayne divided her time between being with Toby in the steering house and standing at the tug's bow. Every so often she turned and smiled at him, but he could tell she was in the midst of a struggle in her mind.

But it soon disappeared when they came into sight of the city and saw the "new" buildings. Jayne kept turning to look at Toby, and her face showed her amazement at how big the buildings were getting. When she'd been here last, none of them had even been reconstructed up to the first level yet. Now some of them were on their third story.

Toby steered wide at the juncture of the Ohio and Monongahela Rivers and headed for the warehouse, which seemed to appear sooner than usual. Toby hadn't been looking forward to Jayne and Gina's reunion, but it was going to happen. With a little maneuvering, they unhooked from the barges and shut down the tug at the dock.

Toby gathered up his log book, and he and Jayne climbed the long wooden staircase along the side of the building. When they reached the top landing, Toby turned and went inside. He looked back and saw Jayne looking at the buildings down the street. He shrugged and went to the counter, loudly announcing his arrival.

The door to the apartment/sleeping room opened, and Gina stepped into the counting room. She looked a little disheveled, and her hair was a mess. When she saw him, she turned quickly and made sure the door was closed tight.

She seemed embarrassed to see him, but she smoothed her hair and greeted him. "Oh, hello, Toby. I guess I didn't hear your whistle.... I was napping, well, reading and I guess I dozed off.... Did you have a good trip?" She had regained her composure and was more self-possessed now. She went to her usual place behind the counter and put on the glasses that sat snugly on her nose as she opened the ledger book before her.

"We had a great trip, and it was profitable," Toby said. "Ella told me to say hello, and Ernie should be here in two days." He was putting down his own log, and opened it to the marked page.

They went over some of the figures and made new entries as they adjusted for items he needed. He lifted his hat off and laid it on the counter. Gina looked up and studied his new hair growth. "It's coming in a little," she said. She reached for his head to turn it when she was startled by a movement to her left. Her hand near his face didn't look too good to Jayne as she stepped up to the counter.

"Jayne...I, I didn't know you were here!" It suddenly dawned on Gina where her hand was, and she dropped it to the counter.

"Hello, Gina." Jayne stepped closer to Toby and stood at his side. Her face held a genuine smile, but Toby wasn't sure it was friendly.

Toby felt the tenseness in the room and tried to lighten up the mood. "We have stories! Lordy! We have stories to tell ya.... Gina, we nearly got killt yesterday, and there is a lot to tell...." He started to think of the right words to tell the story when he heard the door to the apartment open.

He turned and looked; it was the older kid Toby had seen on the street with Gina! He looked like he had just awoken and was fastening his shirt buttons. When he looked up, he was surprised to see Toby and Jayne. Gina's face went crimson in color, and she was speechless.

Toby looked at Jayne, who now had a genuine smile on her face as she looked back at the young man. For some reason, Toby was relieved to see him, yet he felt a pang of jealously. He stepped forward and heard Gina give a slight gasp. "Toby?" she said. He could tell she wasn't sure what he was about to do, but he reached out and offered the other man his hand.

"I'm Toby, and this here is Jayne...." The man nodded and shook the offered hand a bit tentatively. He eyes shifted to Gina and then to Jayne. He nodded to her as he looked at her half-bald scalp.

"I, er, was just leaving. I gotta make it down the hill, to...."

"Don't leave. We're gonna load up some stuff and get ready to head downriver. Goin' to see my family!" Toby smiled at him, but glanced at Gina to see what her response was. She quickly looked at the ledger and tried to busy herself.

Toby continued to press the issue and said, "I haven't seem my family for nearly six months, and I want to spend some time with them. Jayne and I are gonna be gone some weeks...."

The other man was now edging his way to the door and saying to Gina, "I'll see you later?"

"Yes." That was Gina's total reply, and she didn't look up or wave to him.

"Goodbye...." Jayne called to him as she turned back to smile politely at Gina.

There was a long pause without words as Gina wrote out a receipt and then counted out six hundred dollars in gold and silver into Toby's waiting hand....

Jayne and Toby climbed the ladder back to the top deck of the tug. From shore, Gina watched Toby as he steered the Bea back out into the river. The pair looked back once and waved to Gina. She slowly waved back. When they were far enough away, she pounded the doorframe with her fist and used both palms to push out the tears that welled up in her eyes....

"Oh, Baby Grape," she moaned in a whisper. "I'm gonna miss you. I'll never really love another man as much..."

$$\Diamond \; \Diamond \; \Diamond$$

This ends Toby's second adventure. Now is the time to go to www.babygrapebooks.com to see what the "crew" is up to in *Baby Grape's Southern Exposure*, the third adventure.

$$\Diamond \; \Diamond \; \Diamond$$

Author's Notes

I sincerely hope the word "fiction" covers the latitude I took in writing this story for your entertainment. Often, characters and events write themselves, and even I sit in amazement watching the story take turns I didn't expect.

For now it's enough to warn you that Toby and the "crew" are on their third adventure, as Toby continues to look for his mother and sisters. So join in and watch for the sequel, *Baby Grape's Southern Exposure*. And be sure to check in at www.babygrapebooks.com to see the next release date.

At this point I'd like to thank my own "crew" as I extend my sincere thanks to Jennifer McGuiggan (www.thewordcellar.com) for her fine editing. And I'd like to thank Emily Zuzack for her unbelievable artwork—again. If you would like to reach her, she's at emzuzack@gmail.com. All of Emily's work, herein, is copyrighted 2008 with all rights reserved.

◊ ◊ ◊

Thom Rogers lives in Western Pennsylvania, with his dog Annie. In addition to his many other interests, he spends a lot of his time putting together ideas for Toby and the gang's next adventure.

Printed in the United States
206851BV00006B/1-3/P